Second edition, professionally copyedited 2014

Copyright 2011 Larry LaVoie

Visit Larry LaVoie online
http://www.larrylavoieauthor.com
http://larrylavoieauthor.blogspot.com

ACKNOWLEDGEMENTS

I would like to thank my wife, Anna, for the many hours of support she has given as I write and for her review and input on the book, the characters and the story itself. It goes without saying, this book would not be nearly as well written without the editing talent of Sharon Shafa.

This book is a work of fiction. All characters, names, places, and events are products of the author's imagination. Any resemblance to actual people, places, or things is coincidental.

Threads of the Shroud

By Larry LaVoie

Facts

Fact: The organization Grand Orient de France (GODF) exists and is an international organization with lodges around the world including the United States.

Fact: On December 4, 1532, the Shroud of Christ, known today as the Shroud of Turin, was in a fire that nearly destroyed the sacred cloth.

Fact: On April 16, 1534, the Shroud was given to Chambery's Poor Clare Nuns for trimming and repair of the burned areas of the Shroud.

Fact: Poor Clare Nun convents exist throughout the world and the members currently number about 20,000.

Fact: The characters and events depicted in this story are purely fictional and are the creation of the author's imagination.

PROLOGUE

Walter Tait awoke gasping for air and frantically feeling his face for his oxygen mask. In desperation the old man opened his eyes to the blurred image of a man standing over him. He tried to scream, but decades of heavy cigarette smoking had weakened his lungs and his voice had lost the energy for more than a raspy whimper. The intruder was dressed in black, including a ski mask and a hooded sweatshirt covering his head. When his eyes focused, Tait could see the man was holding his oxygen mask in one hand and a gun in the other. Walter Tait thought the man was the grim reaper and in a way he was. The man in black was known to his boss, the Grand Master, as the Assassin.

"Where is the crucifix?" the Assassin demanded. He spoke in English, but his accent gave away his French heritage.

Walter Tait focused his eyes on the French made M1935A handgun, one he recognized from many years ago, and he tried to put more distance between it and his trembling body. *Am I going to die like this?* "Crucifix?" He pointed above the nightstand. "It is hanging on the wall." His voice was shaky and barely audible.

"Croix de Chapelle Chambery," the Frenchman said, waving his gun. "I am certain you have it."

The words of the infiltrator churned like a whirlwind in Walter Tait's mind as he tried to make sense of the Assassin's demand, but he was slow to comprehend due to his 87 years and a touch of dementia. His once sharp mind was foggy. *Crucifix, Croix de Chappell Chambery?* He struggled to breathe, every breath was labored and seemed inadequate. If he was going to get away from the intruder he would have to do it before he lost all his strength. He made his move and rolled off the bed, away from the gunman, and fell to the floor. As he hit the floor, the room lit up from the flash of the muzzle, and he felt a searing hot pain in his side as the thunder of the gunshot filled his ears. He lay motionless on the floor, feeling the life slowly drain from him and his fear turned to calm. His mind began to clear. He knew what the Frenchman was after. He remembered a date from long ago, June 6, 1944, the day he'd been given the crucifix.

It was 0300 hours. The drone of the engine of the C-47 troop transport aircraft was too loud for most of the men of the 82nd Airborne to engage in small talk. Instead, they silently prayed as they contemplated what was about to befall them. He remembered the words of the chaplain, Lt. Joseph Lacy, "What you are about to do today will be a prayer in itself," but he'd decided to pray anyway.

His feet were numb from the constant vibration as he stood with nineteen other paratroopers and fastened his ripcord to the overhead wire. He was ready, at least that was what he told himself, ready for the nightmare he was about to jump into. The door to the aircraft was open and the cold moist night air stung his face.

Suddenly the sky lit up with exploding German anti-aircraft rounds and the plane shook violently. Shrapnel pierced the side of the C-47 and whistled past his helmet. The man in front of him fell to the deck screaming in pain. All he could do was unhook the soldier's ripcord so he wouldn't be pulled out of the aircraft. *Lucky bastard, at least he knows his fate*, Tait thought, but the rest of them were about to jump to an unknown destiny. The plane's engine coughed, sputtered and went quiet. The compartment of the C-47 filled with black smoke. He only knew they were somewhere over Normandy, behind enemy lines. He was scared and prayed a silent prayer. There were ten paratroopers in front of him and they had to get out. Now!

"Come on, move it," Walter Tait yelled, as he crowded up to the door.

The crippled aircraft was affectionately known as the "Gooney Bird" by the men in his outfit. But at this moment he thought, *this "Gooney Bird" is a dying bird*. He could taste the acrid smoke filling the cabin. The plane pitched at an awkward angle and he lost his balance. He steadied himself with a hand on each side of the door. The cold wind attacked his face. The sky was black and foreboding, lit up intermittently by shell bursts and fire balls. It was the last place he wanted to be at this moment, but it was his turn to step out. He reminded himself he had a job to do, *better to jump to uncertainty than die in a crippled airplane.* There was a standing joke among the men in his outfit; a person would have to be stupid to jump from a perfectly good airplane, but in this case, it was the prudent thing to do. Walter Tait stepped into the blackness. A moment of free-fall passed before he let out a sigh of relief as his parachute harness jerked against his torso. His freefall was reduced to the speed of a person leaping from a two-story building.

The darkness beneath him was broken by flashes of small arms fire. Even at this altitude he could hear the crack of rifles. There was a battle raging below. His commander had said they would take the Germans by surprise, but he was wrong. He was jumping into a firefight and until he landed he had no defense. The white parachute against the dark sky made him a perfect target.

As he sank toward the firefight below he could make out buildings, trees, and a church with spires. He barely managed to steer his parachute past the steeple and landed hard on the cobblestone street. He managed a summersault to ease the shock and got to his feet, facing the stone wall of the church. His back was to a graveyard.

He pulled in his chute and wrapped it up while assessing the chaotic scene around him. There was gunfire everywhere. He couldn't tell the enemy from his own men. He slipped into the dark shadow of the church and unclipped his Thompson machine gun. Above him he could see a paratrooper, apparently dead, dangling by the nylon cords of his parachute, caught on the very spire Tait had just managed to avoid. He stuffed his chute under the steps leading to a side door on the church. The air reeked of smoke and gunpowder. He needed to find cover. He climbed the steps and cautiously entered the side door of the church. The inside was dark except for the intermittent explosions of mortar rounds flashing through the blown out windows.

"You are American?" the voice of a woman whispered from the darkness within the church. She had a French accent.

He leveled the machine gun in her direction and, as his eyes adjusted to the darkness, he could see she was not wearing a uniform and lowered his weapon.

"Sergeant Walter Tait, 82nd Airborne." He saw a petite woman with a thin face, high cheekbones, and dark hair, in her mid-twenties. Her clothes were dirty and ragged, as if she had been on the run for awhile. He was startled by the unexpected nature of her presence, maybe it was a trap, either way they hadn't trained him for this. He needed to know if he could trust her, but before he could determine anything more than appearance, she spoke again.

"I am Adele de Savoy, part of the Resistance. You must come with me, we are not safe here."

"I need to join my unit," Walter Tait said.

"Your unit is under heavy fire. You can help them more if you come with me." Adele de Savoy grabbed his arm and led him behind the towering altar, pausing briefly to make the sign of the cross. She stopped in front of a marble casket. "Help me with this," the woman said, pushing on the ancient crypt.

He helped her slide the end of the coffin aside, revealing a trapdoor in the floor.

She pulled open the door and disappeared down a wooden ladder to a tunnel, and called up to him. "*Fermer la porte.* Close the door."

He climbed down the ladder and pulled the trapdoor shut. The tunnel was unlit and Adele de Savoy pulled a match from her pocket and struck it on the stone wall lining the hidden passageway. Tait could hear the faint sound of gunfire and feel the ground shake from heavy mortar fire. It looked as if the tunnel had been there from ancient times, perhaps an escape route. As they moved, hunched over along the dank passageway, the stench of human waste assaulted his nose. He followed the young woman, not knowing where he was headed or what he might face at the other end. It took less than a minute before she dropped the match, climbed another ladder, and lifted a hatch. She disappeared for a moment. He looked up and could see faint light. She appeared again.

"Hurry, we must move quickly."

Tait stuck his head through the opening and could see a room with stone walls like the church. When he was standing in the room, he saw there was a window with shattered glass and rusty iron bars, looking much like a jail cell. There were double wooden doors at one end and a polished wooden plank floor that seemed to magnify the sound of every footstep. He made a brief assessment of his surroundings. The room appeared to be some type of church or meeting room. There were four podiums, one centered on each wall. In the center of the room was a small table with a black cloth draped over it. Another mortar round burst outside causing his ears to hurt from the concussion.

Adele de Savoy went straight for the table, ripped the black cloth from it, and threw it to the floor. She lifted the table top. He could see it was the lid of a large chest. She reached inside.

A mortar shell hit the roof of the building in a deafening explosion and debris rained down from everywhere. Tait grabbed his helmet and hit the floor. He heard the girl scream and looked in the direction of the sound.

"*Dieu aide-moi, s'il vous plait!*" Adele de Savoy was trying to get up from the floor.

Tait did not understand French, but from the cry he knew she was injured and in a lot of pain. He rushed to help her, but she was already struggling to her feet. She had lost her right hand and with her good hand was gripping the chest for support. He grabbed her, but she shrugged him off.

"I must get the crucifix," she said.

He thought she was in shock and tried to reason with her. "You're injured; let me put a tourniquet on your arm."

She reached in the chest and pulled out a crucifix. It was made of wood about eight inches long and black. She handed it to him. "Take it with you. It is the Crucifix de Chapelle Chambery. Protect it and it will protect you."

As he took the crucifix, she collapsed at his feet. He tried to revive her, but she was dead. Another mortar round hit the far end of the building and the room burst into flames. He stuffed the crucifix inside the deep pocket of his fatigues and ran for the door. He cautiously pushed the muzzle of his machine gun through a crack in the door, saw three German soldiers backed up against the building and opened fire. He had joined the raging battle outside.

Now, sixty years later, he lay on the floor. *You will not get the Crucifix de Chappelel Chambery,* he promised himself.

As he lay bleeding, Walter Tait wondered what his life would have been like, had Adele de Savoy not taken him into her trust and given him the crucifix.

A sharp pain struck him like lightning and he gasped for breath when the Assassin's boot struck his side.

"Where is it, old man?" The Assassin yelled, kicking him in the side again.

Tait let out a moan and stirred. Although he was barely clinging to life he resolved to keep the whereabouts of the crucifix from the Assassin. He gritted his teeth each time the boot found its mark, but he did not answer. He would not speak, he would not breathe, and he would not give the man the satisfaction of finding what he came for. *So this is how you are going to take me Lord,* he prayed and a peace came over him. When the intruder finally left the room, the old man was certain he was close to death. *I have to let Daniel know.* Carefully, and with resolve to let his grandson know the secret, the old man dragged the palm of his hand through the pool of his blood on the hardwood floor and started writing a message.

Chapter 1

September Gale fluffed her short red hair, put on light lipgloss and took a final look in the mirror. She was wearing no makeup or eyeshadow, but her fine facial features, opal-green eyes, dimples, and hint of freckles, made it difficult to hide her natural beauty. The soft green suit jacket and matching slacks, silk scarf, and low heel shoes were not required attire, but preferable to a dress or skirt in the rough and tumble world of law enforcement.

From the first days as a detective at the Portland City Police Department, September had found it favorable to minimize her feminine appearance. Unlike her younger sister who could easily pass as a fashion model, September preferred plain and simple clothing, and was more comfortable in blue jeans and a sweatshirt than a dress and high heels. She was unlike her sister in other ways also. From an early age, she could be found on the school-ground playing football or kickball with the boys, instead of the more ladylike sports of jump rope and hopscotch. At twenty-eight, she had never been married and had yet to find a man she was comfortable enough with to date more than a few times, and marriage was not at all in her future plans.

September and her biological sister, Tiffany, were adopted before either could remember. September had bonded with her adoptive father and enjoyed fishing or sailing, while her sister liked nothing more than going shopping at the mall and wearing pretty dresses. When they were in college, Tiffany found a husband in a young archeology graduate student, while September went on to get her degree in Criminal Justice. The girls were opposites in nearly every way, but still they were sisters and were there for each other when needed. Today September was mentally prepared to sit with the family and engage in small talk. She could handle it; after all, she only had to endure it a few times a year.

Before she headed out the door she slipped a Beretta PX4 9MM handgun in her vest holster, and a back-up weapon, a Sig 239 9MM, in an ankle holster. She was on her way to her parents, house for Thanksgiving dinner, but never left without her protection. She checked her watch and was fine with the thirty-two minutes she had for the half-hour drive. She was in her Toyota Prius Hybrid and out of the parking lot of her east-side apartment, when she took a call over her hands free phone.

"Gale here," September answered.

"Sorry to bother you on Turkey Day, but there's a homicide at 4302 S.W. Crestline Dr. You're the one on call."

"No problem. I'm twenty minutes away."

September did a U-turn and headed across town. She called her parents and apologized. She had work to do. She let out a long sigh, as if a weight had been lifted from her.

In the tiny coastal town of Waldport, the morning had been gray and rainy, but the smell of the turkey roasting in the oven and the final preparations for a Thanksgiving meal promised a better end to the day than the way it had started. Daniel Tait stepped out of the shower and wiped the terrycloth towel across the rippling muscles of his stomach and along his muscular arms. He still had the physique of ten years earlier when he had played halfback in high school. As he combed his short, dark mahogany hair, he was still thinking about the e-mail he had received earlier that morning. *Was this what the digital age was coming to?* Elizabeth, his girlfriend of six months, would not be joining him, as they had planned. She had dumped him, on a holiday no less, and when his parents were expecting her for dinner.

The annual Thanksgiving dinner had been a tradition for the Tait family. They had been doing it for as long as Daniel could remember. He knew someday he would be expected to carry on the tradition, but he was two years shy of his thirtieth birthday and had yet to marry, let alone establish a home, and with the events of the morning, any hope of a wife or family seemed a distant dream. *What is it with me and women*, he wondered?

As an only child, Daniel Tait had a childhood many would envy. In high school, he was the star halfback and led his team to the 1A quarterfinals his junior year and to the State Championship his senior year. He was the class president and a 4.0 student. In high school he never had problems with girls, yet it seemed, as he entered college and later the workplace, good female companionship was getting harder to find. He had tried internet dating and it had always ended poorly. He was about to disappoint his mother again.

At his parents' house, he was under constant pressure to live his life as his parents had planned. It was why he had left home his first year in college. Since then, he'd only returned on major holidays. His parents had moved from Portland to Waldport shortly after he graduated from high school, so it wasn't like returning home when he visited. If at all possible, he filled in his family obligations over the phone. This trip to his parents was, however, supposed to be different. He felt it was time he introduced Elizabeth to them. But now it would just be the three of them again, and a hundred questions as to why Elizabeth wasn't there as he'd promised. It was getting so he would rather eat alone in a restaurant than face another day with his parents.

As the three of them sat down at the table, Daniel felt uneasiness in his gut. They bowed their heads and his father blessed the food as he always did. After the blessing Daniel looked up to the voice of his mother. *She didn't waste a second*, he thought.

"I wish you would shave that beard," Marian Tait said. "You're starting to look like a bum. Men don't wear beards any more."

"Mom, I've been wearing it this way for almost ten years. What makes you think I would shave it now?"

"Well, then, you should let it grow longer. You look like you forgot to shave this week. I think it's a sign of ..."

"It's okay, Son," His father interrupted. "I think it looks cool. It covers up that scar you got playing football in high school. I think it looks rather distinguished."

Daniel leaned back in his chair and rubbed the short dark beard. It was just past the point of being stubble and had turned to soft velvet, a length he had kept for several years to hide the scar his father had mentioned. It was an unsightly ell-shaped gash in his lower cheek, caused by an illegal tackle when his helmet had been ripped off and a dozen players piled on top of him. It had required thirty stitches. It was a bad day for him. The knee injury that accompanied the gash on his face required him to give up his athletic scholarship to Linfield College. At the time, he'd grown the beard for his high school sweetheart, who complained incessantly that the scar grossed her out. The romance had gone south after that, but the beard had remained. "I guess I could shave my neck," he said to his mother.

"Daniel, it's too bad Elizabeth couldn't be here this year," his mother said, passing a bowl of mashed potatoes.

Ignoring his mother, Daniel tried to change the subject. "I wish Grandpa was here, but he insisted the drive would be too much for him." He did not want to get into the details of his e-mail breakup with Elizabeth.

"Son, you know he's not welcome here," his father said. "You're a grown man, and if you want to spend time with him, it's your business, but you are not to bring him into this house."

Every year, from the time Daniel was old enough to drive, he had brought up the subject of his grandfather joining them, and every year his father had answered the same. This year Daniel had tried to talk his grandfather into making the trip with him and just showing up at the house, but his grandfather was as stubborn as his dad. It looked like his yearly attempt to resolve the family feud would forever be in vain.

"Daniel, you know that's not what I'm talking about," his mother said.

"Mom, why don't you come out and ask why Elizabeth isn't here?" He wondered why his mother expected him to read her mind. It was pretty obvious that Elizabeth was not there with him. He may as well tell the truth and get it over with. She would grill him relentlessly until she got the full story. "Liz and I broke up. She's in Hawaii or Mexico or somewhere with another guy, okay?" He had barely spilled the news when his cell phone rang and he anxiously answered it. "Daniel Tait here."

The voice on the phone was that of a young woman. "Mr. Tait, this is Detective Gale, Portland Police. We found your name listed as next-of-kin in Walter Tait's possessions."

"Walter is my grandfather. Is he okay?"

"I'm sorry to tell you this over the phone, but your grandfather was found dead this morning."

"That can't be. I saw him just last night."

"How soon can you come down to Central Station, we need you to answer some questions and identify the body."

"I'm in Waldport. I'll leave right now. Can you tell me what happened?" He felt his throat closing up. *Grandpa dead?*

There was a hesitation. "Mr. Tait, please ask for Detective Gale. How long do you think you'll be?"

"Three hours...I'll leave right now." Daniel hung up and pushed away from the table. His mother and father both stared at him. "Grandpa died last night. The police want to talk to me."

The look on his father's face was neutral. "I'd go with you, but...well, you know."

Daniel's mother got up from the table and hugged him. "I'm sorry, honey. I know how close you were to Walter. I'll fix you some turkey to take with you."

"That's okay. I'll get my things and be on my way." He ran up the narrow stairs to his bedroom. A small lamp dimly lit the room. Outside a break in the clouds showed the setting sun over the ocean. As he gathered his clothes and hurriedly stuffed them into a suitcase, he nearly broke down, but fought back the tears. *Grandpa was old; maybe too old.* He tried to remember his grandfather's age. *Was his last birthday 87 or 88?* Either seemed very old to him, especially when he considered the poor health of the man. *He lived a good life.*

He kissed his mother on the cheek and shook hands with his father. "I'll call and let you know what happened." He said the words, but knew his father felt little for the old man. He couldn't remember a civil conversation between his father and grandfather and the last time they had all been together was at his grandmother's funeral. Even that was awkward and he had to separate his dad and grandfather to prevent a fist fight from breaking out.

The trip from Waldport, along the Central Oregon Coast, to Portland was always a slow one. There are no freeways and the winding roads along the Pacific, while great for spectacular views, made the trip trying in bad weather. Daniel turned the radio up against the steady slap of the windshield wipers. He pushed his Jeep, going as fast as he dared in the wet weather on the curvy road. Already he was concerned that the trip might take longer than the three hours he had told the detective.

I can't believe he is dead, Daniel said, over and over in his mind. He thought about his meeting with his grandfather the night before. His grandfather had been in good spirits. He had not even considered the man might be dead in only a few hours. Maybe he took a fall or had a sudden heart attack or a massive stroke. Any of those things would be possible for a man his age. Tears came to his eyes; he wiped them away and concentrated on the road. Nightfall had come quickly and the headlights burned a narrow tunnel through the steady downpour. It was typical weather for this time of year; he might even see snow on the pass in the Van Duzer Corridor. He was traveling through a stretch of Highway 18, where the forest had been purchased by the State of Oregon to prevent logging. The Van Duzer Corridor was designated a Scenic Drive, but today was anything but scenic. The tall Douglas fir trees hugged the road, making it a narrow black ribbon with turns and twists that threatened to be too tight for modern day vehicles to take at highway speed. Daniel had driven the road many times, but this trip seemed unusually long. He was two hours into the trip when he finally entered the I-5 freeway at Salem.

"Damn you, Elizabeth Marten," Daniel said thinking out loud about the message left on his cell phone.

Daniel had met Elisabeth in a college study group at Oregon State. He had been immediately attracted to her, but she was in a serious relationship that she said would last forever. For two years they kept an arms-length friendship. They both graduated with engineering degrees and went separate ways, not to see each other for the next three years; but, as fate sometimes works, they ended up working at the same company, in different divisions, and their paths crossed again. They agreed to have coffee and when Elisabeth told him her college fling had ended and Daniel was between relationships, they decided to date. They had been dating six months and suddenly, out of the blue, she runs off with...maybe she was back with her ex. She was probably using him to get back at her former lover. As the thoughts rolled around in his head he became too depressed to be angry anymore. He was too good for her. If she wanted to run away with someone and leave him without so much as a "Sorry," then so be it.

Portland City Police Central was located on SW Second Avenue, three blocks from the Willamette River in downtown Portland. The building was an imposing, odd-shaped structure, stretching about twenty stories into the city skyline. The building housed the Justice Department and, on the 16th floor, the Portland City Police Museum. Daniel went through the security screening in the lobby and proceeded to the Detective Division and approached the receptionist, a uniformed officer busy talking into a headset. The officer looked up at Daniel.

"Daniel Tait to see Detective Gale," Daniel said, giving the officer his driver's license for identification.

The officer pointed to a young woman standing by a cubicle. The detective's name was prominently displayed on an engraved placard attached to the side of the cubicle. He read the sign, September Gale, Detective, Homicide. The Detective was talking on the phone and Daniel waited, trying to make sense out of why he was meeting with a homicide detective. His grandfather had been nearly bedridden. *Who would want to kill him?* He stared at the young woman. She wouldn't have fit into his workplace dressed in her business attire. The dress code at his company had been relaxed and engineers and office personnel weren't required to wear suits except on special occasions. He was surprised to see the detective on a holiday dressed in a business suit. She was medium height and had a slender, but athletic build. She ran her hand through her hair as she talked. He couldn't tell if it was a personal call or she was in trouble on the job, but she looked concerned. She glanced at Daniel and put a finger up letting him know it would only be a minute. Her eyes were alert and she had a small dimple in her cheek that showed when the corners of her lips turned up. It was hard not to stare. He sensed mystery about her. He had never met anyone named September, and with a last name of Gale, he imagined her parents were free spirits, or at least had a sense of humor. At one time he had heard that the name of a person could influence their personality. If so, he might expect September to have a feisty personality with enough power to wreak havoc. *Was September really her first name?* Now that he thought about it, she did look like September, that time of the year when the season was starting to change and fall was approaching. He was still lost in thought when she spoke to him.

"Mr. Tait." She stretched out her hand to greet him. "I'm Detective Gale. You can call me September, if you wish. I'm sorry to interrupt your holiday."

"You're a homicide detective?" Daniel asked. "Was my grandfather murdered?"

"Follow me, Mr. Tate. I need to show you something."

They went into a rectangular-shaped room with pale green walls and a large white board, which was covered with crime scene photos and a dozen sticky notes. In the center of the room was a table with several manila file folders stacked on one end. Two chrome-trimmed chairs were on opposite sides of the table.

September went directly to the marker board and pulled off a picture. "This is how we found your grandfather after receiving a 9-1-1 call early this afternoon." She handed the photo to Daniel.

"Who found him?" Daniel asked taking the photo.

"Meals on Wheels became concerned when Walter Tait didn't answer his door." She pointed to another picture on the board.

Daniel's jaw dropped. He saw the man he had respected and loved all his life, dressed only in his underwear, lying face down in a pool of blood. His arms were stretched out over his head. Daniel couldn't tell from the photo that it was his grandfather, but he recognized the room and furnishings. He saw the statue of the Virgin Mary his grandfather always kept on the nightstand, broken on the floor, and recognized the distinctively carved headboard of the bed. Daniel couldn't hold it in any longer and burst into tears. "Who would do this? He was a helpless old man. Who would want to kill him?"

"That's what we want to find out," the detective said. "Was your grandfather a member of a cult or any religious organization?"

"No, he was nearly bedridden. He could barely make it to church on Sunday."

"What church?"

"Saint Clare Catholic Church. He's been a member for a long time. You think this is connected to the Church?"

September Gale let out a sigh and picked up another photo. She stared at it for a moment and set it on the table. "I think we need to visit the crime scene so you can get a better feel for what we're dealing with, but first you'll have to answer some questions. Mind you, this is strictly routine. We'll also need a statement from you as to your whereabouts last night."

"A statement? What kind of statement?" Daniel noticed that he stood a good head taller than the young detective.

"Mr. Tait, may I call you Dan?"

"My friends call me Daniel, that would do just fine," Daniel said. "Is your name really September?"

She smiled at him and Daniel saw a dimple in each cheek and a pretty mouth. He was disarmed immediately.

"I was born in September, but it was near the end of the month. Thank God I wasn't born in October." She motioned toward a chair. "Have a seat and we'll get this over with. I'm afraid it's a necessary process, but it should be painless. No waterboarding or any eyeball gouging." She laughed and it came out almost a giggle.

Daniel sat and leaned his elbows on the table looking across at her. She set a small digital recorder on the table. "Aren't you supposed to read me my rights?" he asked.

"If we were booking you, we would need to do that. I'm assuming you are a willing participant in this investigation. Am I correct?"

Daniel sat back in his chair. "Why wouldn't I be? Okay, let's get this over with."

September had already read the sheet on Daniel Walter Tait and thumbed through it while she asked him questions. The Tait family had moved from Boston twenty years earlier. Daniel had gone to Duke Grade School on the east side of town and attended Marshall High School. He was active in school politics and sports and was class president his senior year. He had earned a football scholarship to Linfield College, but after losing the scholarship to an injury the last game of his senior year, decided to attend Oregon State in Corvallis. He graduated fifth in his class with a BS in Mechanical Engineering. Hardly the profile of a murderer, but she was paid to be suspicious. She continued to ask questions for another two hours.

Chapter 2

The Assassin dreaded answering the phone in his small motel room. He had been waiting for the call and had rehearsed what he would say at least a dozen times. The Grand Master was not one to lie to, but what else could he do? He had failed to get the item they sought. The old man was too feeble and had died before speaking of the crucifix. He had ransacked the house looking for its whereabouts and could not find any evidence of the cross. He would now have to look elsewhere. He was deep in thought and it startled him when the phone rang.

"*Qui.*" The Assassin answered.

"*Vous êtes Amérique, parlent l'anglais.*" The Grand Master said. "You are in America, speak English. Do you have news?"

The Assassin hated the English language and didn't understand why the Grand Master insisted on speaking English when he was talking to a Frenchman, but he didn't dare question him. "The old man is dead and I have no information concerning the relic, but he has family who will tell me."

"I have called on our Portland Chapter to assist. A man named John Fleming will help."

"But Grand Master, I need no help." *Why do those in power insist on helping when they have not the slightest idea whether I need help or not?*

"Do not be a fool. This is too important. It was a stroke of good fortune that we found out about the whereabouts of the Chambery Crucifix and you have killed the only person who knew precisely where it was. John Fleming will be contacting you."

The Assassin heard the phone go dead. He didn't like being at odds with the Grand Master. He was a powerful man, and his power stretched across the oceans to nearly every nation on the planet. Though he was upset, he was upset with himself, not the Grand Master. He would gladly give his life for the man who had raised him from the time he was a small child. Through many years and countless sessions, the Grand Master had taught him the rituals and the history of the organization. Without the Grand Master he would have been lost to the back streets of Paris and surely a death from drugs and crime. He would forever be grateful to serve the Grand Master. He was like a father to him, the only father he had ever known.

Chapter 3

Still tired from a restless night's sleep, Daniel Tait stood in the driveway of his grandfather's house in the Burlingame area of Portland. His grandfather had purchased the house right after the family had moved to Portland. His grandparents had been retired several years when they moved to Portland to be with the family. Daniel was not yet old enough for school at the time. The house was a Forties vintage brick structure with a sharply-pitched cedar shake roof. A detached two-car garage did double duty as his grandfather's woodworking shop. Several century-old oak trees stretched their branches out across a large front lawn giving shade in the summer, but in the dreary morning light looked like dark ganglion monsters rising from a sea of brown leaves. For the past several years he had looked after his grandfather; visited him every day and on weekends helped to keep the place up, but it had become an impossible task with his job as an aerospace engineer and his frequent trips to Europe to assist company sales personnel. He wondered what would become of the place now that his grandfather was dead.

Yellow crime scene tape was attached to a sawhorse and stretched across the driveway all the way to the front door of the house. Daniel debated ducking under it, but had second thoughts and waited for Detective Gale to show up. He checked his watch. She was late. A few raindrops hit him and he looked up to see a dark cloud blocking out the last remnants of blue sky.

Earlier that morning, Detective September Gale woke with a start. She was gasping for air and covered in a cold sweat. Usually murder cases didn't get to her, but she had not been able to put the old man's death out of her mind. He had been murdered in a particularly gruesome way. The shot to his side had severed a blood vessel that supplied blood to the right kidney and Walter

Tait had bled out slowly. It had the look of a ritual murder and, if it hadn't been for the blood on Walter Tait's hand and the position of the body, she would have assumed as much when she'd first seen the crime scene. But the coroner had said it had taken over thirty minutes for the old man to die, and with the fingerprints in the lettering, the conclusion was the writing had occurred as the life was ebbing from Walter Tait. Still she couldn't get past the thought that the murderer could have used the victims hand to send the police in a false direction. She had taken the time to search for any other crimes that fit the MO, but had found nothing. For now she was searching for someone who wanted something and was willing to kill for it. The condition of the house told her the killer, more than likely, had not found what he was looking for and would probably be back. In her dream, the killer had returned; that was the nightmare that had startled her from a sound sleep.

Seeing that it was early and she was wide awake, September decided to attend morning Mass at Saint John's in Milwaukie. The service went longer than anticipated and she was running late for her appointment with Daniel Tate. On the way to the crime scene she contemplated her meeting the night before with Tait. Even though Daniel Tait had an alibi and appeared shocked at the scene, it wouldn't be the first time a person with a clean record committed a heinous crime against a family member. Daniel Tait was the only member of the family who had a motive and opportunity. They had found a copy of his grandfather's will and Daniel Tait was to receive the entire estate, that alone was enough for some to commit murder. She would have to remember to find out more about the handsome engineer and his relationship with his grandfather. She pulled her unmarked police issue Dodge Charger into the driveway and saw Daniel Tait was waiting.

Daniel heard a vehicle pull in the driveway behind him and turned to see Detective Gale, in an unmarked white Dodge, pull up beside his Jeep. She stopped just short of the crime scene tape which crossed the driveway a few feet in front of the garage.

Detective Gale got out of her car and walked toward him. "Sorry I'm late. I hope you haven't been waiting long."

Daniel looked at his watch again. "Three minutes and twenty-seven seconds, but who's counting. You know it's starting to rain." He saw she was dressed in a light-gray business suit with loose fitting slacks and black penny loafers. She had a flowered silk scarf over her head and removed it as she approached him.

"Come on, let's get inside," September said, lifting the crime tape. Daniel ducked underneath and followed her to the front door.

Inside, Daniel surveyed the mess in the living room and turned to September. "Did the murderer do this?"

"It's just like we found it. The body has been removed, of course." She handed him a pair of latex gloves. "Put these on."

"Was it a burglary?" Daniel asked, looking around. From where he stood in the entry he could see the living room on the right, beyond that the dining room and a portion of the kitchen, on the left was a hallway leading to three bedrooms. Daniel had once stayed in the house for a week when his grandfather had come down with Asian flu. He thought he had lost him then. "Is it all right to enter?"

"Don't touch anything, but if you see something of interest let me know. This may be difficult for you, but I want you to see where we found him." She started down the hallway. The soles on her shoes squeaked on the hardwood floor. She pushed open the door to the bedroom and took a few steps inside.

Daniel stood in the doorway. The large ornate bed was a mess. His grandfather's oxygen mask was on the floor. There was an outline of where the body had been on the floor and the picture of his grandfather sprawled on the floor in a pool of blood flashed in his head. The blood stains were dark and nearly all dried.

September moved to avoid some small flag markers on the floor and went to the far side of the room. She pointed to the bed. "Your grandfather was on the bed. The gunman was over here. He fired at near point-blank range as your grandfather rolled off the bed to get away." She looked at Daniel's face to see how he reacted.

She walked around the bed to where the heavy pools of blood had congealed. "Look at the floor under the bed and tell me what you make of it."

Daniel moved beside her and looked at where she was pointing. "What am I looking for?"

She removed a penlight from her jacket pocket and shined it under the bed. Daniel crouched down, then got on his hands and knees, taking care not to kneel in the blood. He looked up at September and she handed him the light. He shined it on the floor and saw what she was referring to. Beyond the outstretched outline of his grandfather's arm, far from the big pools of blood, nearly hidden under the bed, were additional blood stains. He had not been shown a picture of this. There were words written on the floor in blood, but the words didn't make sense. "I think it says "Adele de Savoy" with an asterisk."

"Does it mean anything to you?" September asked.

"It might be the name of someone." Daniel got up and handed the flashlight back to September. "Can I borrow a piece of paper and a pen? I want to write it down."

She ripped off a page from her notebook and handed it to him. "I've already written it down. What does it mean?"

"You got me. It looks French. Are you sure it isn't someone's name?"

September shook her head. "I ran a search and we can't find anyone with that name. Maybe it's a place. Was your grandfather associated with anyone from France?"

Daniel shook his head. "As far as I know he hasn't been out of the country since World War Two."

"Your grandfather was dying, face down in a pool of his own blood, and he writes something on the floor and it doesn't mean anything to you?" Her tone was incredulous.

Daniel shook his head again. "I told you it doesn't mean anything. I can't imagine why he would write something that wasn't important. I'm just saying I don't know what it means. Maybe it's the name of the person who murdered him."

They both turned when they heard a knock at the front door.

"CIA," a man's voice said, and they went out to the hallway to see a tall man with his credentials held out in front of him.

"You're a little out of your jurisdiction," September said approaching him. She took his credentials and studied them.

"I'm here unofficially. I have a few questions for Daniel Tait."

"I'm Daniel Tait," Daniel said approaching the man. "You are?"

The man put away his ID and offered his hand. "Agent John Fleming, Portland office, CIA."

"I still want to know why you're at my crime scene," September said.

"When we got word of the murder we thought it might have been committed by a foreigner. We think this may be a murder with international significance." Fleming gave her just enough information to pique her interest.

"Excuse me," September said. "We have a murder in the jurisdiction of the Portland City Police. How does that affect the international community?"

The CIA Agent towered over the Detective and was even taller than Daniel. The way he held his shoulders back and raised his head made him even more of an imposing sight. He spoke with a deep, authoritative tone. "Walter Tait may have been involved in drug smuggling. That's all I'm at liberty to say. I can get the FBI in here, too, if you want."

"Whatever," September said, shaking her head and backing off. "We don't know what's going on anyway. Maybe you can shed some light on it."

"Just a minute," Daniel protested. "My grandfather was an old man. He wasn't involved in anything illegal, domestic or international. He was on oxygen. He could hardly talk. He had to have oxygen just to walk across the room. You've got your poker in the wrong fire if you think he was involved in anything other than trying to live out his life in peace."

"I'll tell you what I know," September said ignoring Daniel's outburst. "The body was found down here." She went down the hall to the bedroom.

"I heard he left a clue on the floor," Agent Fleming said.

September put up her hand and stopped the agent at the door to the room. "Who has been sharing information about my case with you?"

"Lieutenant Terrell Gordon, ring a bell?" Fleming asked, smiling. Terrell Gordon was the Portland City Police division Chief and September's boss.

"I'm glad to see we have such good communication between agencies," September said. She handed him a pair of gloves, turned around and let him enter the bedroom. She pulled out her tablet. "Walter Tait wrote "Adele de Savoy" on the floor under the bed. It was written in his own blood, so we thought it might mean something. Mr. Tait seems to think it's French."

"Actually, it's Italian, but you'd find that out with a little research."

"Okay, what does it mean?"

The agent got down on his hands and knees and looked under the bed. He got up. "I'm not sure. There was a royal family in Italy who were the descendents of the Duke of Savoy at one time. They lost power around the time of the Second World War. Maybe that will help." He reached in his shirt pocket, pulled out a business card, and handed it to Daniel. "When you're finished here, I'd like for you to stop by the office. It's the holiday, so I'd appreciate a call first to make sure I'm in."

Daniel took the card. At this moment he had no intention of calling. The man seemed arrogant and condescending, and he'd had enough questions without trying to answer a bunch more from the CIA. Besides, Fleming's contention that his grandfather was involved in drugs was so far out in left field that it didn't merit his cooperation.

September followed the agent down the hall. "You mean to tell me you know about some Italian person who kills like this?"

"I did my research, but couldn't find a killer with this MO; don't bother trying to make sense of it. We have the best computer people in the world and it doesn't make sense to us."

"If you knew that, why come here?" September still didn't feel comfortable with the CIA in the middle of her case.

"I thought you may have learned something from the family. Give me a call if I can be of help." He walked across the lawn and got into his car, a metallic blue Dodge Durango and backed into the street.

"That's strange," September said to Daniel. "He isn't driving a Company car."

Daniel didn't know what to make of her comment.

After he left his grandfather's house, Daniel went to the morgue to identify the body and spent the rest of the afternoon making funeral arrangements. He had never been through the process before and found there were, what seemed like, another thousand questions concerning his grandfather. The more questions he was asked, the more he realized how little he knew about Walter Tait. He called his father hoping to get more details.

"Dad, what do you know about Catholic funerals?" Daniel asked.

There was a long pause at the other end. "Son, why don't you save yourself a lot of grief? Cremate him and give him a secular burial or pour his ashes in the Ganges, if that makes sense to you. He didn't warrant a Christian burial, at least in my opinion."

"Dad, how can you say that? Grandpa went to church every day of his life."

"Going to church doesn't make you a Christian."

Daniel decided to cut the conversation short. The last thing he needed was another lecture about true Christians and how his grandfather didn't qualify. "Are you and Mom coming to the funeral?"

"You don't need us to put him in the ground. You can handle it, son."

Daniel let out a long sigh. "Tell Mom I love her." He hung up.

He called St. Clare Church and found they had a person who knew his grandfather, and would take care of all the arrangements for a Catholic funeral and a proper burial. It was a relief to him. Daniel had never considered himself to be a spiritual person, but at least he knew his grandfather would want to be buried in a cemetery with like-believers, now he hoped his checkbook would hold out long enough so he wouldn't have to file for bankruptcy when it was over.

The funeral mass was scheduled for Wednesday at St. Clare's Catholic Church in the West Hills. Daniel felt conspicuous as the only person in the front pew. His parents refused to set foot in a Catholic church for any reason and his father's longstanding feud with his grandfather could not even be broken by death. To his surprise the church was nearly full and several people spoke of how his grandfather had touched their lives. There was even a teenager who stood at the podium and spoke of how Walter Tait had changed his life. This was all a life his grandfather had led that Daniel was not familiar with.

At the graveside ceremony a dozen members of the local VFW held a ceremony to bid their brother farewell. Daniel was touched by the love of those who knew his grandfather. To Daniel it added to the mystery of the man. As the casket was lowered into the ground he vowed to find out who the man really was and why he had been murdered. As the small crowd dispersed and Daniel started to walk across the grounds toward his car, he felt a hand on his shoulder and expected it to be another well-wisher, but turned to see the smiling face of the priest who had presided over the ceremony.

"I'm sorry for your loss. I'm Richard Hays, your grandfather's minister."

"You're Father Hays," Daniel said. "I met you about ten years ago. My grandfather thought highly of you."

"I wanted to express my condolences. We will all miss Walter."

"Thank you for the beautiful service. Mrs. Westcott took care of everything. My grandfather would have been very happy with the service."

"I will leave you to your grief, but I just wanted you to know that I'm available anytime if you need to talk."

Daniel looked at the priest and couldn't help but smile. The man had an infectious smile and a compassionate face, and in spite of his thinning gray hair, Daniel could feel the energy radiating from him. He could see why his grandfather liked the man. "That's kind of you."

Fr. Hays handed Daniel a card. "My personal number is on here in case I'm not in the office."

Daniel stuffed the card in his pocket and thanked Fr. Hays again. Before he got to his car he stopped again as he heard his name called.

September Gale ran to catch up with him. "Mr. Tait, hold up a minute."

Daniel was surprised to see her at the funeral. He watched her awkward gait in high heels running across the cemetery lawn. He guessed she didn't wear them often.

"I wanted to let you know we'll get the person responsible," she said.

"Thanks," Daniel said. "I know you're working on it."

"I got a call from Agent Fleming this morning. He said you haven't called him."

Daniel shrugged.

"I know this isn't a good time," September said. "When you're free I'd like to buy you coffee. I'm hoping you can help me with the case."

"I'm going home and change," Daniel said. "How about I fix you coffee at my place?"

September checked her watch.

Daniel, sensing a hesitation added, "Or, if you'd rather, I can meet you somewhere else."

"Actually your place will be fine," September said. She lifted her phone. "I've got to call in."

The apartment complex Daniel called home was in the West Hills overlooking the city. He had already slipped into a pair of blue jeans and a black-and-orange Beaver's sweatshirt when he heard September at the door.

"It's open," he called from the kitchen.

September walked in and looked around as she came through the carpeted living room. "Engineers must get paid well," she said looking around. There were large picture windows looking over the Willamette River. Mount Hood, covered with snow, was visible under high clouds in the distance. "Must be pretty at night."

"Four years at Oregon State and another four years at the foundry. This was a present to *me* when I paid off my student loans. May I take your coat?"

September was still wearing the full length, black nylon, overcoat she'd been wearing at the funeral. He was surprised to see she was wearing a black dress and a light-gray silk scarf. He had assumed she had attended the funeral as part of her official responsibilities.

"You're off duty today?" Daniel asked taking her coat.

"I took funeral leave; part of the perks working for the City."

Daniel draped her coat over the back of a chair at the kitchen table. "Have a seat." He poured two cups of coffee and offered one to her. He sat down across from her and opened a laptop computer. "I've been doing a little research on the puzzle my grandfather left." Earlier she had been wearing the scarf over her head, but now it was draped gracefully around her neck. He thought she was quite striking out of her business attire.

"You found something interesting?" she asked, sitting across from him.

"I'm not sure," Daniel said. "I found Savoy and, sure enough, it was like Fleming said. They were royalty in Italy until after the Second World War. There also is an area of France with the same name only spelled SAVOIE."

"Was Adele de Savoy royalty?"

"I couldn't find anything on her, but The House of Savoy goes back to the 11th century. It controlled a small section of Europe between France and Italy. I can't figure how my grandfather would have anything to do with them. Our family is Anglo-Saxon. Tait means 'bright.'" Daniel smiled. "Actually, my great-grandfather came here from Ireland."

"Bright, I can see that," September said. "So Mr. Bright, what else have you found out?"

"I know you probably thought of this, but if you were dying why would you go to the trouble to make an asterisk unless it was important?"

"For emphasis, I guess so we would be sure to check out the word."

"That's what I thought, too, but what if it's a symbol? What if it has a bigger meaning, a clue for us, but one my grandpa didn't want the murderer to understand?"

"With that imagination, you're going to make a bigger mystery out of this than it already is. Why wouldn't an asterisk be just an asterisk?" September sipped at her coffee waiting for him to come up with more, but Daniel fell silent and typed on his computer.

"We've been through his things, believe me. If there was something with the word Savoy in it we would have found it."

"Did you find the hidden safe," Daniel said, eyeing her for any hint of surprise.

"Safe? Your grandfather had a safe?"

"I'd heard him speak of a safe, but I don't have any idea where it's located. Can we go back and spend some time there?" Daniel asked. "Maybe we can find it."

Chapter 4

Agent Fleming turned off the headlights and pulled his metallic blue Durango behind the warehouse in the industrial district along the Willamette River. The area was secluded this time of night. The silence was occasionally broken by the rumble of a slow moving train and the wind whistling through overhead power lines. From his vantage point he could see the Assassin approaching in a Hertz rental car.

The Assassin pulled up to Fleming with his car pointed in the opposite direction of Fleming; their driver's side windows were no more than a foot apart. He lowered his window and Fleming did the same.

"Turn off your headlights," Fleming said.

The Assassin turned off his headlights, and they were in darkness with only the soft glow of the city across the river providing background light. "Brother Fleming, have you got good news, I hope?"

Fleming had been surprised when he'd received the call from the Grand Master. It had been several years since he had spoken to him personally. He didn't like using his position in the CIA to help solve a problem that was clearly outside the scope of his official duties, but when the Grand Master asked you to do something, it was not wise to refuse. "The Detective and Tait are going back to the house to look for a safe. I'm surprised you did not find it in your initial visit."

The Assassin lit a cigarette, took a long drag, and blew out a cloud of smoke. "A safe? This is interesting. I found no safe. How do you know this?"

"I've got this nifty laser listening device. We might as well let them find it," Fleming said. He waved a hand in front of his face. "Can you blow that smoke in another direction?"

The Assassin ignored Fleming's request and exhaled another cloud of smoke toward him. "But the Grand Master is getting impatient. We should go find it ourselves."

"Patience is a virtue, even for the Grand Master. If we tail them from a distance they will lead us to the crucifix."

"You Americans do things in a strange way. I could get the information much faster my way. A bullet in the right place and they will talk."

Fleming raised his voice. "Like the bullet you put in the old man? You are not in France; get used to doing it my way."

The Assassin removed the cigarette from his mouth and crushed it on the side of the car before flicking it to the ground. "You will place bugs on both of them?"

"Too risky. I only have a bug in Tait's vehicle. I don't expect the detective to be much help. Daniel Tait seems to want to get to the bottom of this as much as we do."

"But knowing his grandfather died for the object, he may want to keep it for himself."

"Then we kill him," Fleming said. "Give it a few days and we'll watch this play out."

The Assassin lit another cigarette. "My brother, I am not joking when I say this is too long. The Grand Master desires the crucifix for the reopening of the Grand Lodge in Sainte-Mère-Eglise."

"We'll do it my way," Fleming said, raising his window. He was halfway across the deserted lot before he turned on his headlights. "Damned French are all alike. They'd be speaking German if it wasn't for us, and they come over here expecting to make a mess and have me clean it up. It ain't gonna happen."

It had been a full week since Daniel Tait had first found out about his grandfather's death. He had been wrestling with the grizzly vision of his grandfather sprawled on the floor and couldn't imagine the effort he had gone through to leave the message in his blood. He tried to put his mind into that of his grandfather. Why would he write something unimportant if he knew he was dying?

The answer, of course, was he wouldn't. Whatever was written on the floor had profound significance. He had to break the code. As an engineer, he had been taught to solve problems in a methodical manner, break each part of the problem into its simplest element, and carefully piece the puzzle together, but this was a tough one. He was dealing with elements he didn't understand. He felt like his hands were tied. He needed more information than a few pictures and a few words, and he wasn't even certain what the clues were supposed to lead to. Was Adele de Savoy the person who had killed him? What was the significance of the asterisk? Why would a dying man paint an asterisk on the floor in his own blood? The questions kept turning over in his mind as he drove toward his grandfather's house. He felt the asterisk was more significant than they had first given it credit, but what that significance was, he didn't have a clue.

He was surprised to see Detective Gale was already in the house when he arrived. She met him at the door.

"You haven't been in here since we talked yesterday, have you?" September asked.

"Good morning to you, too," Daniel said. "We agreed to meet today. What's the problem?"

"Someone broke in and ransacked the place. They turned the bed over and slashed the mattress. They even broke through the plaster in the walls. You didn't mention the safe to anyone did you?"

Daniel looked at her and shook his head. "I'm not sure I like your tone. You think I would ransack my grandfather's house. Why would I do that?"

"Maybe you know something you're not telling me."

"There you go again, blowing steam out of your butt. You don't have the slightest idea what you're talking about. Find someone else to beat on." Daniel turned and walked back toward his car. He heard September calling after him, but ignored her. He got in his car, started the engine, and put the Jeep in reverse. September caught up with him and started pounding on the car as he was backing up. Before he had reached the end of the driveway she was on the hood of the car with her gun drawn, pointing it at the windshield.

"Stop, police!" she yelled at him.

Daniel hit the brakes and the Detective slid toward the windshield and rolled off the side and landed hard on the driveway. He was fuming. Why would she think he would do something to hurt the investigation? Daniel turned off the engine and took a deep breath. He could see she wasn't hurt and was glad for that, but what kind of a maniac was he dealing with? Daniel got out and helped her to her feet. "Are you completely nuts?" He jumped back in the Jeep, before she could answer.

September dusted herself off. She put her gun away and came up to his window and motioned for him to roll it down.

"Roll down the window," September said.

Daniel lowered the window and glared at her.

"I'm sorry, it was a stupid move on my part, but I had to make sure you weren't playing games. If you didn't do that to the house, then we have bigger problems."

"Really?" Daniel wasn't buying her lame excuse for confronting him. "My grandfather was murdered and we have bigger problems?"

"Whoever killed your grandfather didn't find what they were looking for," September said. "The murderer has come back."

"For what?" Daniel asked, still fuming.

"That's what I need you to help me find out."

Daniel got out of the car again. He kept his distance from her. "You're wrong about me," Daniel said as they walked back toward the house.

"I said I was sorry," September said. "I had to make sure."

"Hold up a minute," Daniel said. She stopped and he caught up with her and looked in her eyes. "We need to do this together. My grandfather left a clue that he thought I could solve, but I'm finding out I didn't know my grandfather as well as I thought. What's worse, I didn't know him as well as he hoped." Daniel felt his throat tighten as he said the words and knew he had to quit talking before he began to cry, and he didn't want to do that in front of her.

"I'd like for us to work together on this," September said. "My interest only lies with your grandfather's murder. If the murderer was searching for something, it's in both of our interests to find out what it is."

"I don't care what it is the murderer is looking for, it can't be worth killing for." Daniel said.

September started walking toward the house. "Your grandfather may not agree with you. He didn't give up the information or the murderer wouldn't have come back."

Daniel joined her. Neither was aware of the car parked down the street and the man watching them.

"They really did make a mess," Daniel said looking at the overturned furniture and the drawers dumped on the floor. "Logic tells me he's looking for something that is not too large, maybe a foot or so long."

"What kind of logic can you make of this mess?" September asked curiously.

"Well whoever did this cut openings in the chair back and pillows. That tells me whatever he's after is small enough to fit inside of them."

"What about the holes in the walls? It looks like they used a wrecking bar on the place."

"Isn't this supposed to be your job? I didn't tell anyone we were going to look for a safe. I think someone took out their frustration on the walls, kind of like my buddy Dick when we play golf and he makes a bad drive."

September tilted her head sideways and gave him a disgusted look. "This is a lot more serious than a bad day on the links."

"Sorry, bad analogy, but someone is just as stumped as we are, and that's good, right?"

"You mean maybe the perp will make a mistake?"

"Sure, overplay his hand because things are not going his way, kind of like---"

"Not another sports analogy. Let's get this over with. Where was your grandfather's safe?"

They walked into the bedroom and saw the overturned mattress which had been ripped open with a knife. Daniel stood the mattress on edge and started to put the box springs back on the bed frame when he saw something he had missed. He bent down and looked at the floor under the bed. "Have you seen this?"

September looked at where he was pointing. "Now this is beginning to get my goat," she said taking a picture with her cell phone. When she saw the smudged writing did not show up on the digital image she pulled out a penlight. "Douse the lights," she said.

"What's that?" Daniel asked.

"It's a black light." She placed the light source close to the floor. "Can you make it out?"

"I think it says "gods", or "G-O-D-S". My grandfather was crying out for help."

"Maybe," September said. "My forensic team missed this. I'm going to have a word with them," September said lifting her cell phone.

Daniel stared at the floor. Adele de Savoy, an asterisk, and G-O-D-S, it must have taken a dying man a lot of effort to write these things. He had run out of blood for the last letters and GODS was written in smudges of blood and dust. None of it made any sense to him. Maybe his grandfather was having a senior moment, and it was all meaningless babble. When September hung up the phone Daniel turned to her. "I'm not certain my grandfather had a safe. He might have said, 'safe place'. I could have been mistaken."

Outside, across the street, the Assassin hit the dashboard with his fist. The bugs he had planted in the house were working perfectly, but he had missed the message on the floor and it could mean things would have to happen much faster. He would have to tell the Grand Master the organization had been exposed.

Chapter 5

The Grand Master stood at his fourth story office window overlooking the quaint village of Sainte-Mère-Eglise. He looked out toward the church which had been heavily damaged in the war, but had long-since been restored. Below him on the ground floor was the lodge room he had restored to its former splendor, recreated to the exact look of the past using family photos taken before the war. It had been a labor of love for the Grand Master and the fulfillment of a promise made to his dying grandfather. Now with the restoration complete, he reflected on the history of the order and contemplated the resurgence to power the Grand Orient de Savoy would see once the relic was returned. *GODS is not a cult*, he mused, recalling the criticism the press had given his order throughout the ages after the order split from the Grand Orient de France. GODF, as the French Free Masons was known, disavowed GODS in the 16th century after a bitter schism within the ruling House of Savoy. To the Grand Master, GODS was the true order. After all, they had a direct line of descendents to The Duchy de Savoy. The other members of the House of Savoy that had remained loyal to Rome and the Catholic Church had given up the throne and were no longer relevant. They had proven their weakness when they moved the Holy Shroud to Turin and later surrendered it to the Holy See.

The Grand Master frowned and turned back to his desk and picked up the e-mail from Walter Tait that had been printed in the local paper. He had read the letter a hundred times and his heart beat faster each time he read the words. The crucifix had been found and its secrets were still not known to the possessor of the holy object.

When his cell phone rang the Grand Master was suddenly back in the reality of the day. The retrieval of the crucifix had not been as easy as he had imagined. He looked at the name on his phone and answered.

"Hello."

"I am sorry that I have bad news. We have been exposed," the Assassin said. "The old man left the organization's initials written on the floor."

"Then you must act quickly and without mercy," the Grand Master said.

"You mean...."

"Do what you have to do. The crucifix must not stay in America. Find it and return it to its proper place."

The Assassin disconnected his phone and got out of the car. The bugs he had planted within the Tait house had helped him to hear all that was going on, but he had no way of tracking them when they were not in the house. He would have to bug Daniel Tait if he wanted to know what was going on at all times. To do this he must get close to the young man.

September Gale was having a caramel latte while she waited for her sister to arrive at a Starbucks in the Washington Square Mall Shopping Center in southwest Portland. She had promised her sister she would help her with some early Christmas shopping for their parents. Tiffany Gale was her only sibling. Henry and Susan Gale had adopted the two when they were both toddlers and they had always been close. When Tiffany had married, September felt she had lost her best friend, so after the wedding, they made a pact to never let their lives keep them apart. In truth it was becoming increasingly more difficult for them to meet, and they had to plan their meetings weeks in advance. As the years moved on, it also became more difficult to find things in common to talk about. The two, who had once been as inseparable as Siamese Twins, were struggling to keep close. September saw Tiffany forging her way through the crowded mall and closed her laptop as she reached the table.

"I got you what I'm drinking," September said, handing her a cup.

"I hope you haven't been waiting too long. I hate the traffic this time of year. Everyone off work and all the kids out of school, I don't remember it being this bad when we were young. Do you?" Tiffany removed the top from her latte and took a sip. "It's cold. You have been waiting. I'm sorry, I lost track of time. Have you been thinking about a present for Pops?"

September smiled. Tiffany had always been the talkative one in the family. She let her talk herself out before trying to answer. "I was thinking about a watch, maybe one of the atomic ones that never need a battery and keep the precise time."

Tiffany nodded her head. "I didn't know they made such a thing. I was thinking about a wool blazer with a silk scarf. Something to make a statement at the Coast Guard Ball."

"That would work, too," September said.

"What's wrong? Aren't you feeling well?"

"I'm fine. I've just got a lot on my mind. Maybe we could each buy our own presents this year." September ticked her head to the side and waited to see what Tiffany's reaction would be.

"Now I'm sure something is wrong. Have you met a man? That's it, you have a boyfriend."

"Sorry to disappoint you. I'm working on a case that has me preoccupied."

Tiffany reached over and put her hand on her sister's arm. "September, you really need to take some time off from your job. There's more to life than work. Mom and Pops were devastated that you didn't show for Thanksgiving."

"I'm just thinking, if I can spend some more time on this I could clear it up before the holiday."

"Is there anything I can do to help?" Tiffany seemed genuinely concerned.

"Unless you can figure out why an old man would write an asterisk on the floor in his own blood, I doubt you could be of much help."

"It must be awful to have to look at those dead bodies and deal with all the lowlife in the world. I don't understand why you do it."

September smiled again. Her sister had never really had a full time job in her life. A year out of high school, she had met her future husband while attending a lecture on anthropology. She wasn't interested in anthropology, only in the instructor, who she soon married. Maybe her husband would be able to help, but Tiffany...she was a study of human behavior all by herself. "I really need to do this another time. I'll buy my own presents this year."

"Okay, now I'm really getting worried," Tiffany said.

September got up from the table and put her laptop in its case. "I'm sorry little sister, but I have to go to work. I'll call you next week. Maybe we can wrap presents together."

Tiffany pushed her chair back and stood. "I guess I don't have a vote in this. I'll ask Milton what an asterisk means and call you." September was already walking away.

September had promised Daniel Tait that she would not rest until the person who had murdered his grandfather was brought to justice. The clues written in blood were the only thing she had to go on. Clues were not always as apparent as they seemed. As a Catholic, she had been raised around symbols. The church had a symbol for nearly every occasion, but she had never seen an asterisk used in any church function. Words were understandable and could be researched, but how do you read a dead man's mind when it comes to symbols. She recalled a symbolism class she had taken in college and, at the time, thought it would have little meaning in her life, but now she wondered. She tried to remember if any of the symbols looked like an asterisk. The closest would be the symbol for Christ made up of a large X with a P superimposed over it, but even stretching her imagination she could not make an eight-pointed asterisk out of it. She decided to mull it over for awhile. She knew if she were dying she would not write something in her blood if it wasn't important. She was thankful that she didn't have anything but the Tait murder on her agenda. She could concentrate full-time on the case and wrap it up quickly, at least that was what she hoped.

Daniel was exhausted. He had not had a full night's sleep since Thanksgiving and was groggy when the phone rang. He was surprised that it was September Gale. "Don't you ever sleep?" he asked, "I mean, it's Saturday."

"And it's nearly noon. I've already been to the mall and had a double-shot latte. Would you mind meeting at your grandfather's place again?"

"Sure, what time?"

"I'm on my way there now."

"Have you learned anything new?"

"Nothing, and that's why we need to look through the house again. Every murderer leaves something behind."

"Give me thirty minutes." Daniel's feet hit the carpet and he made a beeline for the shower.

Chapter 6

Daniel Tait and September Gale spent the rest of the morning searching under every rug and behind every picture for a safe, then they started looking in unlikely places. They moved dressers and end tables and searched under the bathroom and kitchen cabinets. Finally Daniel, looking very discouraged, said, "There's a ladder in the garage. I'll go get it and check out the attic."

When Daniel returned, he set up a small stepladder in a bedroom closet and climbed through the opening into the attic. It was soon obvious that no one would put a safe in such an inaccessible space. Now totally discouraged, he was ready to give up. He looked at September standing at the bottom of the ladder and said, "We haven't checked the garage."

"You go ahead," September said. "It's not part of the crime scene, but if you find anything, please let me know. I'll be in my office trying to find out if GODS has some meaning other than the obvious."

Daniel walked out with September. The sky was gray and fast turning even darker. He watched September drive off, wondering if they were ever going to figure out what his grandfather was trying to tell them. The rain that had been threatening all morning began to fall and from the chill in the air would probably dampen things for several days. He pulled up the collar on his jacket and reached in his jeans pocket for a set of keys. He headed to the garage.

The garage was a stand-alone brick structure that matched the house, but had been built when Daniel was in the fifth grade. He remembered the summer stay at his grandfather's, right after the structure was completed. They were pouring the sidewalk that led to the house. *I wonder if it's still here.* He stood at the side door and looked down at the handprint in the cement just outside the door. He squatted down and put his hand in the impression. "You've grown a lot," he said smiling.

The impression was put there the summer after the garage had been built, the summer he first learned about his grandfather's faith. As he thought about that summer he could not remember a better time in his life. Every morning they would get up and head across town in his grandfather's Ford pickup to attend mass at The Grotto. As a twelve-year-old boy he had never thought about the quiet sanctuary in the middle of the city, but his memory of it was fond. The Grotto was a beautiful garden with paved paths, mysterious statues, and a church with beautiful paintings and elegant statues with devotional candles everywhere. They would hike the winding trails lined with rhododendrons. He remembered the pink and red flowers and the small lakes where they would stop and sit. His grandfather would pray before the grotto, a natural stone opening at the bottom of a monumental rock cliff. After mass his grandfather would fix a big breakfast of pancakes, eggs and bacon. During that summer, he didn't realize it would be the last summer he would spend with his grandfather for nearly ten years, until the summer of his graduation from Oregon State.

He felt the rain dripping off the roof and running down his neck. He fumbled through the keys, trying to remember which one fit, but ended up trying one after the other until he finally found the one that allowed him to turn the doorknob.

He flipped on the lights and stood inside the door. The garage was cluttered with boxes of his grandfather's things stacked without regard for order. Conspicuously missing was an automobile. The last car his grandfather had owned was a '57 Chevy that he gave to Daniel for his sixteenth birthday. His grandfather's health was already failing and his license had been suspended. Daniel spent hours restoring the car, removing dents and prepping it for new paint. He drove it until graduation. He looked at the place the car had once been parked and wondered what his car would be worth today. It had been hard to part with it, but it had helped finance his years at Oregon State and that was priceless.

Daniel looked around. *Not much chance of me finding a safe in here*, he mused as he made a path through stacks of dusty boxes. A workbench sat along the entire length of a wall and above were shelves containing the hand tools of his grandfather's trade, now mostly covered with rust from years of non-use. *A shame*, he thought looking at them. He had once thought he would like to have the antiquated hand tools, but now wondered if they would only remind him of his grandfather's terrible death.

Outside the garage, with his overcoat buttoned up against the rain, the Assassin watched Daniel through a window. He leaned into the glass as he saw Daniel fumble through a box, set it aside and open another. *He is looking for the crucifix.* He watched and waited, breathing shallow so as not to fog the glass and silently cursed the rain. He was impatient to move in on Daniel, but remembered what had happened with the old man. If he moved now, would he be able to extract the location from the man? He didn't think so. Why else was he going through so many boxes? His best strategy at the moment was watch and wait.

"Put the gun away," A soft voice behind the Assassin said, and the Assassin bolted upright and turned.

"You should not do that," the Assassin whispered.

Agent Fleming reached out and pushed the Assassin's gun down. "I told you I would handle this. You keep insisting on screwing things up."

The Assassin tightened his lips and slipped the gun into its holster. "Fine. The weather was beginning to get to me. I don't think he knows what he's looking for."

Fleming motioned for the Assassin to leave. "I'll talk to him. You leave. You and that gun are going to get us in trouble."

"Fine, but the Grand Master is becoming impatient. Sooner or later he will have us do it my way." The Assassin ran down the driveway and along the street and disappeared.

Daniel was growing frustrated. He wasn't sure what he was looking for. The boxes contained old clothes, discarded household items and books and magazines. It was obvious there wasn't a safe in the garage and the boxes were all that was left. *Didn't Grandfather ever throw away anything?*

Daniel glanced up as an overhead lightbulb flickered and went out. The garage was now too dark to continue searching. Daniel debated opening the main door for more light, but it was now raining a steady drizzle and already cold enough to see his breath. The cold air would make the garage even more miserable. He remembered the drawer in the workbench where his grandfather had kept lightbulbs and wondered if they were still there. He decided to change the bulb and continue the search. He found a lightbulb, slipped it in his pocket, and cleared a spot for the stepladder. While he was setting up the ladder he noticed something in the garage ceiling that made him curious. He was half way up the ladder when he heard a voice.

"Daniel, you never got back to me."

Daniel was startled and slipped on the ladder and caught his balance before turning to see Fleming. "Geez, don't you know enough to knock?"

"I didn't mean to startle you," Agent Fleming said, "but I left you several messages on your cell phone."

"Give me some slack. I've been busy trying to find out who killed my grandfather."

"I know. I spoke with Detective Gale and she told me you were here." Fleming was lying, but he was trained to lie. Anything to get the information he wanted. He had been keeping close contact with the Assassin and knew Daniel's every move. "I hear you uncovered a new clue."

"Did she tell you that?"

"How else would I know?"

"I'm not sure it is a clue. I'm beginning to think my grandfather was delusional. He was suffering with the early stages of Alzheimer's, you know."

"I'm sorry to hear that. Even so, you would think a dying man would speak with clarity if he wanted you to know something. What are you looking for?"

Daniel climbed down and used a box full of clothes for a chair. "You don't know what GODS would stand for, do you? Maybe an anagram or initials of someone? I thought he might be praying but he would probably not use God in the plural."

Fleming shook his head and feigned concern. "Maybe it was a prayer. You know Father, Son and Holy Ghost, that's plural."

Daniel shrugged. "You came all the way over here to talk to me. Was there something specific?"

"The CIA has uncovered evidence that your grandfather may have acquired an artifact from the Second World War, a cross with Jesus hanging on it."

"A crucifix," Daniel said. "There is one hanging on his bedroom wall."

"That's not the one," Fleming said.

Daniel wondered what was so important about a crucifix, but the tone of Fleming's voice told him he should be careful. He wasn't sure why, but he didn't trust the man. "Let me call Detective Gale and see if she knows anything about a crucifix," Daniel said reaching for his phone.

Fleming pumped his hands. "No, that won't be necessary. This is between us, a matter of international concern, not the worry of a city cop."

"You want me to keep quiet to the Portland Police?" Daniel narrowed his eyes in concern.

"I'd rather you did. It's a sensitive matter." Fleming turned to leave and in doing so clumsily tripped over a box. He landed against Daniel.

"Are you okay?" Daniel asked, helping Fleming to his feet.

"I'll have to learn not to be so clumsy," Fleming said, dusting himself off. He started out the door and turned. "You find an old hand-carved cross, you give me a call." *A Perfect plant*, Fleming thought, as he walked to his car.

Daniel watched Fleming leave the garage. He couldn't help but think the meeting was strange. *Should he be looking for an old crucifix? What significance could that have in his grandfather's death?* As soon as Fleming was to the street, Daniel went back inside and looked up at the panel in the garage ceiling. Daniel moved the ladder aside and cleared a space in the center of the garage floor. There was a short length of rope dangling from the panel and Daniel pulled on it. He heard the sound of springs that hadn't been stretched in a long time. *Could this be the hiding place,* he wondered? The panel swung down like a trapdoor on hinges. Attached to the panel, out of sight when it was in the up position, was a set of folding stairs. *Why had Fleming been so interested in a crucifix? Maybe that was what the killer was after.*

Fleming met up with the Assassin again, this time a mile from where he had talked to Daniel. They stood outside their cars in the parking lot of a mini-mart, each checking his phone. "Is yours working?" Fleming asked.

"These newfangled gadgets you Americans possess are truly wonderful. You say this device will tell me where he is at all times?"

"I also have a plant in his car. I think he's hiding something, but he can't go anywhere without us being able to find him."

"*Sacre bleu,*" the Assassin said, and smiled.

Daniel ascended the stairs and poked his head into the dark space of the attic. There was just enough light coming from a screened air vent at one end of the attic to see that the floor and the walls had been finished. The ceiling was low, leaving only enough height to stand in the very center of the room. It wasn't a likely place for a safe, but he decided to look anyway.

He had heard his grandfather mention a safe only once. Flat on his back in bed and weak with illness, his grandfather had pulled Daniel's ear close to his mouth and said, "If I die, find the safe hiding place." He hadn't thought anything about it until now, but it may not mean a safe at all. *Was he really looking for a safe, or could it be a hiding place?*

A safe or a hiding place, it didn't matter, either way he had no idea what he would find, if anything. Maybe it would hold clues, but then again, if it was so important why didn't his grandfather leave a reference to it in his final seconds on earth? Final seconds on earth...Daniel let the words play over in his mind. Maybe there wasn't enough time. Maybe the seconds had run out.

As his eyes adjusted to the dim light, Daniel could see from the dust on the floor that the attic hadn't been visited in years. His grandfather had probably stopped using the space when he became too feeble to reach the cord and pull down the stairs. Daniel climbed the rest of the way into the attic, and with the absence of anything in the room, wondered if all the boxes in the garage had been destined for the attic, or possibly had been in the attic and removed to the garage. He walked along the center of the room hunched over to keep his head from hitting the rafters. When he reached the far end, he ran his hand along the wall and felt for any sign of a safe. The wall was smooth and painted a light tan as best as he could determine in the poor light. He turned to inspect the wall at the other end of the room and noticed an indent in the floor not far from his foot. It was unusual since the floor was finished in hardwood planks. He stared at it. It was too perfect to be an imperfection in the wood. It was in an obscure place, normally in the shadows, where he would not have noticed it. Except for the light at this moment and the angle of his eyes he might have easily passed it up. He got down on his knees and felt the indented area with his fingers and found the indent was undercut and fit his fingers perfectly like a hidden drawer pull. He tugged at it and dislodged a set of floorboards. The boards were so precisely fit to the opening that they could not be detected under the heavy layer of dust.

Daniel set the board aside and put his hand into the opening. He felt something cold and smooth. He ran his hand along the surface wondering what it was. As his fingers found a corner and moved along the side he realized it was a box; a metal box. On the end was a handle, which he grasped. He pulled the box from its resting place. By the dust covering it, it was evident it had been there for a long time. He wiped the dust from the top with the sleeve of his jacket. He could barely make out lettering, printed in white and wondered why a U.S. Army ammo box would be stashed away in such an obscure location. If he didn't know his grandfather had built the garage, he would have thought it was put there ages ago by a previous owner, but he was certain it was his grandfather's and must be the elusive safe he was searching for. His stomach fluttered in anticipation and he stood up too quickly. "Ouch!" He dropped the box and rubbed the spot on his head that had hit a rafter. After telling himself how stupid he was, he picked up the box again.

Daniel was pulling on the latch at one end of the box when he got a call from September.

"I found out something you need to know," September said.

"I found the safe," Daniel said. "Or at least what I think my grandfather was referring to."

"Let's not talk over the phone," September said. "I'm on my way to the crime scene."

"You're on the road?"

"On Macadam, I'll be there in five minutes."

"I'll be in the garage," Daniel said. "Did you hear? I found the safe." His phone went dead and he stuffed it in the holster on his belt. He carried the box down the ladder and was headed toward the workbench when he sensed he was not alone and the hairs on the back of his neck bristled. Daniel spun around. A man's dark silhouette was blocking the door. He was holding a gun.

"I'll take that," the Assassin said.

Daniel had been to France enough times to recognize the man's accent as French. He froze and slowly let the ammo box drop to his side, but still hanging on to it by one of the handles.

The Assassin stepped into the garage. "It is of no use to you. Give it to me and you will not have to suffer the same fate as the old man."

"What's in it that you would kill an old man for?" Daniel asked, trying to control his rage. *This is the man who killed my grandfather.* He considered the weight of the metal box. *Is it too heavy to use as a weapon?* If he could lure him close enough he might be able to knock the gun away. Then again, he could end up like his grandfather.

"You are right, I will kill for it," the Assassin said. "You will set the box down and back away."

"You murdered my grandfather!" *This better work*, Daniel thought showing his outrage. "You don't even know what's in the box."

The Assassin took another step forward. "I did not want to kill him so slowly. His defiance made it necessary. Had he given me what I asked, he would have died in peace. Instead he drowned in his own blood. The question is, will your defiance bring you the same fate?"

Daniel's feigned outrage became genuine anger and he couldn't hold it back. He was face to face with the man who had murdered his grandfather.

The Assassin raised his weapon. "I am going to kill you anyway. You might as well cooperate."

Daniel lunged at the Assassin and swung the box in a fit of rage. He felt the impact of the bullet before he heard the sound from the gun. The force knocked him backwards and his head hit the floor with a dull thud.

September pulled in the driveway and stopped just short of the crime scene tape. She heard what might be a shot, but with the slapping of the windshield wipers and her windows rolled up she wasn't sure. It could have been the dropping of a box or the business end of a hammer hitting a nail, but she turned on her flashing lights and drew her weapon as she exited the vehicle. What she had learned and needed to tell Daniel had alarmed her enough that she wasn't taking any chances. She approached the garage with care, taking snapshots of the area with her eyes as she put her back to the house and moved across the breezeway to the garage door.

"Daniel, are you in there?" she yelled, slipping her weapon through the door before she made herself visible. There was no reply, so with her weapon at the ready, she quickly moved into the garage. She saw Daniel sprawled on the floor with his hand grasping the handle of the ammo box. He wasn't moving. For a moment she thought he had fallen and that had created the sound that seemed like a gunshot. Then she heard noise upstairs and stepped over Daniel and pointed her weapon at the opening to the attic. "Police, drop your weapon and come down." She waited a moment. "Throw down your weapon. There's no way out. Give yourself up."

She heard a crash and debated rushing up the stairs, but decided she would be a perfect target when her head entered the attic area. "Police!" she yelled again. "Come down with your hands up!" She stood with her weapon trained at the opening. She heard another crashing sound from upstairs and all went quiet. With her gun trained on the opening, she squatted down and felt for a pulse on the side of Daniel's neck. She called for backup and an emergency response team. She heard a noise outside and ran out the door. She saw a man running across the lawn. He disappeared into a hedge along the property line. She saw splintered wood scattered on the driveway. The attic vent had been kicked out, leaving a hole the size of a small window. She heard tires squeal and turned in time to see the tail end of a car speeding away. She went back inside to tend to Daniel, but first climbed the stairs to make certain the attic was clear. Whoever had been there had made a clean escape.

Daniel felt fingers probing his face. He opened his eyes and saw September's blurry image. He smiled. She was leaning over him and checking his eyes with a penlight. "My head hurts," he said, trying to lift his right hand, but something was holding it down. He struggled and let go of the ammo box.

"Who was that man?" September asked.

"What man?" Daniel felt groggy and his mind was fuzzy. He tried to sit up and September helped him to a sitting position.

"I heard a shot and must have surprised him." She kept her hand on his back helping to steady him.

Daniel rubbed the bump on his head. As he turned his head toward September, in the closeness she smelled of lilacs, and her warm breath touched his face. He felt like he was in a dream, but reality set in as she stood up.

"Come on. Let's get you off the floor. Can you stand?"

"I may need a little help," Daniel said, but his sheepish grin gave him away.

"You're going to live. Do you know who shot at you?"

"The man who murdered my grandfather," Daniel said, rubbing the lump on his head. "He had a French accent."

"I was coming to warn you," September said. "I think your grandfather was mixed up with some bad hombres."

"The man was French," Daniel said, reaching down for the ammo box. "He wasn't Hispanic."

"So...I don't know the word for a bad Frenchman. You can thank God he was a bad shot." September said.

Daniel held up the box. "Yeah, he was mad at the box, I guess." He pointed to a hole, dead center, through one side of the ammo box.

"Give that to me," September said, reaching for the container.

"My grandfather was killed for what is in this box," Daniel said. "He seemed to think it contained some kind of treasure worth killing for. You want to open it with me?"

"Okay, but not here," September said.

"Then my place. You want to ride with me or follow me?"

"I'm not letting that box out of my sight," September said.

"Let's go then," Daniel said.

They walked out of the garage as a patrol car pulled up with its lights on. Close behind was an Emergency Response Vehicle. September talked to the officer while two EMTs checked Daniel. They gave him leave once they were certain he didn't have a concussion. They repositioned their vehicles so Daniel's Jeep could leave. September gave the officer a description of the vehicle she had seen leaving the area and joined Daniel in the Jeep.

The Assassin had circled the area and parked in a nearby grove of trees and low-lying brush. He watched through binoculars as they got into Daniel's red Jeep Cherokee. He had no reason to doubt that he would be able to gain possession of the relic and very soon. He checked his handheld tracking device. It would not be difficult to find them, wherever they were going.

Chapter 7

"Lock the door," Daniel said to September from the kitchen of his apartment.

September set the deadbolt and fastened the security chain, although she knew it was a worthless device if anyone wanted in. She was thinking the box held a bullet that may be a match with the one that killed Walter Tait. She needed to tell Daniel what she had learned on the internet. It seemed Walter Tait had gotten himself mixed up in something that could also get Daniel Tait killed. She joined Daniel in the kitchen.

"Your first instinct concerning the name on the floor had been correct, but Fleming was also right," September said. "Savoy was an area between France and Italy with ancient origins, if that's any help, but I don't believe in coincidence, so it has to be the French connection. What the connection is to my murder case remains a mystery. Let's hope the box holds a clue."

He pulled on the latch and the lid on the box sprung open. "Whatever is in the box, the Frenchman wanted it enough to kill for," Daniel said. He peered inside and saw only pieces of paper. He turned the box upside down on the table and the contents spilled out.

"Better put on gloves," September said, handing Daniel a pair.

"You carry those things around like normal people carry Kleenex," Daniel said taking the gloves.

"I hope you're not expecting me to be normal."

"I would never accuse you of being that. Not many people would do what you do for a living."

September spread some of the contents across the table and the slug fell out of a folded newspaper. She picked it up and held it up to the light. "It's remarkably intact," she said. She pulled a Ziploc bag from her pocket and dropped the bullet in.

Daniel looked at the items scattered on the table. Most noticeable was the yellowed newspaper in which the bullet had been lodged. The paper had been folded several times. Daniel put a pinky-finger into the hole where the bullet had been. The bullet had completely obliterated much of the writing. He opened the paper. It was a French newspaper for a place called Sainte-Mère-Eglise, "This is the headline. FRANCE AMERICAINS LIBERATE".

"Americans liberate France," September said. "What's the date?"

"25 August, 1944," Daniel said. "D-Day. The Allies invasion of Normandy was June 6, 1944. This was about nine weeks later."

"They teach you that in engineering school?" September asked.

"I'm a history buff. My grandfather was part of the invasion. He celebrated that day every year with a birthday cake. He talked about going back there, but his health was failing."

"His birthday was on D-Day?"

Daniel looked at her. She was smiling again and he liked that. "Grandpa wasn't sentimental about much, but he would choke up when he remembered D-Day. He said he got a second chance at life the day of the Normandy invasion."

September frowned. "It seems a strange thing to say if he was in the war with the fighting and all."

"He was in the middle of it all right. He was with the paratroopers..." He stared at the paper again. Something caught his eye even though he couldn't understand French. On the same page as the headline was another story and a name in the article caused the hair on the back of his neck to bristle.

"What is it?" September asked, leaning into him to see what he was staring at. He turned his head and their faces were inches apart. He held his eyes on her for a moment too long and became embarrassed. He cleared his throat. "This is the same name Grandpa wrote on the floor." His finger was shaking as he touched a line in a column of names.

September stared at the name he was pointing to, Adele de Savoy, 6 Juin, 1944. "It appears to be a list of those from Sainte-Mère-Eglise who lost their lives in the war. She died on the day of the invasion."

"I think I know how to make sense of this," Daniel said, going to his laptop that was setting on the kitchen counter. He opened Google Translate and typed in the French and they both read the English translation as it appeared on the screen. Afterwards they looked at each other, confused. "This is it?" Daniel asked. "How can an old newspaper article be worth killing for?"

He picked up a copy of his grandfather's will. It had escaped the bullet. He read the several pieces of paper. The date was a week after his grandmother's death. "He left everything to me."

"I know," September said. "We found a copy in your grandfather's things in the bedroom. I was really hoping this box would answer more questions," September said. "Maybe your grandfather was in love with Adele and that's why he kept the newspaper."

"I doubt that," Daniel said, "but we now have the French connection. When you talked to Agent Fleming this morning did he mention anything about a crucifix?"

"Fleming? I haven't spoken to him since that day at your grandfather's house."

"Really? When he came over to my grandfather's earlier, he said you told him where I was."

"You saw him?" September gave Daniel an incredulous look. "Today?"

"How much do you know about Fleming?" Daniel asked. "He seems a bit spooky to me."

September frowned and narrowed her eyes in thought. "I checked him out, if that's what you're getting at."

"Is he legit? A real CIA Agent."

"As far as I could get information. The CIA isn't too keen on city cops asking about their agents. But from what I could gather he checks out 100%, the real McCoy, why?"

"He didn't want me to mention my meeting with him. He seemed like he didn't want you to know he came by."

"What did he want?"

"Well...he showed up at my grandfather's place claiming my grandfather was involved in some kind of international smuggling operation. He wanted to know if I'd seen an old crucifix."

September laughed. "Your grandfather, a smuggler? I don't think so. By the way, I almost forgot. I think I found out something else that, if we put it all together, might make some sense."

"I hope so," Daniel said. "I need to go back to work next week and we don't seem to be making much headway."

"There is a French organization that's part of the Free Masons. They call themselves Grand Orient de France. They abbreviate the organization with all caps, GODF."

"Free Masons? My grandfather was a Catholic. I doubt he would be a Mason. If I remember my history, the Free Masons are alleged to be remnants of the Knights Templar, formed after the Catholic Church put them on trial for heresy, and disbanded the order in the 14th century. The Knights Templar were from France though, you don't suppose...."

"I'm not suggesting anything. There seems to be a definite connection to France. Maybe your grandfather had something that belonged to the French Free Masons."

"You mean something from the war?"

"A crucifix, perhaps?" September lifted her eyebrows.

Daniel typed GODS in his computer and didn't find what September was suggesting.

"You need to tie it to France," September said, leaning over his shoulder. "There are a number of branches, GODF is the main one. The Paris branch is GODP. Suppose there's a Grande Orient de Sainte-Mère-Eglise, GODS."

Daniel looked up at her and smiled. "That would be GODSME. Sounds like we're grasping at straws. Everything is pointing to France. Especially with this newspaper article, but I don't see a crucifix."

September began excitedly pacing around the room. She turned and faced Daniel, who was still sitting at the table and held up two fingers. "We have two pieces of a puzzle that tie your grandfather to France over sixty years ago. We have Adele de Savoy, a person your grandfather obviously knew, and she was killed on the day of the invasion, the very day your grandfather was there. What if someone is avenging her death? GODS could be a French organization that is seeking to avenge her death. Maybe your grandfather killed her. If we can find out how the two are connected, we may solve this crime."

Daniel stood up and stretched. "My grandfather isn't a murderer and besides, if Adele de Savoy was killed by my grandfather, whoever is avenging her death must be ninety years old. I wouldn't get too excited about solving this, just yet."

"You don't understand," September said. "Until you found the newspaper, none of this made any sense, but now we have the possibility that someone in the French Free Masons killed your grandfather. Maybe he isn't avenging her death, maybe she gave something, like a crucifix, to your grandfather and they want it back."

"Before we go any farther, let's see if there is such an organization," Daniel said, moving his laptop to the table and sitting down in front of it. In less than a minute he turned the screen toward September. "You almost nailed it. "Grand Orient de Savoy" is a non-recognized faction of the French Free Masons. According to this, the group was founded by a disgruntled member of the House of Savoy back in the 16th century. The House of Savoy was located in Chambery, France until the 16th century, when they were attacked by French troops and forced to move to a more secure location in Italy, where they ruled until after World War Two. It also says the House of Savoy had possession of the Shroud of Christ, known today as the Shroud of Turin."

September's eyes lit up. "The name Savoy again. It can't be a coincidence. Somehow Adele de Savoy and Grand Orient de Savoy are connected... and the House of Savoy." September removed her jacket and folded it over a chair. Her gun was in a holster that fit neatly in a shoulder holster under her arm.

"You ever shoot anyone with that?" Daniel asked.

"Not yet," September said, grinning. She pointed a finger at Daniel. "Better not try anything."

Daniel got up from his computer. "Adele de Savoy...a French Free Mason off-shoot called Grand Orient de Savoy...the Second World War, and a killer with a French accent; why on earth would all of this be coming together today?"

"It may be why the CIA is involved. Fleming may not be telling us the whole story."

Daniel shook his head in defeat. "I can't think when I'm hungry. Can we continue this over dinner? I'll buy."

September eyed him suspiciously. "I could eat, but we go Dutch."

"A cheap date. I like it," Daniel said getting a jacket from the entry closet.

"It's not a date," September said, putting on her jacket.

"Where would you like to go on this non-date?"

September adjusted her jacket and ran her hands through her hair. "I look a mess. Someplace that's not fancy."

Outside Daniel's apartment the Assassin stared into the dark afternoon sky and grimaced at the bad news. He had bugged Daniel's apartment and listened to the conversation through a pair of ear phones. He, like Daniel, was disappointed with what he had learned. If the crucifix was not in the box, it meant his worst fear might have been realized, and the crucifix was on its way back to Chambery, France. It appeared the old man had not had the crucifix after all. He dreaded breaking the news to the Grand Master, but it was not the first time they had been disappointed. He was sure the Grand Master would not give up his search and this would not be the last stop on his quest, but he also knew the time to retrieve the crucifix was growing short.

Chapter 8

Jake's Crawfish House was an historic restaurant on 12th Avenue in downtown Portland. It had been in the same location for over a hundred years and was known for its fine seafood and rustic atmosphere. Daniel and September parked a block away and walked through the aged wood and glass doors and waited for their table in a bar with standing room only.

"I'm surprised we got in here without reservations," September said as they were being escorted through a crowd of people standing in the bar. They were seated at a table next to a window that looked out on the busy streets of Portland. They ordered drinks and looked out at the people walking by on the street outside. There were some with open umbrellas and others with their overcoat collars turned up against the cold November rain.

"It looks like we made it here just in time," September said, noting the rain had started falling in a steady drizzle. She rocked on her chair that didn't quite set flat on the ancient wooden plank floor.

"Here let me fix that for you," Daniel said, leaning down with a piece of folded napkin and placing it under one of the legs of the chair.

"I guess you never stop being an engineer," September said. She tested the fix and was satisfied that it worked. "You like being an engineer?"

"My job's a lot like yours, if you think about it. We both get paid to solve problems."

"I suppose you're right. I never thought of my job being like an engineer. I always pictured engineers designing and building things."

"We do that, but there is a branch of engineering that dismantles things to see how they were built. Reverse engineering, if you will. You deal with unraveling mysteries, and I deal with figuring out how a mystery was designed. It's nearly the same thing except you have to deal with the human element of the mystery and I only have to deal with how it functions mechanically. I think your job is tougher."

"Oh," September looked genuinely interested in his analogy, "why's that?"

Their drinks arrived and September stirred her Tequila Sunrise with the swizzle stick.

"You have to figure out how people think, and what makes them tick. I only have to figure out how things work, using the specific and predictable laws of Physics." Daniel lifted his Dewar's on the rocks. "Here's to unsolved mysteries, without them neither of us would be employed."

They touched glasses and sipped their drinks. September opened her menu to avoid an awkward silence. She looked up and saw Daniel was staring at her. "What?" She asked, touching her face. "Do I have something on my face?"

Daniel shook his head and grinned. "I was just trying to figure out what must have happened to bring a Frenchman to the United States and take my grandfather's life?"

September took a sip of her cocktail and thought for a moment. "We know it's connected to something that happened during the Second World War. A lot of things were brought back from WWII. I remember my grandfather showing me a German Luger he said he took off of a Nazi officer. Maybe your grandfather took something with special significance from someone."

"But why now? The war was over forty years before I was born. He was an old man. To tell the truth, I didn't expect him to live another year anyway."

They were interrupted by the waiter, a college-age man in black slacks, a white shirt, and a dishtowel wrapped around his waist. He looked at September.

Daniel said, "I hope you like fish."

"It's a little late to ask me now, don't you think." September handed her menu to the young man. "I'll have baked halibut with green vegetables and young potatoes."

"Bring me the grilled marlin, rice and green salad with blue cheese dressing." Daniel held the menu up for the waiter. "Oh, and since we both are having fish, a bottle of Chablis, Tualatin Vineyard, 2000, if you have it."

"Do you still want it if we don't have that exact year?" the waiter asked.

"Sure. Surprise me."

"What's so special about 2000?" September asked.

"Nothing," Daniel said, grinning. "I was just showing off."

"You mean you don't have the slightest idea what you ordered?"

"Tualatin Vineyard is a very good Oregon winery. I'm sure we won't be disappointed." Daniel offered the bread basket to her and she broke off a piece of sourdough bread and handed it back to him.

September put the piece of bread close to her nose. "I love the smell of fresh baked sourdough bread."

"What made you become a police officer?" Daniel asked.

"Detective," September said. "My uncle was a police officer who was killed in the line of duty."

"Wow," Daniel said. "That must have been tough."

"I was a teenager and he was serving as a street patrolman. He was shot by a gang member. He didn't even have time to draw his weapon."

"But they caught the ones who did it?"

"The camera on his dash captured the event. They brought him in the next day."

"So you decided you wanted to follow in his footsteps."

September waited until she finished swallowing a piece of bread before answering. "I was in high school and didn't have a clue of what I was going to do once I got out of school. I suppose the exposure to the police and the court and everything surrounding his death gave me a boost. The investigating officer was female."

"Weird how things that happen outside of our control can have a defining influence on our lives," Daniel said. "Where did you go school?"

"Coming from a Catholic family, I went to school at St. Mary's of the Valley."

"You were raised Catholic? My grandfather became a Catholic. Boy did that cause a riff in the family."

The waiter brought the wine and showed the bottle to Daniel. He nodded and the waiter poured a small amount for Daniel to taste. He felt the cork, tasted the wine and said, "Very good." When the waiter had left, Daniel showed the bottle to September. "2000 must have been a good year; they still had some in the cellar."

"Or a very bad year, because they still had some left," September said showing her dimples again.

"They'll probably charge me rental space for keeping the bottle that long. No kidding you were raised Catholic."

"Have you got something against Catholics?" September said, trying to read his face.

"Not me, but I'm afraid my parents would be a little taken back if I brought you home to meet them...not that that would ever happen."

September shook her head. "I probably will never meet your parents, so you have nothing to worry about, but why don't your parents like Catholics? Are they atheists?"

"No, they are Christian, but my father detests Catholics."

"But you said your grandfather was Catholic. I don't understand."

Daniel refilled September's glass. "It goes way back in our family. My great-grandfather was from Northern Ireland and was not a Catholic. He was a proud British subject and detested the lower-class Catholics and their desire to break away from British rule. Being from the north and proud of it, it became family tradition to wear orange on St. Patrick's Day. You can imagine how that went over in the predominantly Irish Catholic section of Boston where my father grew up. He said he was constantly in fights with Catholic kids. My parents moved to Portland shortly after I was born. When I was about eighteen my grandmother died from cancer and my grandfather announced he had joined the Catholic Church. To this day my father hates my grandfather. I got to know my grandfather a little better after graduating from college. It's been a point of contention between me and my dad, but I figured I didn't have a dog in the fight. My grandfather was doing what he wanted to do. I thought the whole thing was stupid."

The waiter served their food and September was quiet. Daniel wondered if he had made a mistake baring his family history to someone he hardly knew. "I hope I didn't upset you," Daniel said.

September sampled her fish. "I understand where you're coming from. Everyone has a choice to be prejudiced or not. You chose to pretend it wasn't your place to get in the middle of it."

"You think I'm prejudiced?"

"You said lower class Catholics. That sounds a bit biased to me." She raised her eyebrows and looked him in the eyes.

"I was just telling you what my family told me. I don't have to take sides. I could care less."

"Why do you think your grandfather joined the Church?" September took a bite of vegetables and gave him a quizzical look.

"I don't know. According to my father, it was for no good reason."

"Believe me," September said. "Matters of the heart and a change in religion always have a good reason. What did your grandmother think of his conversion?"

"Grandma? She died before he became Catholic, but he had been attending the Catholic Church for some time. She would have had a fit and I think that upset my dad even more. Grandpa waited to be baptized in the Catholic Church until after she had died. He couldn't have pissed off Dad any more if he would have divorced my grandmother and married a Catholic."

They finished their meal in awkward silence. When they were finished and the waiter had put a black folder on the table, "I'll be your cashier when you're ready," the waiter said.

Daniel reached for the bill, but September snatched it up. She studied it. "I'll let you buy the wine. My meal comes to twenty-seven dollars. She opened her wallet and put a twenty and a ten in the folder. "That should cover my meal and my portion of the tip." She handed the folder to Daniel.

"You want to go back to my place or to your car?" Daniel asked, as they pulled away from the restaurant.

"We were on a roll at your place. Maybe we missed something."

"My place it is," Daniel said.

Back in his apartment, Daniel went to the items scattered on the table. "I'm not sure what to do with all this," Daniel said, putting the papers back in the ammo box. He picked up the newspaper and a picture fell out from between folds. September picked it up.

"What's this?" September asked handing a picture to him.

Daniel took the picture and admired the craftsmanship of the wooden sunburst in the photo. He handed it back to her. "My grandfather was a woodcarver, a skill he tried to pass on to me."

"You look like you'd be pretty good with your hands."

"I never had the patience of my grandfather. I like power tools. They get the job done much faster. My things may not be as pretty, but they're just as functional." Daniel paused a moment then added, "my grandfather never agreed with me on that. Probably why I became an engineer."

September continued to stare at the picture. "I think I've seen this before. It's a cross. Any idea why it would be in the box with the paper?"

"I don't even know why he kept the paper hidden away. You call that a cross?"

"It's a starburst cross. See the uppermost point and the points at 90° are longer."

"I guess," Daniel said. "Looks more like a sunburst to me."

"He must have felt it needed safekeeping," September said. "Maybe it has something to do with the newspaper article." September continued to stare at the picture. "I'm trying to remember where I've seen this cross," she said again.

Chapter 9

The Assassin packed his suitcase and debated whether to risk packing his weapon and decided against it. He checked his passport and set it on the dresser beside his gun when the phone rang.

He raised his cell phone to his ear. "I understand you have not found the crucifix," the Grand Master said.

"I'm on the three o'clock to Amsterdam and then to Paris. The package is not here. My job here is finished."

"All the information we have leads us to where you are now. You should not give up so easily."

"I have not surrendered; I believe the item may have been returned to Chambery."

"And why would you believe such a thing? There is no reason."

"There is nothing here. I tell you the old man did not have the crucifix and his grandson hasn't got a clue as to where it is or if it even exists. The detective on the case is a woman and she is even more clueless. What is there but for me to proceed to the next logical place?"

"Very well, but Fleming must continue to watch things while you go on this, what do the Americans say, 'boondoggle'."

The Assassin pulled the phone from his ear and stared at it, clenching his jaw and shaking his head. "I have notified Fleming and he is fine with my leaving."

"Very well, check in with me before you go to Chambery."

The Grand Master set the phone down and stared out the window. He recalled a story he had heard in his childhood; a story that had been past down in his family for generations. He remembered it as if he were there. The year was 1465 and there lived a powerful Duke named Louis I, who ruled over a region of the country known as Savoy, which is now a part of France. The Duke of Savoy was a surviving member of the Ordre du Temple, or Knights Templar, and was the most powerful knight in the kingdom, for he had acquired, through his travels to the Holy Land, the sacred burial Shroud of Christ. It was kept a secret, a secret the family went to great lengths to keep, but the secret got out when the son of the Duke, Amadeus IX, founded an order to worship the Shroud. The Holy Shroud was hidden away in the Sainte Chapelle de Chambery, but the Catholic Church found out its hiding place and desired to gain possession of the relic and add it to their vast fortunes. This caused a great division within the House of Savoy and, on the fourth day of December in the year 1532, a fire was set in the chapel which was located within the confines of the Savoy Castle complex, known as the House of Savoy.

In April of 1534 the Poor Clare Nuns were deemed by the Church in Rome to be devout, holy and innocent, and worthy to handle the Shroud and for the first time, the family surrendered the Shroud to the hands of the Church nunnery for repairs. The nuns trimmed the burned areas and sewed patches to cover the holes, but the sacred threads which were trimmed from the burned area, threads covered with the precious blood of Christ, remained with the Poor Clare Nuns for safekeeping and adoration. It was not the place of the Duke of Savoy to give away the precious threads of the Shroud, so his brother, siding with the French in an invasion of the castle, recovered the threads in a raid of the nunnery, and later founded Grand Orient de Savoy for safekeeping. The threads remained in GODS possession until the German occupation of France when they were lost again. Lost but not forgotten, the Grand Master mused.

Daniel Tait was given permission to enter his grandfather's house, but only with police supervision. As he entered through the front door, he was thinking about the strange visit from Agent Fleming and his mention of a crucifix his grandfather supposedly brought back from Europe during the war. If his grandfather had possession of the crucifix, why was it missing now? Under strict instructions that nothing was to be removed from the house, Daniel sorted through the mess of overturned furniture and scattered belongings. In the kitchen, he found an ancient computer and decided to see what was stored on it. He had never seen his grandfather use a computer and doubted the old computer was any more than an artifact given to his grandfather by a well-meaning friend. It took only five minutes before he had broken his grandfather's password and logged on to his grandfather's e-mail web page. Even more surprising than the discovery that his grandfather had an e-mail account was the old machine was capable of getting on the internet.

He called Detective Gale to see if they knew about the computer and checked the e-mails. September assured him they had gone through it and there was nothing significant. After hanging up, Daniel was not convinced. After all, he was looking for a crucifix and the police were looking for a murderer. When the police checked the computer, they probably hadn't put the two together. He was convinced after the encounter in the garage, that a cross or a crucifix held a clue to why his grandfather was murdered. He already knew the murderer was a Frenchman with a quick trigger and a bad disposition. But he had yet to know why. As he looked through sent e-mails he came across one that caught his interest. It was addressed to Fr. Rick and the subject was Poor Clare Nuns.

Daniel had no idea what a Poor Clare Nun was, but what caught his eye was a question in the body of the e-mail. He read it over for the third time and decided he needed help from an expert. He searched his pockets for the business card he'd been given by Fr. Hays and found it in his billfold. He read the name, Fr. Richard (Rick) Hays, checked the e-mail address on the computer with the one on the card and found they matched. It was clear his grandfather knew more about the electronic age than he had given him credit. He decided to pay Fr. Rick Hays a visit and called for an appointment.

With a copy of the e-mail in his hand, Daniel knocked on the rectory door of St. Clare's Church. While Daniel waited in the office for Fr. Rick to arrive, he looked at a collage of pictures on one wall and saw his grandfather was in several of them. *He must have been quite active in the Church.* One in particular caught his eye. It was a photo with Fr. Rick and his grandfather with the same sunburst he'd seen in the photo from the ammo can. The sunburst that September had called a starburst cross.

"Your grandfather was quite active in the Church," a voice behind him said.

Daniel turned and saw the same intense gray eyes and infectious smile that had greeted him at the funeral. "When was this picture taken?" Daniel asked, pointing to the one of Fr. Rick and his grandfather holding the sunburst carving.

"About ten years ago. Your grandfather presented the cross to us the day he was baptized."

"I thought it was a sunburst," Daniel said.

"Your grandfather was very artistic. He said it was symbolic. It represented the birth and death of Christ. The star of Bethlehem and the cross of the crucifixion are merged into a single entity. Quite clever, I think."

"Where is it now?" Daniel asked.

Fr. Rick thought for a moment. "We didn't have a place for it. As beautiful as it was, it was quite an imposing figure, and if I may say, a bit modern for our more traditional church. I donated it to The Grotto of Our Sorrowful Mother. You should go there; it's truly an inspirational experience."

"I'll do that," Daniel said turning around. "Thank you for seeing me on such short notice."

"I'm happy to see you again," Fr. Hays said, offering a chair to Daniel. "What can I do for you?"

Daniel sat in a mahogany chair with a flowered cushion, while Fr. Hays sat in a brown leather-covered chair behind his desk. "I came across an e-mail my grandfather sent to you about a week ago. He was asking about Poor Clare Nuns."

"Yes, our church's namesake." Fr. Hays leaned forward in his chair and his eyes lit up. "Saint Clare was the founder of the Poor Clare's, and the patron saint of our parish."

"Do you know if they would have anything to do with a lost crucifix?"

"As I recall, Walter was trying to find the origin of a crucifix he had brought back from the war. He wanted to get it back to its rightful owner before he died."

"Did he succeed?" Daniel asked.

"I don't know," Fr. Rick said. "With all the activities surrounding the Thanksgiving holiday, I never got a chance to respond. There was something, though. After mass about a week before Thanksgiving, he asked me another question that puzzled me at the time."

"Another question?"

"It seems he thought the crucifix came from a lodge, Grand Orient de Savoy, and he had e-mailed them, but never got a response. I told him that couldn't be. The Grand Orient de Savoy is an atheist organization and I'm sure wouldn't possess any religious artifacts."

Daniel's eyebrows raised in interest. He leaned forward. "My grandfather wrote GODS in his own blood on the floor where he was murdered," Daniel said. "I can't help but think there's a connection."

Father Rick nodded and rubbed his chin. "The medieval church chose to distance itself from the Society of Free Masons. Grand Orient de Savoy was an offshoot so radical that the Free Masons expelled them from their affiliation. I can't imagine your grandfather having anything to do with them. If it was Grand Orient de Savoy that killed Walter, you could be in grave danger."

"You seem to know a lot about the organization," Daniel said. "Why are they so dangerous?"

Father Rick leaned forward in his chair and looked intently into Daniel's eyes. "History tells us there was a time when the ruling family of Savoy had possession of the Shroud of Turin. Sometime in the mid-sixteenth century, the brother of the Duke of

Savoy, said to be an agnostic, tried to destroy the Shroud by setting fire to the church where it was locked in a secure location. That brother is said to have founded Grand Orient de Savoy. The organization has been banned from meeting in Italy because of their radical demonstrations against Christianity. The Catholic Church, understandably, has condemned the organization."

"You told my grandfather GODS would have no purpose for the crucifix."

"I did, but on second thought, if they did have possession of a religious artifact it would be for nefarious purposes."

"Such as?"

"I don't want to get into the disgusting, wicked immoral things they would do with a religious artifact."

"I understand, but what kind of an artifact would be worth killing for?"

"Whatever it is, it must be of great significance to the church. The Grand Orient de Savoy exists to desecrate all that is considered holy in Christianity."

Daniel thought about his encounter with the Frenchman in his grandfather's garage and the strange conversation he'd had with Fleming. There was definitely a radical group of people out there. Why else would the CIA be interested?

Fr. Rick stood and gave Daniel a warm handshake. "Your grandfather was a devout man with a pure heart. I'm certain he was not mixed up with a cult like Grand Orient de Savoy. I've told you all I know. Please be careful. You have Walter's spirit in you. I can see it. God bless you in your search."

"Thank you, Fr. Hays," Daniel said.

"You can call me Rick," Fr. Hays said. "I hope we can talk again."

As Daniel drove back to his grandfather's house, he reflected on the words of Fr. Rick. Was his grandfather mixed up with a cult and not even aware of it?

"Detective Gale, in my office," Lieutenant Terrell Gordon said, standing by September's desk. She turned and walked back to her corner office.

"Close the door," her boss said as September entered. "Don't bother to sit, this won't take that long." The lieutenant was a stocky woman with dark- almond skin and shiny-black, shoulder-length hair without even the hint of a curl. She wore the dark blue uniform of the Portland Police and was proud of the silver bar on her collar. She had been a veteran of the force for seventeen years and was known not so affectionately as, 'The Enforcer,' by those under her.

Terrell thought September had used her degree in Criminal Justice to land what some felt was a cushy job with flexible hours and a sloppy dress code. Terrell Gordon thought detectives should sweat more and think less. It was good old police work, the beat on the street, that solved most crimes, in her opinion, and Detective September Gale was nothing but a pretty face with a badge.

"What is it, Ma'am," September said, standing in front of the lieutenant's desk.

From her chair her boss looked up at her. "September, that ritual murder over in Burlingame, how's it coming along?"

"We haven't got a suspect yet."

"Why not?"

"It's a complicated case. There was no DNA and the only clue we have is what the man left scrawled on the floor in his blood."

"I got a call from a friend the other day who said you were getting too close to the prime suspect, the man's grandson."

"Excuse me," September said. She clenched her fists and gritted her jaw to maintain composure. "Daniel Tait is not a suspect and he's cooperating in the case."

"Don't get your panties in a twist. I don't have to remind you a family member is the perp 80% of the time."

"Well, this case is one of the twenty-percent. All the family members have alibis."

The lieutenant gave her a condescending stare. "The entire family claims they were together at the time. How convenient is that? You'd do good to look into Daniel Tait's alibi a little closer. He could have murdered his grandfather and driven back to Waldport. He was the last one to see the old man alive."

"I don't know what Fleming's been telling you, but there was an attempt on Daniel Tait's life the other day. Someone is still out there with a French accent and I think Fleming knows more than he's telling us."

Terrell went back to some paperwork on her desk. "That will be all. Keep your distance from the suspect, ya hear?"

September went back to her desk. She felt like breaking into tears, but held on until she was down the elevator and out the front door. "That witch," September ground out through clenched teeth, loud enough she got a few stares from people on the sidewalk. She called Daniel Tait. "Where are you?"

"Nice to here from you, too," Daniel said.

"I don't have time for games. Are you at the house?"

"Just pulling in the driveway."

"Wait for me. I'm on my way."

Daniel was about to mention the meeting with the priest, but the phone went silent and from the curtness of September's voice, he doubted she'd be interested. He glanced in his rearview mirror and saw a gray sedan drive past. He had seen the car before and thought it must be someone who lived on the street. He went to the front door and waited for September to arrive.

Fifteen minutes passed and Daniel wondered what was keeping the detective. When an hour passed and she didn't show, Daniel called her cell phone.

"Detective Gale, Homicide," September answered.

"I thought we were going to meet," Daniel said.

"I'm sorry, on the way over I was called out on another case."

"Do you want me to wait?"

"No, this could take a while. I'll catch up with you later."

"I'm going to be out and about. Call me on my cell." He hung up and walked back to his car. It was turning dark and rush hour traffic was about to start. He figured he had just enough time to drive across town without getting caught in traffic. He hadn't been to the Grotto since he was a kid. He decided to pay his grandfathers starburst cross a visit.

The Grotto was lit up with a million tiny lights for the Christmas season. Fortunately it was the dinner hour when he arrived and there was ample parking. Daniel got out of the car and put on a heavy jacket. The east wind had picked up and the windchill was considerably below freezing. He tried to remember where his grandfather had taken him, but this night, with the Christmas lights, nothing looked familiar. He found himself wandering up a path to an elevator and a turnstile that required a token to operate. He turned to leave, but a man in the dark robe of a Servite friar handed him a token and smiled. Daniel thanked him and rode up the elevator with him in silence. When he got out, he was standing on a bluff that overlooked the Portland Airport and he could see planes coming and going, as well as the lights of the city. He stopped to reflect. He could see there was something spiritual about this place. Christmas music was playing in the background from overhead speakers. He didn't know how long he had stood there reflecting on his grandfather when he heard a group behind him talking about the meditation chapel. He followed them along the path to a building that seemed to be made of glass, and, as he entered it, he thought it must be hanging out over the cliff. This was truly a spectacular view, he thought. He stood by the enormous plate glass windows and wondered what the view would look like in the daylight hours. He was looking north over the Columbia River and could imagine Mount Saint Helens in the distance beyond the city lights of Vancouver, Washington. Another hour had passed before he decided to continue along the lighted paths and see where he ended up. He wandered through what seemed like an endless number of paths with periodic stops and benches for rest and reflection. He was trying to find his way back to the elevator when he found himself lost on a path which wasn't lighted. He tripped on a swelled area of the pavement and fell, catching himself on his hands in a grassy area. He picked himself up and looked around. He could see lights ahead and started along a fence until he emerged on a well-lit path and stopped at a stone monument that rose straight up for as high as he could see. He leaned his hands against the obelisk and hung his head. He was standing at the high point of the cliff and at the base of a hundred-foot-tall stone edifice, which was topped with a bronze statue of the Blessed Virgin. He could feel the cold rock taking the heat from his hands. He listened to Silent Night playing softly in the background. He felt like the entire weight of the world was on his shoulders. *What am I doing here? How is this helping to solve the murder of my grandfather?* He wondered why Elizabeth hadn't returned his calls. *Could she be this cold and calloused?* He wandered back to the elevator and rode down by himself. At the base he walked back through the turnstile and stopped in front of the grotto, a huge cave in the side of the rock cliff he had been at the top of. The lights were bright and numbered in the thousands. Above the grotto opening he saw the cross he had been seeking. In a strange way he felt close to his grandfather at this place. He remembered those days in the summer of his eleventh year when he and his grandfather had visited this place so often. He found a bench and broke down and cried.

When September pulled into the parking lot of St. Clare's Church she was approached by a uniformed officer who pulled her aside before she made it to the door of the rectory.

"Detective, I know you are Catholic and this could be difficult."

"Just tell me what happened," September said.

"The priest, Richard Hays, was murdered." The officer checked his notes. "It's pretty gruesome."

"Thanks," September said, turning back toward the rectory.

"There's one more thing," the officer said.

September stopped in her tracks.

"The last one to see the victim was Daniel Tait," the officer said.

"We better find out where Tait is and get him in for questioning. I'll try his cell, but first I want to see what happened here." She entered the rectory.

Daniel mulled over his conversation with Fr. Rick. His grandfather had presented the church with a six foot high symbol of the birth and death of Christ. Someone wouldn't put that kind of effort into a project and give it away unless they felt strongly about their faith. His grandfather had never pushed his conversion on Daniel, but he had included him in his spiritual life when he was around. Maybe that was why he didn't feel as strongly as his father about his grandfather's choice of religion. He thought about the picture of the starburst cross and how it had led him to this place and the newspaper from France with the name of a war hero, Adele de Savoy, a woman who had died defending her country. They were hidden, all together, and somehow connected to his grandfather's dying message on the floor of his bedroom. As he looked up at the starburst cross, he thought, *maybe the asterisk wasn't an asterisk at all, but the starburst cross*. He closed his eyes and visualized the asterisk as his grandfather had written it. *What would a cross constructed more than fifty years after The War have to do with Adele de Savoy or the rogue organization GODS?* He felt like he was at a standstill. If there was a connection and the cross his grandfather had given to the church had something to do with his murder, the killer would also know it by now. Still, all indications were that the killer had been looking for a crucifix, not a modern-day cross.

September Gale stared at the grotesque look on the face of the priest. He had been tortured and disfigured and from the extent of the wounds, it appeared the killer had acted with intent and without mercy. She did not know Fr. Richard Hays personally, but she'd heard of him. Some friends from high school were members of St. Clare parish and had spoken highly of Fr. Rick in the past. It was a time when the Catholic Church and all priests were under attack for the indiscretions of a few bad priests, and Fr. Richard Hays had been outspoken in his criticism of abusive clergy, no matter what religion they were. He had made enemies both within the religious community and outside. Still, she couldn't imagine anyone being so upset to do this. In her mind, the Church had lost a priest and gained a saint. As she went over the crime scene, she became more and more convinced that this particular priest had been targeted, and the fact Daniel Tait was the last one to see him was of particular concern. *Whoever did this might be after Daniel.*

As she checked the office for anything that might have been missed by the forensic team, she reviewed the pictures on the wall and immediately recognized Walter Tait with the starburst woodcarving. She considered it carefully and took the picture for evidence. She had learned not to believe in coincidence. She had to find Daniel Tait before the killer found him.

It started to rain. Daniel looked up from where he was sitting and wiped the tears from his eyes. High up inside the cave, almost obscured by the shadows, he saw a replica of The Pieta, a work by Michelangelo, if he remembered his art appreciation classes correctly. It was the statue of Mary with the crucified body of Christ across her lap. It was enough to bring many to tears through the ages, but Daniel was all cried out. As he looked at the statue, he could relate to the terrible loss she must have felt. He had to solve the mystery of his grandfather's death. His cell phone vibrated on his belt holster and he reached for it. He wiped his eyes again and checked the caller ID. "Hi, September, are you ready to meet?"

There was a long silence on the other end. "September?"

"Where are you?" September asked softly.

"I'm at The Grotto."

"Stay there until I get there."

"Sure, but what's going on?"

"I can't talk now. I'll meet you in front of The Grotto. Don't move."

September knew she'd have to bring Daniel Tait in for questioning; there was little she could do about it. He was the last to see his grandfather alive and the last to see Fr. Richard Hays; at least that was what the evidence showed. She would be accused of neglecting her responsibilities if she didn't bring him in, and worse, if Daniel were guilty of the murders through some clever ruse, she would be negligent for allowing the perpetrator to get too close to her. In addition, there was something else bothering her. She put the politics of the investigation out of her mind and decided to follow her gut; whoever killed Fr. Hays wanted to know what Daniel Tait had learned. The tortured condition of the priest told her the killer had been after information, possibly information that would lead him closer to the alleged crucifix. As these thoughts streamed through her mind, she considered that the killer may know Daniel was at The Grotto and he was at least an hour ahead of her. She flipped on her flashing lights and hurried down the freeway maneuvering through bumper-to-bumper traffic on the Banfield Freeway.

Agent Fleming was stuck in traffic on Sandy Blvd. not far from The Grotto. He was cursing the outcome of his visit with the priest. He had wanted to have a civil conversation with the man, but he had not been cooperative. He'd even been rebellious. Fleming had had little to do with any church and especially Catholic priests. He considered the Catholic Church and its age-old traditions the great hoax of the ages. He believed the religions of the world were the cause of most of the turmoil in the world. Fleming believed that man was perfectly capable of solving the world's problems without the help of a deity, but religion always got in the way. Yet he hated that he had killed a priest; not because Fr. Rick was a holy man and God might rain fire down upon him, but because clergy were in a special category of individuals, like police officers and firefighters. Untimely deaths of priests got way too much media attention. *Why did he resist giving out information? Hadn't he given the man ample time to give up his secrets? Principles shouldn't be worth dying for.*

Fleming checked the GPS location he had placed on Daniel Tait's vehicle and the tracking device he'd put in his jacket when he'd faked falling against him in the garage. The device told him precisely where Tait's vehicle was. He watched it for a moment, and seeing it did not move and wasn't on a street, decided it was in a parking lot or a vacant lot in northeast Portland. The tracking device he had placed in Daniel's jacket was not as powerful as the device in Daniel's Jeep and he would have to get closer to see exactly what Tait was up to. If Tait had found the location of the crucifix he would have to wait for him to retrieve it or extract the information from him first. He pulled into The Grotto parking area and pulled his car into the shadows on the far end of the lot, away from the Gift Shop. He saw Tait's Jeep, but no Daniel Tait. He checked his weapon, and seeing that the grounds were starting to become busy, screwed a silencer to the nose of his weapon. With the Assassin on his way back to Europe, Fleming had assured the Grand Master he would handle things on this end. He felt victory was close. The crucifix was somewhere in the park, and the cross Daniel Tait was after was somehow the clue.

Fleming slipped the gun in his shoulder holster and headed down a path. He looked at the hand-held locator. It showed Daniel had stopped somewhere in the park and it was just a matter of time before he would find him.

Chapter 10

The Grand Master waited for the Assassin to check in before proceeding to Chambery, the only other place the crucifix could be according to the Assassin. He looked at the e-mail he'd been given by a lodge brother who was the editor of Paris-Normandie, published in Sainte-Mère-Eglise. It was asking about a crucifix removed from a hall in 1944 and if the paper knew who it belonged to? Of course Walter Tait could not have known the Croix de Chambery originally resided in the nunnery in Chambery, a fortunate break for Grand Orient de Savoy. The Grand Master held up a photograph of the crucifix. It was removed from the nunnery ages before he was born. *A crude carving,* he mused, *done by unskilled hands.* It was made of wood, that through the ages and hundreds of years of handling, had been worn smooth and turned black from the oils of the hands of those who believed the cross held the power to cure. The first Grand Master of GODS, Charles I, de Savoy, was a direct descendent of Umberto I Count of Savoy who was the founder of the House of Savoy.

There was a knock on the door. *"Enterer dans la sale,"* the Grand Master said rising from his desk and walking in front of it.

The Assassin strode into the room. He was taller than the Grand Master and out of respect hunched slightly so as not to appear superior.

The Grand Master looked at the haggard condition of the Assassin. His eyes were ringed with dark shadows from too little sleep. He felt empathy for the man. After all, it was simply a matter of fate that the Croix de Chambery was even being pursued. Until a few weeks earlier the existence of the crucifix was a legend, a story the octogenarians told around a bottle of single malt Scotch or a bottle of fine wine. Until the e-mail from Walter Tait had gloriously been handed to him, the existence of the crucifix had been all but forgotten. But now that it was known, it was paramount that it be returned to the lodge and made part of the opening rites. "I have spoken to Brother Fleming in America and he believes la Croix de Chambery is still in his country. If your hunch, as you call it, is incorrect, you will go back and complete your assignment."

The Assassin gave him an exhausted gaze. "I tired myself trying to find it. The old man may have had it at one time, but he did not have possession of it. Before I left, I thought his grandson might have found it hidden in a metal box, but even that led to a dead end. My belief is the crucifix has been returned to the nuns of Chambery. There is no other explanation."

The Grand Master gave him a look of incredulity. "What would bring you to that conclusion? I can think of several other possibilities." The Grand Master picked up a gold cigarette case from his desk and offered the Assassin a cigarette. The Assassin took a cigarette, and the Grand Master picked up a gold lighter engraved with the family crest, lit the Assassin's cigarette, and then lit his own. "You see this crest. It has been in my family from the time we were royalty. There is a reason why I am Grand Master and you serve me."

The Assassin drew in a long breath and exhaled a plume of smoke hoping to calm his nerves. He was aware that his normally steady hands were shaking as he removed the cigarette from his mouth. "The old man, Walter Tait, could hardly speak, but in his last breath he drew a symbol on the floor with his own blood. At first I thought it was an odd sign. The symbol he drew was an asterisk. Do you know the meaning of an asterisk?" He did not wait for a response from the Grand Master. "It means something has been left out, omitted. I looked it up in an American dictionary. He did not want us to know something and I think he did not want us to know the cross has been returned to the nuns in Chambery. He left the asterisk as a sign to his grandson to look somewhere else, only his grandson is not that bright. He has no idea what he is looking for."

The Grand Master sat down and leaned back in his chair. He took a long drag on his cigarette and let out a white cloud of smoke. "If you do not find the cross in the nunnery, what then?"

The Assassin did not look the Grand Master in the eyes. "I will go back to America and do whatever is necessary. If Brother Fleming needs my assistance, I will cooperate." He hung his head and studied the artwork on the carpet of the Grand Master's office.

"I hope you are prepared to do that. We must have the crucifix for the opening ceremony early in January. Do not disappoint me again."

Daniel Tate got up from the bench and walked around to get his blood circulating. *What was taking September so long?* The rain was falling in earnest and he looked around for shelter. He could feel the dampness and cold soaking through his jacket. He put his hands in his pockets to warm them from the cold. If September was on her way she was certainly taking her time. He let out a sigh and the fog from his breath rose in a small cloud.

"Hello Daniel," Agent Fleming said.

Daniel was startled by Fleming's voice. It was as if he had appeared out of nowhere. "Agent Fleming, what are you doing here?"

"I could ask you the same question," Fleming said. He pulled his collar on his overcoat up around his neck. "How is the search for your grandfather's killer going?"

"Not good," Daniel said. "Actually you may be able to help. My grandfather made a cross and presented it to a church and the pastor of the church said it was in The Grotto. "Check it out—" Daniel felt his phone vibrate and answered it. He turned away from Fleming. "September, where are you?"

"I'm just pulling in the parking lot."

"Good, take the path to the grotto. We'll wait for you."

"Someone is with you?" September asked.

"Agent Fleming."

"How did he know where you were? Don't say anything to him. I'm right down the path."

Daniel looked up. Fleming was gone.

"Daniel!"

Daniel saw September running toward him at full speed with her gun drawn. "It's about time you showed up. A few more minutes and I would have come down with pneumonia."

"Where is he?" September asked.

"Fleming? I don't know. He was just here."

"Come on, we have to get out of here."

"Do you mind telling me what's going on?"

"Come on." She grabbed his arm. "We need to go."

Daniel stood fast. "I'm not going anywhere until I get an explanation."

"Fr. Hays was murdered," September said.

Daniel gave her an incredulous look. "That's terrible. I was just there. What happened?"

September pulled on his arm again. "Daniel, I'm not asking. We're leaving now."

Daniel looked up and saw the starburst cross. "Wait, my grandfather's cross is right here." He pointed to the huge cross above the grotto.

"We'll come back." September said, nearly pulling him off his feet.

Fleming saw Daniel point at the huge cross above the grotto. He had the object in view from his hiding place in the shrubbery. He was certain the cross held the final clue to the location of the crucifix. He had access to all the data and he had gleaned enough information from the priest to know that the crucifix had not been seen from about the same time the starburst cross had appeared. He'd also figured out the meaning behind the asterisk; a cross within a cross. He would have to eliminate Daniel Tait and the nosy detective. There was no other way of covering his tracks. Daniel was the one who had put the puzzle together and he couldn't have him giving the clues to the police. If he didn't eliminate Daniel Tait he would never be able to get at the cross before the authorities put it under surveillance. He took aim and fired. The silencer muted the sound to a whisper that blended in with the background music and the steady din of the rain.

"What was that?" Daniel asked, grabbing his arm. He felt a burning sensation near his shoulder.

September heard the bullet ricochet off the grotto wall. There wasn't time to argue with Daniel any more. She tackled him to the ground. "Are you hit?"

"It went through my jacket," Daniel said. "Is someone shooting at us?"

September was on top of Daniel with her gun pointed into the bushes lining the assembly area in front of the grotto. The lights were so plentiful on the shrubbery lining the area that the darkness beyond the bushes gave perfect cover for anyone not wishing to be seen. Several people were milling around, but the park was still not crowded. From where she was, she couldn't tell from which direction the shot had come. "Now are you ready to get out of here?" September asked.

"I kind of like it here," Daniel said, putting his hand on her waist and looking into her eyes.

September rolled off him and under a park bench. "Take some shelter," she said, still trying to see where the gunman was.

Another bullet hit the back of the bench she had rolled under and fragments of splintered wood hit Daniel in the face. He rolled under the same bench next to September.

"What are you doing? It's a little crowded under here," September whispered.

"You have the gun. I'm sticking close to you," Daniel said.

"When I say go, we need to get out from under here and run."

"But we'll be exposed."

"Are you going to argue with me now?" September pushed him. "Get out there and hightail it toward the parking lot."

Daniel rolled out and jumped to his feet. He headed up the first trail he spotted and didn't look back until he was at the top of the trail and realized the parking area was off to his right. Another bullet hit near his feet and he immediately turned left and headed up the steep embankment. It was dark. He had wandered outside the normal boundary of the park. He continued up the slope grabbing bushes and small trees to help keep his footing. At the top he climbed some large rocks and jumped over a short fence. He stayed on the ground wondering if he had lost the gunman. When all seemed quiet, he found a paved path and ran along the fence line. He recognized the area from his earlier exploration of the grounds. He could see lights of the city off in the distance and knew he was heading toward the elevator.

Completely exhausted and soaked to the skin, he stopped to catch his breath. He stood hunched over and realized he was in the same place he had been earlier at the base of the monolith at the peak of the grotto cliff. At this point, the fence was no more than a foot in from a sheer drop to the assembly area in front of the grotto. He turned and nearly ran over September.

"Come on, we have to get back down. What part of parking lot don't you understand?"

"I took the wrong path and he was shooting at me. How'd you know where I was?"

"I followed you until you turned up the embankment. I figured it would be faster for me to take the elevator, but the gift shop was busy and a token costs...I'm here and we need to go." A bullet ricocheted off the base of the statue they were using for cover. September hit the ground and pulled Daniel down with her. "I don't know what's going on, but this guy seems to know where we are."

Daniel scooted on the ground away from the statue.

"Be careful, there's a drop off there. We're directly above the grotto," September said. She had yet to fire her weapon in the poor light and couldn't figure out how the gunman was able to locate them. She scooted over next to Daniel. "You get any closer to the cliff and you'll be dead from the drop."

"What am I supposed to do?" Daniel whispered. "I'm going over the fence."

"Don't be stupid. That's nothing but a sheer drop and the rocks are wet."

"We can't go the other way," Daniel whispered.

"Empty your pockets," September said.

"What!"

September reached in his jacket pocket and pulled out a pack of gum and his cell phone. She tossed them over the cliff.

"That was my phone," Daniel protested.

September reached in his other pocket. A bullet hit the ground in front of Daniel and he jerked away.

"You must have a bug in your pocket," September said. "Either find it or toss your coat."

Daniel didn't waste any time. He ripped off his jacket and was going to throw it over the fence, but September grabbed his arm and stopped him. She slid the jacket about three feet from her and crawled on her belly away from it. She jerked on Daniel's shirt.

"Be quiet and follow me," September whispered, getting to her feet.

Another bullet hit the jacket with a dull thud. September got up and ran with Daniel behind her. She didn't stop running until they had reached the elevator to the lower level. The area in front of the elevator was well lit and they pushed past the people who were getting off. As soon as they cleared the door, September pushed the button to close the door. Daniel barely made it in behind her.

"What now?" Daniel asked.

"We'll take my car," she said, between gasps for breath. "When we hit the bottom, follow me. No more excursions."

"You make it sound like I did that on purpose."

"Don't get sensitive on me now," September said.

She looked up at him. He thought she looked like a drowned kitten. Her hair was soaked and looked like an eggbeater had been run through it. The door opened. Daniel was hard pressed to keep up with her as she darted toward the parking area.

They got in her car and sped out of the lot. "How am I going to get my car?" Daniel asked.

September glanced over at him. "You are the most argumentative person I ever met. You could have gotten both of us killed."

"I deserve to know what's going on." Daniel said.

"We're going down to the station and I'm going to interrogate you. You're going to tell me everything you know and we'll get it on the record."

"You mean I'm under arrest?"

"That's right. As far as my department is concerned you are being brought in as a suspect in the murder of Richard Hays."

"This sucks," Daniel said. "I didn't do anything."

"I know that," September said, slowing for traffic. She turned on the flashing lights and her siren.

"If you know I didn't do anything, why bring me in?" Daniel asked. "Can you turn up the heater?"

September reached for the controls. "Shut up and cooperate if you want to get to the bottom of everything that's happening. For once, listen and keep your mouth shut. When we get to the station, I'm going to put you in handcuffs."

"What?"

"It's the only way we're going to get through this without both of us dying in the process."

"Can't you tell me a little more?" Daniel glared at her.

"Fleming is part of the conspiracy. He knows what you know and wants to kill us to cover his tracks."

Daniel considered what she had said. "I'm sorry," Daniel said. "I didn't mean to get you in the middle of this. I never trusted that guy. Is he really CIA?"

"It doesn't matter. I would have been in the way no matter what. I just need time to figure out who else is involved."

Fleming picked up the jacket and threw it back to the ground. He put his gun in its holster and picked up the jacket again. He fished out the tiny tracking bug from the pocket. At the fence that overlooked the airport, he dialed the Grand Master on his cell phone.

Chapter 11

The Assassin remembered the Chapelle de Chambery well. He knew the secret passageways that ran under the courtyard to the building that had once been the sleeping quarters for the Duchy de Savoy's armed guards. As a child he had roamed the Chateau de Savoy freely and had marveled at the massive guard towers and the gigantic bell spire. Once he had been given permission to ring the bell for the morning mass and the heavy brass bells pulled him up in the air every time they swung back and forth. He smiled as he thought of that day. His life was simple back then.

Today he was on another mission and he was sure there would not be any bells ringing for this visit. He parked his Citroën rental car outside the walls of the castle complex and walked along the cobblestone street. He passed through the arched tunnel that led to the courtyard. He stood in the early morning darkness and gazed up at the four flights of carved stone steps that stretched across the entrance to the Chapelle de Savoy. As he ascended the steps he wondered how many of the Knights Templar had walked up these same steps. Though he was not a direct decedent of any nobleman, he felt a kinship. Like the knights and the crusades of centuries past, his was on a noble mission. Like the knights, he would kill if he had to, to do what was right by his leader. He felt the morning chill settle on him as he entered the church through the heavy, ornately carved wooden door. That same doorway had been used for centuries by noblemen. In time of siege the common people seeking refuge from the attacking French armies were allowed to use the door.

The Assassin entered the church and let his eyes adjust to the dim light. Along one wall, he saw the statue of St. Francis de Assisi and a few dozen votive candles flickering in red glass containers. He sat in a pew near the statue. The nun would be there shortly. She had never missed a morning in her eighty years. He had only to wait for her.

As a child the Assassin had been amazed at the devotion of the Poor Clare Nuns. He had spent many hours on his knees, until they had turned red and raw, as penance for his schoolboy pranks. In those days he had knelt in the dark confessional waiting for a priest to show up so he could receive absolution for his sins. He looked at the door next to the shrine and frowned. He had told his innermost secrets to a priest on the sworn testimony that his secrets would remain between the priest and God, but it was inside that very door that he had been betrayed. One morning the priest had stepped aside and allowed a gendarme to take his place. As soon as he was released from jail, he made sure the priest did not live to betray a confessor's trust again. That was the first time he had killed.

The Assassin got up from the pew and entered the confessional. He sat on the small wooden bench where the priest normally sat. He adjusted the curtain and while he waited, thought about the priest he had rendered unconscious so he could take his place. Maybe he should have killed him. It was not like him to have doubts or leave witnesses, but he was only here to solicit a confession. He turned on the outside light indicating he was ready for Mother Falerina.

At 93, Mother Falerina had been a member of the Poor Clare convent from her late teens. She loved the history of the Poor Clare's and was devoted to the lifestyle of one who gave up all worldly possessions and devoted their life to prayer. Like Saint Clare of Assisi, the founder of the Poor Clare's, Mother Superior Falerina had come from a wealthy family and her parents had voiced much disappointment at her decision to become a woman of the cloth, but it had been a call from God and, at the age of 13, she had entered the convent as a novice. Now as an old woman, she was sure her decision had been the right one. She was at peace and did not regret dedicating her life to sacrifice, prayer, and devotion to the order of Poor Clares. If there was a character flaw within the nun, it would be the overwhelming desire she had felt since she received an e-mail from Walter Tate concerning a crucifix he had acquired during the war. She felt an overwhelming sense of pride that she would be the one in charge when the holy relic would be returned. It was this sense of pride that she had confessed daily and prayed would go away, but alas, this was why she was going to confession this day. The pride she felt was a sin, plain and simple, it was not welcome in her being and she wished to be absolved of all her sins. She knelt before St. Francis and said a prayer before entering the confessional.

Daniel was led into Police Central with his hands cuffed behind his back. It was not something he wanted and when the press was there with cameras flashing it ticked him off beyond words. He tried to hide his face, but turning away only gave another reporter a shot at him from another angle. He was unable to answer questions because, frankly, he didn't know why September was doing this. He was marched through the building with a police officer on each arm and finally placed in a holding cell. It was over an hour before September confronted him from outside his cell.

"How are you doing?" she asked through the bars.

Daniel looked up from the bunk he was sitting on, his face turning red with anger. He stood up and grabbed the bars. "You tricked me into coming here with you. I trusted you. Do I need a lawyer?"

"I know you're upset and you have a right to be, but I couldn't protect you when you were running around with a hit man on your ass."

"A hit man? I was doing fine until you showed up."

"If I come in there, are you going to be civil, or do I have to remove my gun and beat some sense into you?"

Daniel looked at her. She had dried her hair and cleaned up a little, but still wore the dirty white blouse and jeans she'd worn at The Grotto. "You have a strange way of trying to gain my confidence."

"Okay, let's start over. I'm sorry I had to trick you into coming in, but I am concerned that your life is in danger. You may have found out something and given it to the killer. Now you are just another witness if we ever catch them. And I did tell you I was going to bring you in."

"I thought you were kidding. So I'm worth more dead than alive?"

"Maybe to the killer or killers. What did you learn that led you to The Grotto?"

"I honestly don't know."

September summoned a jailer who opened the cell. "Come on, let's find a room that's more comfortable."

It was close to midnight and most offices were vacant. The halls were lighted with low-energy lights that caused everything to be cast in dark shadows. They proceeded to the end of a long corridor where September turned on a light in a small employee break room. She put on a pot of coffee and motioned to a lounge chair for Daniel to be seated.

"Was there something at Fr. Rick's that caused you to go to The Grotto?"

"My grandfather's cross. The same one you saw in the picture from the ammo box. I found an e-mail and wanted to see if Fr. Rick knew anything about the Poor Clare nuns. Instead he told me about a question my grandfather had asked him about the Grand Orient de Savoy."

"And was he any help?"

"Not really. He said that GODS was a cult and wouldn't have a need for a crucifix, but I saw a picture of my grandfather with the same cross that was in the photo in the ammo box. He said my grandfather had donated it to the church, but there wasn't a place for it at Saint Clare, so Fr. Rick donated it to The Grotto."

"So you went to The Grotto to find it." She poured coffee into two paper cups.

Daniel took a cup from her. "I had just found it when I got your message and bullets started flying."

"I know where the cross is," September said. "I remember seeing it from prior visits. But I think it's only displayed at Christmastime."

Daniel looked up at her and sipped his coffee. "I was at The Grotto cave. I saw a replica of The Pieta. I didn't see the cross until Fleming showed up."

"You needed to look up," September said. She sat in a lounge chair. "I thought I recognized the cross from the picture and then I remembered I'd seen it at The Grotto. They place it above the manger scene during the Season of Advent."

Daniel studied the tile floor for a minute and then said, "Fr. Rick said the cross had a double meaning. The starburst represents the star of Bethlehem at the Birth of Christ and the cross represents His death, kind of like the Alpha and the Omega, beginning and end."

September thought about it for a minute. She couldn't imagine the cross only meaning the beginning and end. What about the resurrection? She didn't want to get into it with Daniel at this time. "The Grotto probably never got the message because they only display it during the Christmas season. They use it for the Christmas star. All this doesn't explain why Fr. Rick was murdered, or why Fleming was using you for target practice."

"You sure it was Fleming?"

There was a tap on the door and a young woman poked her head in the room. "I got that list." She handed a paper to September.

"Thanks," September said. "You can go."

"What have you got?" Daniel asked.

"I had a search run on GODS in the United States. Looks like we got lucky, there's a lodge in Portland."

"But the priest said they were not the ones who would want the crucifix."

"If we can get a list of members we may find out differently."

"I don't follow."

"If Fleming is a member of GODS, he may be more loyal to them than he is to the CIA."

Daniel finished his coffee and tossed the cup in the wastebasket. "Fleming isn't going to like us meddling in his affiliations."

"He should have thought of that before he started shooting at us." September tossed her cup and checked her watch. She opened the door. "We should have enough protection at your place by now, so I can let you go."

"What about my Jeep?"

"They should have it swept by now."

"Swept?"

"For bugs. You don't think I was going to let you drive it with a tracking bug in it?"

"Then I'm free to go?" Daniel was a little skeptical.

September walked him to the lobby and held open the front door.

Daniel saw his Jeep parked curbside in a "No Parking" zone. "I'm not going to get a ticket for this, am I?"

"Get some sleep and I'll call you," September said, still holding the door for him.

"That's what my last date said," Daniel said, grinning.

September smiled. "Get out of here. There'll be an officer at your place. Don't go anywhere and stay out of trouble."

Chapter 12

September rose from a fitful sleep and took a quick shower. She had only half-an-hour to get to the Chapel in The Grotto for noon mass. After the service she met Fr. Anderson in the foyer and asked if she could talk with him over lunch.

"Far be it from me to turn down a free meal," the robust priest said. "But I have to be back by three for religious education classes."

September checked her watch and said, "I can eat pretty fast. I don't think it will take that long."

September, dressed in blue jeans, a blue denim shirt, and a navy jacket waited outside the rectory for the priest to come out. She watched as the big man approached her. He wore a heavy coat over a white shirt open at the neck and dark slacks that had long lost their crease. He was clean-shaven and had a full head of black-wavy hair. His voice was so deep that he sounded like he was talking from the bottom of a well. "There's an Elmer's around the corner. They make good ham and eggs. They serve breakfast all day."

September knew the place and in two minutes they were trying to find a spot in the busy parking lot.

After ordering, September gave a brief history of her family before telling the priest why she was anxious to share a meal with him. "I'm interested in the cross that hangs above the grotto during Advent. What can you tell me about it?"

"Not too much. We had a star placed over the manger scene until we received the cross as a gift about ten years ago. One of our parishioners suggested we use the cross. She said she knew the man who carved it and that it was a star *and* a cross so it had special significance. Personally, I liked the star, and by the time Mrs. O'Malley passed away it had become a tradition. You know how the church is about tradition."

September nodded and smiled. "The reason I was asking is we would like to have the cross for awhile to examine it."

"I can't imagine why you would want to do that," Fr. Anderson said. "What on earth would you be looking for?"

"Frankly, I have no idea," September said. "I know it's an inopportune time with all the Christmas visitors and the season, but when Fr. Rick at St. Clare's was murdered...well, we think it had something to do with the cross."

"Like I said, we've had that cross for several years. What could possibly be learned by taking it down?"

September leaned into the table. "Father, the reason I'm here is to see if we can examine the cross without the formality of a search warrant. We may be able to clear this up and there will be no need to keep the cross. It would only be a matter of hours."

The priest looked at her from across the table and nodded. "We can take it down this afternoon and you may examine it on Grotto property, if you promise to release it before the evening lights are turned on. Without the star the manger scene loses some of its significance."

"I understand," September said.

"Do you really?" Fr. Anderson asked. "Without the star how would the Magi find the Christ Child?" He winked at her.

"We better get going, if we want to get this done," September said. On the way out to her car she called Daniel Tait on her cell phone.

"Get over to The Grotto," September said. "We're taking the cross down."

There were a lot of things Daniel had forgotten about his grandfather, but now that he was gone, little things kept triggering his memory. As he drove against traffic along the East Bound Freeway, he looked up at Providence Hospital and a memory of the place flashed in his head.

His grandfather had been in intensive care for a week and not expected to live. He was in the waiting room with his father and mother when his grandmother came out and whispered something to his father. His father nodded and left with his grandmother. Daniel was ten or eleven years old at the time. He sat with his mother waiting for his father to return. An hour passed and then another. His mother took him down to the hospital cafeteria and they had lunch. After lunch they returned to the waiting room and a nurse came to get them. They were led down a hall through locked doors to his grandfather's room where he lay dying.

Daniel's eyes narrowed as he remembered the crucifix his grandfather was holding. It was made of a dark-colored wood and smooth. The figure of Jesus was nearly rubbed away, but you could tell it was a crucifix and not just a cross. It looked like it had been hand carved and at the time, Daniel thought his grandfather must have carved it.

Could this be the crucifix they were looking for? The thought hit him so hard he nearly lost control of his Jeep. He slammed on his brakes to prevent rear-ending the car in front of him. He couldn't remember seeing the crucifix after that day. It was about a year later when his grandmother passed away. If he remembered correctly, his grandfather had started building the starburst cross shortly after he recovered. Suddenly he felt a burst of energy as he moved through traffic toward The Grotto. *Was there a connection between the crucifix and the starburst cross?* He couldn't wait to tell September.

September and Fr. Anderson took advantage of a break in the weather and strolled along the path toward the grotto. She noticed the park was not nearly as lush and pretty this time of year. She remembered it much prettier from her former visits. But the annual evening Christmas lighting made up for the lack of color during the winter months. As they ambled along Fr. Anderson filled September in on the history of The Grotto.

"The Grotto is a shrine and a sanctuary," Fr. Anderson said, as they sauntered along the paved path. "A sanctuary because it is a place where people come to get away from the hustle and bustle of everyday life and a shrine because it honors Mary, the Mother of God. There are God's wonders around every corner. Those who drive by are hardly aware of the beauty that is hidden in this 62-acre site in the middle of the city."

September felt herself growing impatient. While she was interested in the beauty and history of the site, she was not here as a tourist and wished they could pick up the pace. She tried to walk faster, but the robust priest had his own pace and wouldn't be rushed. "Fr. Anderson, I don't mean to be disrespectful, but I'm trying to investigate a murder."

Fr. Anderson looked at her with scorn. "You are walking amongst some of the most beautiful artwork in the world. Do you realize that the bronze statue of Our Sorrowful Mother that sits atop that cliff was blessed in the Vatican by Pope Pius XI in 1934?"

He stopped and pointed at the top of the cliff, high above Grotto cave and September gasped, "The cross is gone!"

"Don't panic," Fr. Anderson said. "I'm sure there is an explanation."

"I'd like to know what it is," September said.

Fr. Anderson pulled a cell phone from his pocket and spoke on it. He turned to September. "The cross is in our maintenance shop for repairs. It seems it was vandalized last night and they found it on the ground at the base of the grotto." He shook his head. "I'm deeply concerned with the younger generation as of late."

"Were there any witnesses?" September asked.

"Let's go to the maintenance building. I'm sure they can answer your questions."

To her amazement, the priest picked up his pace as they walked toward the chapel. They took two flights of stairs down to the base of the church. The maintenance building was at the far end of the administrative parking lot. September called Daniel to let him know they would be in the maintenance building and to take the driveway north of the exit. Daniel was less than a mile away so she decided to wait outside until he arrived. "Father, you go ahead. I'm going to wait for Mr. Tait."

Daniel entered the driveway as September had instructed and pulled into a parking space only a few feet from where September was standing. He opened the door as she walked toward him. "What's happened?" He asked.

"Follow me, I'll explain on the way."

They walked into the building and saw Fr. Anderson with a tall, lanky man in coveralls toward the rear of the building. As they approached they could see the starburst cross laid out on a makeshift bench made up of two sawhorses and a sheet of plywood. Even as they approached they could see the cross was heavily damaged.

"How bad is it?" September asked.

"I'm afraid it's a complete loss," Fr. Anderson said.

September introduced Daniel to the priest. She leaned over the cross and Daniel picked up one end. The points of the starburst were shattered and the bottom of the cross had been broken as if someone had used it like a baseball bat.

"Who would do such a thing?" Fr. Anderson asked, shaking his head. He tapped the maintenance man on the shoulder. "We'll have to replace this with the old Star," he said to the man in coveralls.

"I've got a pretty good idea," Daniel said.

September nudged him. "We're not here to speculate. Can we take this for our investigation?"

"It is no longer any use to us," Fr. Anderson said. He turned to Daniel. "I understand your grandfather built this cross. It served a useful life with us. We will miss it."

"Thank you," Daniel said. "I'm sure my grandfather would have appreciated your comment."

September tried to gauge the length of the cross by stretching out her arms. "It's much bigger than it looked hanging on the cliff."

"It'll fit in my Jeep," Daniel said.

"We'll bring it back when we're done," September said, reaching for one end of the cross.

"No need," Fr. Anderson said. "It looks like it's beyond repair. Unfortunately, it wasn't insured."

As Daniel and September carried the cross, the maintenance man held open the door. They carried the cross through the parking area and Daniel opened the back of his Jeep.

"The maintenance man seemed a little strange," Daniel said.

Fr. Anderson heard him and said, "Herman is a deaf-mute, but bless his soul, he thinks God has given him a blessing."

"Seems more like a curse to me," Daniel said.

Fr. Anderson smiled, "To some it would seem that way, but Herman can enjoy his world without the bickering and arguing that we must endure. God has provided for his needs as he has all of ours."

Whatever, Daniel thought. Right now he didn't feel like God was providing much for him. Immediately he acknowledged he had all his senses and maybe that should be enough to be thankful for. "You hold it here and I'll fold down the seats," Daniel said to September.

After he closed the hatch, Daniel and September bid Fr. Anderson goodbye.

"Where to now?" Daniel asked.

"Back to your grandfather's house," September said. "We already know who did this and I doubt he would leave any fingerprints."

"Good idea, we can check it out in my grandfather's workshop."

"You think he found what he wanted?" September asked.

"I don't think this is the cross he was looking for," Daniel said. "My grandfather had a crucifix. It's got to be hidden somewhere and I think I know where it is."

The Assassin had gotten the news he had wanted from the old nun and was disappointed. He had left Mother Falerina slumped over in the confessional. She will not talk, the Assassin mused. The morning light was still an hour away as he made his way down the ancient stone corridor toward the nunnery. The Mother Superior lived in a simple private room at the end of a hallway with twenty other rooms of the same size and shape. *It is a dismal existence*, the Assassin thought moving silently and swiftly to the door of her room. None of the doors were locked; a rule of the order and none of the rooms contained more than a cot, a crucifix on the wall, and a small table. The floors were wood planks worn smooth through the ages. The Assassin was not concerned about his invasion of the private space of the nuns since he had left the church during their morning prayers. He doubted the crucifix was in the nunnery. The nun would not lie, even if it meant saving a precious relic.

The Assassin lifted the thin mattress and slit it open and shook out the cotton stuffing. He checked the room for anywhere else the cross might be hidden and resigned himself to the fact that he had been mistaken and the crucifix must still be in the United States, probably among the old man's possessions. Though he was concerned about the call he would make to the Grand Master, he was sure that he was much closer to finding the location of the crucifix and another possibility had been eliminated. If it wasn't here, then it had to be back in America.

Detective Gale wasn't sure where the investigation would go from here. She had evidence that Agent John Fleming was involved in the attempt on Daniel Tait's life, but did not have enough evidence to have him arrested. If she brought him in now, it would tip her hand. If Fleming was found to be a member of GODS, they would have to bring in the FBI. The murder of two citizens in her jurisdiction could turn into the international conspiracy Fleming had first mentioned, and she still didn't have a clue as to why.

As she drove toward the Burlingame area, she wondered at the way the cross was damaged. It looked like it had been smashed in a fit of rage and her gut told her Fleming was behind it. There was no reason for Fleming to be at The Grotto, and to have the cross destroyed the same night was just too much of a coincidence.

She got on her phone and called her office to see if her assistant had been able to obtain a membership list for GODS.

"Megan, what have you got on Fleming?" Megan was the intern yet to graduate from the academy and assigned to September in a work-study program. She was a whiz on the computer and had done an exhaustive job of searching. "I'm so sorry. I've run down every site I could find and there is nothing on the internet regarding members. It appears GODS really is a secret organization."

"I thought they were an offshoot of the Free Masons. Don't they have to register with the government?" September came to a halt on the freeway and contemplated turning on her flashing lights then thought better of it. In the bumper-to-bumper traffic she would probably cause an accident and this wasn't an emergency.

"The organization is registered as a non-profit, but it seems the members don't have to register for anything."

"See if you can find anything on Poor Clare nuns in France. Walter Tait sent them an e-mail."

"The nuns have entered the digital age?"

"Believe it or not, even the nuns have discovered the value of saving our trees." September disconnected and called Daniel, who had disappeared in the traffic on the expressway. "Wait for me when you get there," she said. "I'm stuck in traffic."

"Somehow I missed the mess. I'm turning on Terwilliger now."

"I'll call the officer on duty at the house and let him know you're coming."

Chapter 13

The Assassin had driven for twelve hours from the church in Chambery and was back in Sainte-Mère-Eglise, in his room at the Hotel Le Sainte-Mère. As he cleaned his weapon he could still smell the powder residue from the gun he had used to put a bullet in Mother Falerina's head. An hour later the Assassin stowed his weapon in the gun safe in the Grand Master's office and waited for the Grand Master to return. It was time for the noon meal and for the Grand Master, like many Frenchmen, the noon meal was the biggest meal of the day. They do not know the value of deprivation, the Assassin mused. Pain was something close to him and he all but worshipped the suffering he had endured in his life. He rarely ate more than one meal a day and considered it glutinous to eat in excess of one's need for existence. He worshipped his body and felt that its existence on the earth was for bettering mankind, and to be true to that cause was to deny oneself of those things that would distract from the main purpose.

The one vice the Assassin engaged in was tobacco. He admitted it had a hold on him and he did little to deprive himself of the simple pleasure of a cigarette. He lit a cigarette and waited to share the news of his visit to the convent with the Grand Master. He wondered if they had found her body. She would be missed, he knew, but not by him. He looked at the scar on the palm of his right hand and grimaced. He had failed to cry when the ruler had found it's mark and the blood had flowed from his hand. Sister Falerina was shocked that the metal edge had drawn blood and she had tried to wrap his hand in a cloth bandage, but he had licked the wound and held it up to the rest of the fifth-grade class in defiance.

He blew smoke rings as he waited and chuckled. After her confession, Mother Falerina had been surprised that he was in the confessional instead of the parish priest. He had made sure she remembered him before he extracted his revenge. *A pity she had not yet received the crucifix from Walter Tait,* he thought. He would have to return to America and this time he knew for certain the Croix de Chambery was still there. He immediately stood when he heard the leather heels of the Grand Master's shoes on the marble floor outside the office. As the Grand Master entered, the Assassin said, "Grand Master, I have great news."

As September pulled into the driveway of Walter Tait's house, she parked directly behind Daniel's Jeep and waved at the officer sitting in his car next to the jeep. She got out of her car and helped Daniel pull the cross from the back of the jeep. They carried it into the garage.

"I can make room for it over here," Daniel said. They leaned the cross against the workbench and Daniel cleaned off the boxes that were stacked on the bench clearing an area large enough for the cross to rest on.

"Not that way," Daniel said as they lowered the cross on the bench. "Turn it over." The back of the cross was now facing up. Daniel retrieved a bulb from a drawer in the bench and replaced the overhead light that had burned out. "This cross, if it the one my grandfather made, will have his mark on the back."

"He had a mark?" September asked surprised.

Daniel went over the cross from top to bottom looking for the three letters of his grandfather's mark.

"What exactly are we looking for?" September asked.

"The initials WDT," Daniel said. "Walter Daniel Tait. And before you ask, I have my grandfather's middle name."

After what seemed like an exhaustive inspection, September said, "It doesn't look like it's here."

"It has to be. Check the broken piece."

September lifted the broken end of the cross from the floor and set it on the table. "What if we don't find it?"

"If we don't find it, my grandfather didn't make it."

They went over the back and then turned the cross over and checked the front. There were no markings.

September stepped back from the cross and sat down on a cardboard box. "You expect me to believe this is **not** your grandfather's work. I saw the picture and I saw him in the picture in Fr. Rick's office."

"You saw a cross that looks like this one, but it is not this one. The cross my grandfather built is missing. This one is of no value to us."

"You seem hellbent on finding your grandfather's cross. What aren't you telling me?" September asked. "First, you said the gunman wanted a crucifix, and now we are looking for a cross. Did it ever occur to you, you could be wrong?" The frustration showed in September's voice.

"We're looking for a crucifix, but some way my grandfather's cross is connected. Why else would Fleming try to destroy it? I was hoping there would be a secret compartment or a hiding place. A cross within a cross, you know, an asterisk."

September shook her head. "Maybe Fleming was just following you. He tracked you to The Grotto using a GPS device and thought you were onto something."

Daniel looked down at her dejected figure. Her face was smudged and her blouse was dirty. Her hair was a mess. "I realize you're trying to solve a murder. That's also what I'm trying to do. Where would an old man hide a crucifix, if he didn't want someone to find it?"

"In a church," September said. "If I wanted to hide a crucifix I'd hide it in a Catholic church."

"Aren't there a lot of crucifixes in a church?"

"You made my point," September said, standing up. "In a Catholic church you could hide the crucifix in plain sight."

"I don't think he would do that," Daniel said. "There is something about this crucifix that makes it special and my grandfather wouldn't put it on display where anyone could get at it. He was trying to return it to the original owners and I think that's what caused the whole thing to blow up."

"I'm going to play the devil's advocate here," September said. "Your grandfather obtained a crucifix that he didn't know at the time was stolen from a ruthless bunch of religious zealots. He's getting old and contacts people in the community where he obtained the crucifix to see if he can return it before he dies. But the people he contacts aren't going to take a chance on him finding out the true origin of the crucifix, and decide to get it back by force if necessary. It's simply a matter of your grandfather getting mixed up in something he didn't understand. It got him killed and if you don't stop this witch hunt it will get you killed, too."

"Whether you like it or not, I'm in the middle of this and I'm going to finish what my grandfather started."

"I'm not fighting you. I'm just saying you need to know what you're dealing with. Whoever wants that crucifix will do whatever it takes to get it and the more you know the more danger you are putting yourself in."

Daniel started toward the door. "I appreciate your concern, but we aren't getting any closer to solving my grandfather's death by standing here. We need to find out what happened to the original cross my grandfather built. If it was given to The Grotto, why wasn't it the one we brought back here?"

"If you're certain this isn't the cross your grandfather built, then I'll call Fr. Anderson and ask him if there is another one." September pulled her phone from her pocket.

After she hung up she said to Daniel, "Fr. Anderson wasn't at The Grotto when the cross was given to them, but there is another cross that looks just like this one. The only person still around who can tell us what happened is the maintenance man."

"Herman," Daniel said. "Great. He's deaf and dumb. How are we going to speak to him?"

"Not speak," September said. "Communicate like this." She signed something that caused Daniel to throw up his hands.

"Where'd you learn to do that?"

"My cousin was deaf. I learned signing when I was six years old."

"You said was. Is she..."

"She died when I was a teenager. She had other problems."

"I'm sorry," Daniel said. "It sounds like you were close."

September grimaced and tightened her lips. "She was the same age as my little sister. We were all blessed by her presence." She walked out with Daniel. "If we are going to find your grandfather's cross we need to get to The Grotto before Herman gets off work.

John Fleming checked his watch. If the flight was on time he had half an hour to kill. He pulled into the short-term parking at Portland International and turned off the engine. As he sat with the radio playing soft Jazz he leaned his seat back and thought how different things would be if he would never have joined Grand Orient de Savoy. *What had he got himself into this time?* His induction into Grand Orient de Savoy came about as a result of a trip to Europe, a graduation present from his proud parents. While visiting the French city of Chambery he happened upon a museum and was enthralled with the history of the area. While he wandered through the medieval armor and weapons, he had been approached by a young French woman with piercing dark eyes and raven hair.

"You are an American, no?" She said in perfect English.

"*Non, je suis un Français avec un accent terrible,*" he had said in his very best French.

"You are most certainly an American. Frenchmen do not dress so casually. You are a cowboy, no?"

He laughed. "No, I am not a cowboy." He pretended to draw a gun and shoot her.

John Fleming was smitten with her beauty and her daring sense of adventure. They shared an espresso and lunch at an outdoor café, if you could call a striped umbrella and four chairs in the middle of a sidewalk with a street vendor's cart, a café, but he was instantly in love and none of that mattered. They spent the day together and that evening dined in the restaurant at his hotel. It wasn't until the next morning that he learned her name was Marie Cuvier. They spent a week together and she introduced him to Marcus de Savoy, the son of the Grand Master. For an American to be knighted into Grand Orient de Savoy by the Grand Master himself was a great honor, Marcus had said. It had all seemed innocent at the time. Now, as he looked back on it, he was trapped in a double life, one which he regretted each night as he stared at the ceiling of his room. He wondered what Marie Cuvier was doing on the other side of the world. He wished she was in his life today and he had never joined the CIA. But that was water under the bridge, a bridge he could never cross back over.

Uncle Sam recruited John Fleming to expand their international fight against terrorism. His family members had no history of activism and his parents were both solid U.S. citizens with no police record or participation in radical activities, even though his mother had been a student at UC Berkley during the radical days of the Vietnam War. His father had served on a nuclear submarine as an officer in the Navy and had met his mother while she was a graduate student teaching English Literature at Portland State College.

John Fleming had been recruited to the CIA while he was a graduate student at Reed College. His major was Nuclear Physics, but it was his minor in French that interested the CIA. He was recruited to go undercover as a spy for international terrorists on American soil. His knowledge of the French language made him stand out as a candidate since many radicals from the Middle East spoke French as a second language, and his lack of a religious affiliation was considered another plus. Church goers, particularly Christians, were not likely to effectively infiltrate radical Islamic terrorist groups. At the time of his induction into the CIA, he was not yet a member of Grand Orient de Savoy, a secret society which would have raised a giant red flag. Once he joined the cult he realized that GODS demanded even stricter devotion than The Company. It wasn't long after he became a member that he was asked to do something that would bind him forever to GODS. "You can only serve one master," John Fleming was told, as he was being shown photographs of him performing the most sacred ritual of the GODS, an act that would ruin his life forever, if it were to be made public. At the time he had thought only of the beautiful French girl and not about the consequences. Now none of that mattered.

John Fleming checked the clip in his Glock 9mm semi-automatic handgun and stored it under the seat in his Cadillac XLR sports car. The Assassin was due to arrive at any minute.

When September and Daniel arrived, Herman was in the back of the maintenance shop putting a coat of paint on the Bethlehem Star that was to replace the cross over the manger scene at the grotto. September was nearly on top of him when he started upright from her presence. As she signed, she spoke and Daniel could hear her words.

"Is there another cross like the one that was destroyed?" September asked.

Herman nodded and responded with signs that September interpreted. "There is another one. It is in the chapel."

"Which chapel?" September asked.

"The Chapel of Our Sorrowful Mother," September said, as she read his response.

September thanked Herman and said to Daniel on the way out of the building, "Come on, we're going to church."

The chapel of Mary was a hewed-stone structure that towered over the other buildings in The Grotto. Its towering presence outside belied the relatively small footprint of the building's interior. The 40-foot-high ceilings, the elegant marble statues, and the painted scenes rising high above the altar made Daniel feel small, almost tiny, as he entered through the golden entry doors. Inside he saw a church that could accommodate over 500 worshippers. The walls were covered with stonework bricks with alcoves housing elegantly-carved statues. Above the altar was his grandfathers starburst cross, suspended high in the air from nearly invisible wires. "Wow," Daniel said. "The architecture has a European flair."

September looked at him and dipped her hand in the fountain of Holy Water and crossed herself. "Makes you glad you're a Christian," she said.

Daniel swallowed. It was a lot to take in. His grandfather's carving among such glorious works of art.

"The statues are carved of Carrara marble from Italy," September said. "They are of the saints and here to remind us of the significant people in our lives."

"It looks like the starburst cross," Daniel said, looking up at the cross high in the air. "How are we going to get it down?"

September stared at the cross with him. "Why do we need to take it down?"

Daniel gave her a quizzical look. "I thought we were looking for clues to my grandfather's murder. So far we have been led to this place. Twice, I might add. The crucifix could very well be hidden inside the cross."

September grimaced and looked at Daniel through tightened lips. Her dimples were showing, but she wasn't smiling. It was more a look of concern. "I know, but we'd need a good reason to get them to take down that cross."

"I thought you got an agreement from the priest."

"Fr. Anderson. That was for the one outside. This presents a whole new problem."

"Give me a ladder and I'll get it down."

September slugged him in the shoulder. "Don't you dare."

Daniel grabbed his arm. "You hit me again and I'll report you for police brutality."

"Really?" September was about to hit him again when she was interrupted by a sound behind them.

"Ahem...Miss Gale, I'm surprised you would be "cutting up" in the chapel." Fr. Anderson's voice filled the empty church and reverberated like he was on a loud speaker. He ambled up the aisle like a penguin on the march, his body swaying right and left, as he slowly made his way to them.

"We were just discussing how we were going to get a closer look at the cross," September said.

"I see," Fr. Anderson said. "You'll never land a fella by beating him up. And you'll never get a closer look at that cross by being disrespectful in God's house." He winked at her.

"Forgive me, Father," September said. "We really need to take a closer look at the cross. If we had a ladder, we might be able to look at it in place."

"That won't be necessary," the priest said. "Follow me." He walked behind the altar and began lowering the cross by turning a pulley hidden behind the large marble monolith that rose high behind the altar.

"That's the way I would have done it," Daniel said.

"I forgot you were an engineer," September said. "Now, tell me what we are looking for."

The cross was lowered until it rested on the floor. Daniel knelt down beside it. The wood was layered in gold leaf and he touched it with reverence. "My grandfather put a lot of work into this." He rested his fingers on his grandfather's initials tucked away in the valley of the star.

"You're sure this is the one your grandfather carved?" September asked.

"Right here. WDT, it's the real thing."

"But what does it tell us?"

"Let's turn it over."

Fr. Anderson helped them turn the cross over. "Son, I didn't know your grandfather, but I spoke to some of our older parishioners and they remember him fondly."

"He spent a lot of time here," Daniel said, "at least at the grotto. He brought me here when I was a kid. I didn't appreciate the beauty of the place. Now it makes me feel like I'm...on holy ground. Why do you think that is?"

"We are all born in the image of God, and we all have a need for him in our lives. Perhaps it's your turn."

Daniel turned back to the cross. He examined the back carefully and turned away disappointed. "It's not here."

Fr. Anderson left for a minute and returned with a soft cloth and started to polish the cross. "It hasn't been dusted for a while. We might as well take advantage of our efforts."

Once the cross was high above the communion table again, Daniel stepped down from the sanctuary and sat down in the first pew.

September sat beside him. "You seem disappointed. What were you looking for?"

"I honestly wasn't sure." Daniel focused his eyes on the cross. "I guess I was hoping my grandfather would speak to me from the cross. I guess I expected there to be a compartment housing the crucifix. I thought the asterisk might be a cross within a cross. It was stupid. Now, I don't know where we go from here."

"You think about it and call me if you come up with anything," September said. "I have to get back to headquarters."

Chapter 14

September got the call early in the morning. It was bad enough that she had missed dinner with her family on Thanksgiving Day, now she was about to miss it again. Her mother had rescheduled because she wanted the whole family together and September was about to make apologies again. She was on her way to investigate another homicide. This one was in a park not far from the Tait murder. She waded through thick foliage and ducked under a string of Crime Scene tape. She saw the medical examiner, Kenny Parson, hunched over the body. "What have you got, Kenny?"

Kenny was the deputy coroner for Multnomah County. He had been on the job 13 months and this was the first time he had been asked to handle a case on his own. His boss was out of town for the holidays. He felt the neck where there were obvious abrasions and looked up at September. "We're just about ready to bag-and-tag. You want to have a closer look?"

September made her way to the body. "How long's she been here?"

"Near as I can tell at least a week. She was a pretty girl. Someone's sure to have missed her."

"What else do you have?"

"For your benefit I'll give you the short version. Her neck is broken so I guess that would rule out suicide. Someone grabbed her head like this, and *snap*. She was middle class. No sign of a struggle. It appears she was killed somewhere else and carried here, not dragged. So we're dealing with a person with some strength, most likely a man. She wasn't molested, has all her clothes on, and no pocketbook or identification. She wasn't married, mid-twenties. I doubt we'll be able to find dental records; she appears to have perfect teeth, a product of the fluoride in the Portland water, so she is probably local. I'll have to get her on the slab to give you an exact cause of death, but the broken neck is my best guess."

September looked around the heavy overgrowth for any signs the killer may have left behind.

"Good job, Kenny. Anything else?"

Kenny closed the eyes on the victim. "Yeah. I hope you find the son-of-a-bachelor who did this and send him to the chair."

"We use lethal injection now," September said.

Kenny looked down at the young woman. "I know, but whoever did this deserves to be fried."

September searched the area, but it was so rugged and wet for the past week there was little hope of finding a clue. In an hour she gave up and decided to go back to headquarters and see if there were any missing persons matching the girl's description. She had spent so much time on the Tait case lately that she almost welcomed another case to take her mind off it. She had started to develop a fondness for Daniel Tait and knew that was not wise. She drove through the heavy traffic wondering where things could go between her and Daniel. She guessed as far as she would let them. It was obvious there was an interest from Daniel. He was a handsome man, a professional and they seemed to like the same things, although they didn't share the same religion; in fact, she was pretty sure he wasn't a Christian, even if he said he was.

She smiled, thinking about her sister. She should have been a cop, the way she had seen through her. She knew there was something blooming between her and Daniel, even when September wouldn't admit it. In fact she had gone out of her way to keep Daniel at arm's length, something that was difficult to do at times. She used the handsfree device in her car to call her parents to relay the bad news, she would miss another dinner with the family. There was a girl without a name that had missed the holidays with her family and she had to reunite them, even if it was under the worst of circumstances.

Daniel dressed, grabbed a travel mug of coffee, and drove to Space Age Metals, his place of employment. It was the first day back on the job since before the Thanksgiving holiday and he knew there would be enough work piled up to keep his mind off the tragedy. He was through the door and in the lunch room refilling his coffee mug, when John Howard stopped him.

He had worked for John Howard for the past three years and got along with him well. Howard was a tall man, about the same height as Daniel, but with a balding head, rimless glasses and a black shirt and tie, a complete opposite in looks and dress. He had over thirty engineers working for him in the Titanium Casting Group of Space Age Metals. To many of the engineers he was an imposing figure to be feared, and there were plenty of rumors to back up the man's reputation of being a hardnosed manager, ready to kill anyone who didn't do his job, but Daniel had gotten to know John Howard and respected the man. He had a tough job overseeing a room full of engineers, many of them fresh out of college.

John Howard put his hand on Daniel's shoulder. "Can we talk a minute?"

They found an empty table and both sat down. John set a handful of manila folders on the table.

"I saw your grandfather's obituary in the paper. If you need some time off, I'm sure we can arrange it."

"Thanks," Daniel said, "but the funeral is already over and there isn't much else I can do. I guess if there is a good side to this, it's that it happened on a holiday and I had vacation time already planned."

Howard removed his glasses and looked across the table at Daniel. "You probably haven't been by first inspection yet, so I'll fill you in before you get blindsided."

Daniel looked him in the eye. "You mean the cracked struts on the fan frame?"

"You've seen it, then. Calvin Rutledge went through the roof when he saw it."

"I caught the first one through the system the day before the holiday and instructed Jim Bloom to have the gas-cooling manifold in the vacuum casting furnace checked for a leak in the ductwork. The part is not cooling uniformly after casting and is ripping itself apart. The struts are the weakest point resulting in the cracks."

John smiled and rose to his feet. "Good, I figured you'd be on top of it. Let me know if you need any help."

Daniel got Jim Bloom on his cell immediately after his boss left. At $100,000 each, he hoped he had put the correction in before any additional parts showed up with cracked struts.

Missing Persons was a separate division in the police department and September had to access their files to see if there were any young women with her victim's characteristics reported missing. She was surprised to find there were three. The body had been dead for a week, but the cold November weather had kept the decomposition to a minimum and September was able to get a reasonable picture of the victim with her cell phone. She compared it to the three pictures on her computer and was sure she had a match. She verified it with the morgue and made a visit to the girl's parents.

"Mr. and Mrs. Marten, I'm Detective Gale, Portland City Police," September said showing her shield.

They invited her in and she sat on the couch in the living room. "I'm so sorry to inform you that we found the body of your daughter this morning. I'm afraid she was the victim of foul play."

September hated this part of the job. There was never a good time to tell a parent they had lost a child. All parents expect their children to outlive them. She waited for Mr. Marten to comfort his wife and hated the next part almost as much. "I need to ask you some questions. I know it's a bad time, but the sooner we get answers, the sooner we can find the person who did this."

Mr. Marten moved his wife to an overstuffed chair, and helped her sit. "What can we help you with?"

September turned on a digital recorder. "If you don't mind, I would like to record our conversation for later reference. When was the last time you saw your daughter?"

Mr. Marten sat on the arm of the chair holding his wife's hand. "She came by last week and said she was going to have Thanksgiving dinner with her boyfriend at his parents' place."

"Do you have a name?"

"They have been going out for a few months, but we haven't met him yet. Elizabeth was not going to bring a boyfriend home unless she was pretty serious about him," Mr. Marten said.

Mrs. Marten got up and walked across the room. "Liz gave us a picture of them. They were such a lovely couple." She removed a picture from a shelf on the bookcase and handed it to September.

September looked at the picture of Daniel Tait with his arm around the murder victim and gasped. She quickly caught herself and swallowed hard.

"Are you okay," Mr. Marten asked. "Can I get you some water?"

September shook her head, "no," and struggled to hold back the tears. "I'm sorry, I have to go. Here's my card. I'll call and make an appointment for you to identify the body." She got up and headed for the front door. "I can let myself out. I'll call you as soon as I can."

September sat in her car a long time before she drove off. She was debating what to do. Should she call Daniel, or send an arresting officer to pick him up. She knew he had returned to work. Her mind was buzzing with conflicting emotions. *Did he not think they would find the body and come after him? Maybe he is innocent. Maybe that was why he was hanging around. No, there are no coincidences. One murder, maybe, but not three linked to the same person. Daniel Tait was a serial killer and a very clever one!* She had been falling for a serial killer. She wasn't going to take anymore chances. She sent an arresting officer to Space Age Metals to arrest Daniel Tait. On the way back to her office September played back the recorded interview with the Martens. *How could I have been so stupid!*

Daniel caught up with the cracked fan frame in the x-ray department. The large casting was sitting on a rack attached to a robotic arm that could position the part at any angle and take digital x-rays of the internal defects, if any. He viewed the digital x-rays over a flat screen monitor.

Two uniformed officers quickly made their way along the marked passageways of the casting plant, led by a security guard who knew Daniel and his way around the facility. As they moved along, they gathered a following of curious employees. They approached Daniel and handcuffed him as they read him his rights.

Daniel saw the crowd that had gathered and gave his co-workers a terrified look. The words of the arresting officer played over in his mind. *You are being brought in for questioning in the murder of Elizabeth Marten.* He still couldn't believe it. *Elizabeth is dead?*

In the interrogation room of the station Daniel sat in a gray metal chair and became increasingly frustrated with the continuous bombardment of questions. "You need to find the person she ran off with." He had said that so many times that he was as tired of repeating it as the detectives seemed to be of hearing it.

"How long are you going to stick with that story," a detective asked.

"She was going to come over to the coast and have Thanksgiving dinner with my parents," Daniel said again. He was aware his temper was starting to show. The detective pressed even harder every time he repeated the story until Daniel decided to clam up. They were not going to believe anything he said anyway.

An hour passed, then two hours. Daniel had memorized the imperfections on the tile floor under his feet and could identify every dust speck on the table in front of him. The clock on the wall above the mirrored windows ticked loudly every time the second hand moved another notch, sixty times a minute, thirty-six-hundred times an hour. It would have put him to sleep except for the chill in the room. Another hour passed and a detective he hadn't seen before entered the room. Daniel looked up at him, a clean-shaven man with bushy eyebrows and a face that had the redness of too many years of alcohol abuse. He pulled up a chair, spun it around and straddled it.

"I'm Falcon Race," the detective said, stretching out a beefy hand.

Daniel had had plenty of time to think about what was going on. He decided he'd had enough. He needed to talk to someone who would listen or demand an attorney. The trouble was, he didn't know an attorney. "I want to talk to September Gale," Daniel said.

"Detective Gale has been removed from the case and is on administrative leave."

"You can't do that, she's investigating my grandfather's murder."

Falcon Race slammed his large hand on the table. It sounded like a gunshot. "You cannot tell us what we can and cannot do. We know what you did. You went over to your girlfriend's apartment because she wanted to break up with you. You two had a little squabble and it got out of control. You calmly went up to her, but she turned away. That made you furious and you grabbed her head and snapped her neck." Race paused for effect. "She went down and you, being an engineer, took a minute to analyze the situation. You lifted her lifeless body and walked out with her holding her waist for support so it would look like she had too much to drink and you were helping her. Yeah, you are big enough to do that. The neighbor who saw you said she looked like she was drunk. You put her in the passenger seat of your car and buckled her in so no one seeing you would be suspicious. It all sounds familiar, doesn't it? Do I need to continue?"

Daniel shook his head. "I'm going to tell you what happened, because you were not in the room when I told it to the other detectives. You've got it all wrong. I was visiting my parents in Waldport and I received an e-mail from Elizabeth saying she was not going to come to Thanksgiving dinner at my parents' and was going to the islands for the holiday. I was upset, but we weren't that close and I figured she wasn't ready to meet my parents. We had been dating for a few months, and I wanted to introduce her to my parents, well...she had actually brought it up. Usually meeting my parents is enough to scare a girl away. If she wanted to run off with someone else that was her choice." Daniel took a deep breath. "You can check my phone records or something. Isn't that what you're supposed to do before accusing someone of murder?"

Falcon Race rose to his feet and went over to the mirrored glass and stood in front of it. "You're in a lot of trouble Mr. Tait. We have three murder victims and you were the last person to see each of them alive. You expect me to buy your alibi that you were in Waldport?"

"You're forgetting one thing," Daniel said.

"And what would that be?" The detective turned around and looked at Daniel.

"Whoever murdered my grandfather and Elizabeth and Fr. Rick was the last one to see them alive, not me."

Falcon Race rushed the table and hit it with both hands causing Daniel to scoot back in his chair. "You think this is some kind of joke?"

"I've had enough of this," Daniel said, standing up. "I don't know what's going on, but I didn't kill anyone. You either charge me or let me go."

Falcon Race was still leaning on the table. "Sit down. I'll tell you when you're free to go."

Falcon Race stormed out of the room and Daniel sat back down. His butt was sore from sitting on the unpadded chair and he was becoming hungry. He figured this whole thing was a career-ender no matter how it turned out. *How am I going to face the people back at work?*

Outside the interrogation room, there were two additional detectives, Stan Ryan and Judy Jacobs. Falcon Race threw up his hands. He was the trump card and they had now played their complete hand and not been able to break Daniel's story. "I don't know. We can hold him for another hour and maybe he'll break, but we really have nothing other than the woman's testimony and that isn't solid either. She described a shorter man and a rental car. She said she could read the Hertz sticker on the bumper." He looked at the other detectives. "Stan it's your call."

Stan looked at Judy and raised his eyebrows.

"I think he's telling the truth," Jacobs said.

"Not you, too." The voice came from behind them. It was the division chief, Terrell Gordon. "I don't understand what you women see in that guy. You let him go and he's just going to go out and kill again."

"You didn't let me finish," Jacobs said somewhat perturbed at the chief's accusation. "I checked his cell phone and he picked up an e-mail early Thanksgiving morning like he said and it was sent from Elizabeth Marten's computer. I called in the FBI and they were able to track the route. Daniel Tait was in Waldport when he received the message. If he figured a way to do all that so he could commit two murders, then we could use him on the force to help us out."

Terrell Gordon patted Judy Jacobs on the back. "Good work, detective. Next time, speak up and we won't have to waste the taxpayer's money. Let him go, but I want a tail on him. Just because we can't figure out how he did it doesn't mean he didn't do it."

September drove to her parents' house in the West Hills. She had called her mother, and her mother in turn had called her sister. September was in the middle of a big mess and they were there to help her. September parked her car in the circular drive and entered the house through the front door. "Don't you ever lock your doors?" September asked, from the entry hall. "There are a lot of people up to no-good out there."

"In here, September," came Tiffany's voice from the kitchen.

Tiffany was two inches taller than September and had the build of a fashion model; slender, on the verge of anorexia and a perfect complexion. She took care to have her flowing red hair perfectly styled and wouldn't be caught dead in the Levi jeans and white, long-sleeved shirt September was wearing. After they downed a pot of coffee and September had clued them in on her plight, Tiffany volunteered a cure for her ills.

"You know what you need?" Tiffany said. "A day at the spa and a complete make over. It will be my treat."

September laughed so hard she choked on her coffee and spilled it on her white shirt. "A day at the spa. I'm suffering enough, already. That would be pure torture for me, and, as for a complete makeover, I'm perfectly happy with my low-maintenance look."

"She was just trying to help," their mother said. Maxine Gale didn't look anything like the two girls. She had dark hair and brown eyes, which had caused a lot of explanation when the girls were young. But the fact that the girls were adopted had always been out in the open and she had figured it made for a healthy relationship. With both of the girls' parents dead and no living relatives she had always felt the girls were as close to her as they would have been to their biological mother. After all, they were both too young to remember the adoption anyway.

September moved her coffee mug away from her. She had had enough coffee and it was starting to give her the shakes. "Mom, why don't you and Tiff go to the spa? They may have suspended me, but that doesn't mean I'm going to forget about the case."

"Oh, that reminds me," Tiffany set her cup down and looked at her sister. "What kind of an asterisk was it you wanted to know about? Milton said there are several kinds of asterisks, five-pointed, six-pointed, eight-pointed. He was really intrigued with the question."

September thought for a moment. "It was written in blood so it wasn't real clear, but I'm sure it had eight points." September looked at her sister expecting a response. "Tiff?"

"Oh, eight points, I got it. I'll tell Milton."

Their mother collected the cups and carried them to the dishwasher. "September, I'm worried about you. How can you deal with dead bodies and clues written in blood? I always pictured you married with three kids and a husband by now, a man who put on a tie in the morning and went to work at a bank or an insurance office. Now you tell us you are falling for a serial killer, and you spend your holidays looking at dead bodies."

"Face it, Mom," September said, not wanting to hear the lecture again. "Your kids don't always grow up to your image of them. I always pictured you and dad in a mansion on the bay with a yacht docked outside; you see how this works, don't you?"

"Listen, young lady, your father and I did a very respectable job raising you."

"And I appreciate it, but every time we get together you two try to pound me into a round hole. You can't seem to accept that I'm the square peg in the family."

"We love you, anyway," Tiffany said trying to dial down the rhetoric. "Now, how about we all get that makeover?"

September slid off the high stool and let her feet hit the floor. "I'm out of here. I'll check back for midnight mass on Christmas, and I don't want any makeover gift certificates in my stocking."

"Darn," Tiffany said. "September, don't go. I want to show you the tie I got Dad for Christmas."

"I want to be surprised," September said, walking out the front door.

Chapter 15

The Assassin focused on the digital clock in his rental car as he waited for Fleming to arrive at The Grotto. It was two a.m. and Fleming was already half-an-hour late. The Assassin was growing impatient. Fleming had found out about the second starburst cross, and while they didn't know how it was connected to the crucifix, they needed to check it out. Fleming had intercepted a conversation between Daniel and September concerning the asterisk and the possibility of it being a cross within a cross. The cross in the church may very well be the hiding place for the crucifix. Why else would Daniel Tait and Detective Gale have examined it? The Grand Lodge opening was to take place in January and time was growing short. The Grand Master had even threatened to come over himself if they couldn't find it. A lot of good that will do, the Assassin thought. Another body in the way. The Grand Master and Fleming seemed to be meddling more and more in the Assassin's affairs. He had never before had such interference in his work. He felt like he was losing control.

He looked six-stories up at the stone walls of the Chapel of St. Mary through the windshield of his car. *We have better structures in France*, he mused. The Americans do not build on the grand scale as we did in the past. Our churches have endured a thousand years of weather and wars. The Americans may be a powerful country, but France prevails when it comes to architecture. He got out of the car and looked around the complex on the lower level. He had traced the electrical lines to the back of the structure and his next move was to cut power to the millions of Christmas lights in The Grotto. He jimmied the lock on the electrical room door and cut the main circuit breaker. As he walked back to his car, snowflakes started falling; large flakes the size of a Euro coin. He stuck out his tongue, leaned back his head, and a flake wafted down and landed to his delight in his mouth. His mind drifted back to his childhood in Chambery. It was 1974 and he was on his way to school. To the delight of a ten-year-old child, the ground was covered with a light blanket of snow and the flakes were falling ever faster. He made footprints in the snow and marveled at how the white powder made an exact imprint of the waffle pattern of the sole of his shoe. He looked up at the sky and was overcome with the beauty of the snow flurry. Everything seemed quiet, even his footsteps were silent and he started singing Silent Night, *"silence de la nuit, sainte nuit"*, he sang, his heart full of joy. He didn't see or hear the priest coming. Suddenly, the priest grabbed him by the collar and marched him into the classroom. He was beaten with a switch until he screamed for mercy.

    The Assassin looked at the darkness surrounding the church. His lips curled down and his eyes watered. That snowy morning in Chambery was the last time he had cried and would never cry again. He felt he was no longer capable of it. Physical pain was something he had conquered, but he still had feelings which he had to bury. The headlights flashed across the lot and the Assassin turned to see a car pull into the parking area. His cell phone ringtone sounded and it startled him.

    "Hello. You were to meet me here," the Assassin said, eyeing the bright lights, slowly creeping toward him. Abruptly the lights were joined by, flashing blue and red strobes. In the darkness the parking area and the entire church was reflecting the lights of the police vehicle. The Assassin closed the phone and slipped it in his inside jacket pocket and gripped the handle of his weapon.

    The policeman waited a long time before getting out of his vehicle. The Assassin stood facing the car. He took care to shield his weapon. The policeman finally opened the door of his cruiser and stepped out.

    "Are you in trouble?" the officer called, as he approached the Assassin.

    "No, I seem to have lost my way," the Assassin said.

    "Where are you headed?" The officer asked?

    "The airport, I have an early morning flight to catch."

    The officer shined his flashlight in the Assassin's face. "You have an accent. Where are you from?"

"Not from around here," the Assassin said.

"Let me see your hands, both of them," the policeman said.

The Assassin showed him his left hand and, with the other hand still in his jacket pocket pulled the trigger and the bullet hit the officer in the gut. The officer fell to his knees grabbing at his stomach. *Terrible waste of a suit jacket.* He watched the man writhing on the ground. The snow was falling steadily and the snow-covered ground turned red around the fallen officer. For a moment the Assassin considered shooting the officer in the head to show him mercy, but immediately changed his mind. It would make too much noise and there were houses close by. He walked back to the policeman's vehicle, slipped on a pair of latex gloves, turned off the strobes and the headlights, and waited for Fleming to arrive.

Fleming was driving toward The Grotto from Gresham, where the snow had been falling for over an hour and had coated the ground and the roads with two inches of slush. The unexpected weather had caused several accidents and traffic was stopped. It had taken an hour for him to make his way through the mess and he was pulling into the service gate of The Grotto when he saw the lights of the police cruiser go out. He turned out his headlights and moved ahead slowly. The snow was a good two inches deep on the surface of the lot. With the snow leaving clear tracks, it was not a good night to break into the church. He got out of his car and walked toward the Assassin.

"It's me, Fleming," he called out, and saw the Assassin dragging the officer toward the police cruiser.

"I know it's you. You are late," the Assassin said. "Help me with this."

Fleming reached in a pocket and came out with a pair of tight fitting rubber gloves. "I'll take care of him. You go back to your car and follow me."

The man groaned as the Assassin handed him over to Fleming. "What are you going to do with him?"

"You'll see." Fleming dragged the officer around the far side of the cruiser. He opened the door and stuffed the man in the front seat. He stripped off the officer's jacket and shirt and threw them in the back seat. He stretched the man out and with a switchblade knife started to probe the bullet hole. The man started to moan louder and Fleming slugged him in the face and continued probing for the bullet with the knife. When he located it, he used his two index fingers to reach into the wound and retrieve the slug. The officer was letting out strange sounds and Fleming hit him again. *This guy just won't give up.*

As Fleming drove off, he checked the rearview mirror of the police cruiser he was driving to make sure the Assassin was following him.

It was before daylight and at this time of the morning traffic was light. The lack of plowed roads made the trip to the Columbia River slow and it took half-an-hour to reach the levy along Marine Drive. Fleming pulled the police cruiser onto an access road and drove along the top of the levy for a quarter-mile before he found the perfect spot. Still on the top of the levy, he turned the car facing the river and stopped. He looked over at the wounded police officer who was nearly dead from loss of blood. "This is where it all ends," Fleming said.

Leaving the car in gear, he rolled down the window and quickly got out of the car. It hesitated a few seconds as it teetered on the edge and Fleming helped it along by pushing on the trunk. It gained speed as it started down the steep embankment and in a few seconds the car nosed into the swift waters of the Columbia River. He waited while the current carried the car downstream and in a few more seconds it disappeared below the surface of the water.

"It will be a long time before they find the car," Fleming said, climbing into the Assassin's car. "Drive slowly along here or we'll end up like the police officer."

The Assassin was still angry for the delay and glared at the man who was supposed to be helping him retrieve the crucifix. "This delay to our plans would not have happened if you would have been on time."

"Get over it. I told you why I was late." Fleming pointed to an access road to the levy that connected with Marine Drive, and they turned on it and were back on their way to retrieve Fleming's car from The Grotto. "Our plans may have been delayed for the time being, but I have other news to share with you that may change our approach. They have arrested Daniel Tait and suspended the detective who was working on the case. They found the body of Elizabeth Marten."

"I was hoping they would not discover her until we had the crucifix in our hands and I was back in France. This is truly a setback."

"Maybe not. They released Tait, but have a tail on him so we need to be particularly vigilant. Tait is still our best bet for solving the whereabouts of the crucifix."

The Assassin smiled. He was developing his own plan. He would dispose of the detectives who were following Tait in a manner that would point again to Daniel Tait, but he would not do this until the time was right. When he did retrieve the crucifix, no one, not even Fleming would be alive to testify against him.

Daniel showed up at Space Age Metals at six a.m. with his empty coffee cup in his hand. His eyes were red from lack of sleep. He had wrestled with the sheets all night, trying to determine who would have reason to murder Elizabeth Marten. When the news hit the workplace that he was a prime suspect, it would be impossible for him to do his job. It wouldn't matter that he was released. He needed to catch his boss before all hell broke lose. He filled his coffee cup and headed upstairs to John Howard's office. He wasn't surprised to see John at his desk. The man was a machine, if there ever was one. Even robots shut down for maintenance once in a while, but not John. Daniel knocked on his door.

Howard looked up from his work. "Daniel, you want to tell me what's going on? The shop was a mess after they hauled your ass out of here yesterday."

Daniel tightened his lips and nodded. "I can explain, but you're not going to like it."

"You're damn right I don't like it. We were already a week behind because of Thanksgiving and now you cause the whole place to stop with speculation and rumors about you being accused of murder."

Daniel knew he was better off letting his boss blow off steam and not cutting in, especially if he wanted to be heard, so he waited until Howard had run down. "You know Elizabeth Marten, the dimensional engineer in Plant Two."

John Howard stared at him. "Give me the short version."

"She was found dead and they thought I might have been the last to see her."

"Why would they think that?"

"We were dating."

"Give it to me straight. They hauled you off in handcuffs. Did you do it?"

Daniel knew his boss would have certainly questioned the security guard that helped escort him out. "She was murdered, but I was at my parents' place when it happened. I wouldn't be here if they thought I did it."

John's face looked grim. "This whole incident has disrupted production too much. I don't have a choice but to suspend you until this is cleared up. I'm sorry, but company rules are you will be suspended without pay. Jim Bloom will be handling your tasks until you return."

"But I didn't do anything."

John got up from his desk and walked over to Daniel and looked him in the eye. "I promise you, if this clears up and you are innocent, I'll give you your job back."

"I might as well be fired," Daniel said.

Howard pointed his hand at Daniel. "You'd do the same thing. I can arrange for you to access your IRA, if you need money."

Daniel let out a long breath. "I'll take care of this and give you a call. In the meantime if you need my help, you can reach me on my cell." No matter how hurt he was, Daniel understood Howard's position. He had learned from hard lessons in the past that life wasn't always fair. The last time he felt like this was when his football scholarship was rescinded. He remembered he'd felt like it was the end of the world, but it had given him the drive to excel in engineering school and land a good job. It wasn't the end of the world, at least, not yet. Not if he could clear all this up.

"Daniel?" Howard was giving him a quizzical look.

"Sorry," Daniel said, "I spaced out for a second. I have a few things in my desk, I need to get. Do you need my security ID?"

"I'll go with you to your desk. Give me your badge and I'll take care of it."

Daniel felt like he was being fired. They didn't trust him enough to get a few items from his desk. *Did his boss need to look over his shoulder to make sure he didn't steal something?* Again he swallowed hard and accepted that it was only temporary.

September called Judy Jacobs, the only other female detective in homicide, to see what was happening with Daniel Tait. She was surprised at how short Judy was with her. They had never worked closely together on a case and she had heard that there was some office rivalry going on, but she had elected to leave it to the rumor mill. Now she needed Judy's help, and Judy seemed to be gloating in the fact she had been suspended.

"I can't talk about the case, you know that," Jacobs said, and hung up.

Judy Jacobs was with Falcon Race, sitting in her car, outside Space Age Metals, waiting for Daniel Tait to come out so they could follow him. They had followed him to work, but had failed to catch up with him early enough to put a tracking bug on his Jeep.

"Who was that on the phone?" Falcon asked.

"That was Gale, trying to find out what's happening with the Tait case."

"I wish the chief would have waited to suspend her until she briefed us. That kid is up to his neck in excrement, if you know what I mean."

"I reviewed the file Gale had on his grandfather. Walter Tait seems to have been tied up with a foreign cult. When the old man died, he tried to pass on some information by writing on the floor, but according to Gale's file, there wasn't enough information to locate what the cult was after. There was even a watch on Daniel Tait's residence for awhile for his personal safety. That's been lifted and we are taking over."

"Hopefully this won't take too long. I like tailing suspects about as much as having my teeth extracted."

The snow was beginning to melt and Daniel trudged across the Space Age Metals parking lot in three inches of slush. He carried a small box containing a few personal items from his desk. He sat in his Jeep letting the windshield defog and felt completely alone as he contemplated his next move. He looked down at the box on the seat next to him and thought about all the boxes in his grandfather's garage. Would his life end up like his grandfather, with a few dozen cardboard boxes in a garage? He decided he needed to start back where he had learned about the cross in the first place; back in his grandfather's garage.

As Daniel pulled out of the parking lot he saw a black Ford Taurus sedan parked across the street. It was an unusual place for someone to park and he immediately thought it looked like an unmarked police car. He checked his rearview mirror and watched it pull out about a block behind him. *This is odd, do they still suspect me?* He decided to see how good they were at driving through three inches of slushy snow. He turned a switch on the dash and his Jeep was in four-wheel-drive. He pressed on the gas and picked up speed. At the next corner he turned up a winding street that had a steep hill. Around the next corner his cell phone rang. He ignored it for a moment, but the voice on the blue tooth came through his radio, "Incoming call from September Gale."

Daniel answered, "September, I'm in the middle of something. I'll call you right back." He hung up and circled back to the street that passed by his workplace. He turned and cruised by Space Age Metals again. The black car was nowhere in sight, but he failed to see the metallic blue Dodge Durango that picked up his tail as he passed his place of employment.

As Daniel headed for the west side of town toward his grandfather's place he maneuvered around stalled traffic and abandoned vehicles left from the night before. He called September.

"We need to meet," September said. "They thought I was getting too close to you and I'm suspended from your case."

"I know," Daniel said. "I asked for you when they were interrogating me."

"You didn't. No wonder I was suspended."

"You're going to rag on me for your situation? I just lost my job. I'm not interested in hearing you whine."

"Whine! I'm not whining. We need to meet and I'm not taking no for an answer. You need to tell me everything that's going on and I mean everything, including why they let you go."

"Well, since you put it so nicely, where do you want to meet?"

"Saint Clare Rectory. I'm on my way now."

Daniel was about to ask her why, but the computer voice on his device said, "Disconnected."

Chapter 16

"Saint Clare Rectory, it is," Daniel said, forging his way through stalled cars and minor fender-benders in the early morning Portland traffic. As he crossed the Sellwood Bridge he glanced down at the boathouses moored on the Willamette River. The sun was yet to rise and the multi-colored Christmas lights reflected off the water. On any other occasion he might have pulled over and taken in the festive scene, but he wasn't in a mood to celebrate anything. His eyes came back to the traffic in front of him and he pushed down hard on his brakes. The tires had no grip on the wet snow and the Jeep slid, in slow motion, toward stopped traffic in front of him. He could see there was no hope of stopping and took his foot off the brake, turned the steering wheel and gave the Jeep's Hemi Engine enough gas to maneuver into the oncoming lane. Fortunately an accident on the west side of the river had stopped all opposing traffic and Daniel was able to gain an additional six-car-lengths of open road, enough to bring the Jeep to a sliding stop alongside several cars. He looked over at the panicked people in the cars next to him and gave them a sheepish grin. He was completely stopped when he heard the crunch of vehicles smashing into each other like dominoes. He glanced to his right and saw the driver of the car next to him brace for a rear end collision.

Daniel put the Jeep in reverse and backed across the bridge. Only then did he notice the cause of the accident, a metallic-blue Dodge Durango, with none other than Fleming at the wheel, had plowed into the back of the car Daniel had avoided by turning into the oncoming lane. Daniel did a double take. *Was Fleming following me?* He gave a short wave and continued backing up until he cleared the bridge and could turn around. As it was, the snowstorm had left Portland traffic a complete mess and his trip to Saint Clare's, which should have been fifteen minutes, would take another hour. He decided to take the 205 freeway, but even that would take half-an-hour to get to from where he was. He called September and told her he would be delayed. "By the way, I think Fleming and another guy were following me."

"I still don't have anything on Fleming. I don't need to tell you to stay clear of him. I'm almost certain he was the one who was shooting at us in The Grotto."

"I thought you were certain," Daniel said.

"He was talking to you before I got there and disappeared just before we were shot at. We didn't actually see him shoot. I'm an officer of the law. Do I have to spell it out for you?"

"You don't have to be so rude about it. You hung up before I could ask you why I'm headed to Saint Clare's."

There was a long silence. "That's where Father Rick was killed. I neglected to check his computer. It would be helpful if you were there. I don't want to miss anything."

"You mean regarding my grandfather?"

"Of course I mean your grandfather. You said he e-mailed Father Rick. There may be something of interest on his computer."

"Gotcha," Daniel said. "I thought you were suspended."

Another long silence. "I am, but there's nothing stopping you from asking a few questions."

"You're using me."

"Are you interested in solving your grandfather's murder, or not?"

"I'm almost to the freeway now. Hold tight until I get there."

Daniel was surprised at how little snow there was in Lake Oswego. The highway that ran along the river was bare and wet. The sun was starting to rise. Most of the traffic was headed in the opposite direction and was moving smoothly. To avoid the traffic jam that had caused him to detour, he cut cross-country and found himself in snow again as soon as he reached the hills. When he arrived at Saint Clare's, he pulled beside September's Toyota Prius Hybrid. September was sitting inside.

"I thought you'd be a Dodge Charger type," Daniel said, walking up to her car. "Hemi engine, rear-wheel drive, zero-to-sixty in five seconds, and you're driving this *"green" machine*. What a disappointment."

September got out and looked at her light green hybrid. "I still have to buy gas when I'm not on the job. I can drive for a month on what you spend for gas in a week."

"Yeah, but are you having any fun?" He saw September wasn't smiling. "Okay, now that we got that out of the way, how are we going to do this?"

September stood close to him and spoke in a low voice. She told him her plan.

Daniel nodded. "The great rectory caper. I get it."

Daniel knocked on the rectory door. It was answered by a young woman about his age. She wore glasses and had shoulder length dirty-blond hair. "I'm Daniel Tait and this is Detective Gale. We were here earlier to investigate the death of Father Rick."

The woman opened the door. "I haven't touched anything in his office. The tape is still across the door," she said, defensively.

"We need to get into the office again," Daniel said, walking to the office. He hesitated at the tape that crisscrossed on the doorway. He turned to the young woman. "We'll take it from here."

"Sure," she said. "If you need anything, I'll be in my office." She pointed down the hall.

Daniel turned to September. "You're sure you want to do this?"

"No," September said. She handed Daniel a pair of surgeon's gloves. "You do the honors. I'll stand lookout."

Daniel took the gloves. "I can't believe I'm doing this. You're going to stand out here and let me break the law."

"Shut up. At the most it's a misdemeanor. The door is open. She let us in. It's not like you were breaking-and-entering."

Daniel ducked under the tape and walked over to the computer. The room had changed little since he had been there. He made his way around the blood stains on the carpet and the outline on the floor where Fr. Rick had been found. The computer was on and all he had to do was log on as the user. It didn't require a password. He opened documents to see if there were any recent letters that mentioned Walter Tait. There were hundreds of letters and what looked like thousands of sermons, or homilies, as they were filed. He doubted his grandfather would be mentioned in any of them, so he went to the letters, from most recent, to several months earlier and found nothing. He looked over at September who had an anxious look on her face. "There isn't anything here."

"Well, it was worth a try," September said. "Let's go."

Daniel went back to the computer. "Just a minute, I want to look at another file."

"Hurry up."

Daniel brought up the pictures and scanned the thumb nails. He came across one titled Tait Crucifix and opened it. His hands started to shake. The item showed a cross with a barely definable image of Christ hanging on it. He sent the picture to his computer and deleted the copy in the computer. He scanned the rest of the photos, and not finding anything, closed the screen.

They were back in the parking area before Daniel told September what he had done.

"You did what?" September asked.

"If the Frenchman is looking for that crucifix, I didn't want him to find it."

"You could have sent it to my place; at least, it's not being watched."

"I wish you would have said something earlier."

"How could I? You didn't...never mind. I'll meet you at your apartment."

"No need. I've got my computer with me."

"Did anyone ever tell you, you are a frustrating individual to be around?"

"My mother," Daniel said. He opened the passenger door on his Jeep and tossed the box into the back seat. "Get in. I'll turn on the heater."

They sat in the car. Daniel picked up a signal and opened the picture on his portable computer. He enlarged the image and turned the notebook toward September. "Looks pretty old, doesn't it?"

September fixed her eyes on the image and her jaw dropped in awe. "This is not old, it's ancient." She tilted the screen to remove the glare and fixed the image in her mind. She had never seen anything like it. "You can see the years of wear. This crucifix was hand carved at least centuries ago."

"I think we finally know what we're looking for. Judging from its size it would easily fit into a shoe box. It's exactly the one I saw in my grandfather's hands as he lay dying when I was just a kid."

"You've see it before?"

"I barely remembered it. I thought my grandfather was dead. He was in the hospital and his hands were clinging to the crucifix. It looked like those old pictures of dead people in coffins."

"Why would your grandfather hide it?"

"Well, you saw what someone would do for it. Maybe he realized its value," Daniel said. "Can you imagine how many people have handled this through the years? And my grandfather had to hide it to protect it, how the world has changed."

"People haven't changed," September said. "The bones of the saints were stolen all the time and they would show up in another church who would claim them as their own. The Arc of the Covenant has never been found. It's most likely hidden away in some ancient church so someone won't steal it."

"I get your point," Daniel said. "If my grandfather was going to return this to the original owners, he may have come across someone other than the rightful owners."

September handed the small computer back to Daniel. "If the church wanted this, they wouldn't kill for it."

"What makes you think that?" Daniel asked.

"For one thing, the Pope just came out with a statement against putting too much faith in relics. They can be easily faked, and it's only in rare occasions that a miracle can be attributed to a relic."

"Miracles?" Daniel thought back to that day his grandfather was given up for dead. "I think this must be the genuine article, because we were all told my grandfather was as good as dead, before my grandmother put the crucifix in his hands."

"Daniel, you're an engineer. Did I hear you right? You believe in miracles?"

"I didn't say that. I just said, when my grandfather asked for the crucifix, everyone thought he was as good as dead. He lived another twenty-three years after that. What would make it a genuine relic anyway?"

"What you just said," September said, smiling.

"Maybe it was carved from the original cross Christ was crucified on," Daniel speculated.

"I doubt that," September said. "The wood of the cross would be way too valuable for anyone to carve a crucifix out of it. More likely, coming from France, Saint Francis of Assisi or an ancient figure of the church carried it with him. It could have been carried by one of the apostles."

"Unlikely we'll ever find out," Daniel said. "We still don't have a clue where it is."

"You want to come over to my place and I can fix some breakfast?" September asked. "We did your place last time. You can tell me what happened between you and your girlfriend."

"You don't ever stop being a detective, do you?"

"You know they aren't going to drop it just because you had an alibi."

"I'm here, aren't I? I'd still be in jail if they really thought I did it....you don't think I did it, do you?"

September leaned into him. "Daniel, it doesn't matter what I think. I'm off the case." She opened the door and got out. "The offer for breakfast is still open."

"If I show up at your place you'll know my decision. Close the door, its cold outside."

Chapter 17

There was no apparent damage to Fleming's Dodge Durango, but the four cars down the line from him had incurred varying degrees of damage and he was clearly at fault. There was an hour's worth of paperwork to fill out and three phone calls before it was taken care of. They lost track of Daniel and went by his grandfather's house. Not finding him there, they proceeded to his apartment, and finally to the church. They arrived as Daniel was pulling out of a parking space in front of the rectory.

"We should go in the church and find out what he discovered," the Assassin said.

Fleming glanced at him. "We all know where that ended up last time, don't we?"

"My brother, I keep telling you, we need to have the crucifix for the lodge dedication ceremonies in January. Sooner or later you will have to do it my way."

"Well, right now, that would be later." Fleming said. "Keep your eye on the target. We don't want to lose him again."

Daniel realized he was sulking as he drove toward his grandfather's house. He thought about September's words and why they had made him angry. What would he have thought under the same set of circumstances? After all, he had been so quick to write off Elizabeth and that message from her computer wasn't even sent by her. *How quick we are to embrace the digital age*, he thought. *We can easily become victims, if we don't watch ourselves.* Of course, as an engineer, he was in the digital age up to his eyeballs. Engineering was a field that used the digital age to the max. Technology was ever-changing and he had to keep up with it. It wasn't until now that he realized there was a downside. A simple message sent from a computer and he had assumed the worst, not even considered it could have been sent by someone else, but why would he suspect that? *What does that say about me?* His grandfather had sent a message innocently, and now he was dead. He had just sent a picture of the crucifix through the internet without thinking twice about it, and it had magically appeared on the tiny notebook computer in his vehicle. The good and bad of digital technology had touched his life several times over the past few weeks and, to tell the truth, most of it was bad. He pulled the Jeep over to the side of the road and stopped. He wanted to go to September's place, but he didn't have the slightest idea where she lived.

"What now?" Fleming asked as he saw Daniel pull the Jeep off the road.
"You know he is taking us on an undomesticated duck chase?" the Assassin said.
Fleming glanced over at the Assassin. "A wild goose chase?"
"If you say so. We are no closer to the crucifix than we were the day I arrived in America. I am getting tired of the awful food and the constant rain. Just last night it was snowing and now it is rain again. Do these people have duck feet and gills?"
They cruised by Daniel and could see he was talking. "He must be calling someone," the Assassin said.
"I'm going to pull over and wait for him to pass again."
The Assassin shook his head. The thought entered his head that it would be good to get rid of Fleming now, so he could do the job right.

On the drive across town to her place, September was having second thoughts about inviting Daniel there. She wasn't certain it was safe to bring him to her apartment; after all, the last information she had was that Elizabeth had been killed in her apartment. Daniel was an enigma wrapped up in a mystery. He had an alibi for everything, an answer for everything. She had never met anyone quite like him. He was good looking, but not handsome, personable yet elusive; smart, but not brilliant;

compassionate, yet at times, emphatic. He was respectful of religion, but not religious. She pulled her Prius into a parking space and stared up at the window on her second-story apartment. She sat there for a long time and the longer she thought about it, the more it seemed reasonable. *Daniel Tait could very well be the perfect description of a serial killer. What better way to put a victim off guard? Be everything a person was looking for and when they least expect it, wham!* She stared at the picture window of her apartment and saw the reflection of white fluffy clouds in a blue sky.

No matter how she thought about it, she couldn't bring herself to the point of thinking Daniel Tait a serial killer. There was the hole in the ammo box, the bullet from a French issue handgun, and the shots fired at The Grotto. She had been with Daniel at the time and it all added up to someone out there trying to kill Daniel. The evidence didn't support the Chief's belief that she was getting too involved with the suspect. She was just doing her job, pure and simple, nothing more and nothing less. Her cell phone rang. It was Daniel Tait.

"I thought I'd take you up on your offer, but then I realized, I don't know where you live," Daniel said.

September looked up at her apartment window again and the blue sky had turned to a dark gray cloud. She had to turn and look out the back window of her Prius to make sure she was not seeing things. "I've changed my mind. Meet me at Elmer's, behind Fred Meyer's in Clackamas."

"I know where it is, but it'll take me fifteen minutes or so to get there."

"Take your time. I'll be inside having coffee." She lived less than five minutes away, but didn't want him to know.

September picked a corner booth, ordered coffee, and waited for Daniel. A man was sitting at the counter and he looked familiar, even though she could only see his back. He had dark curly hair and a jacket with a Clackamas Gun Club logo on the back. A twinge of fear swept through her. She remembered the firing room in the basement of the gun club. She had been practicing for a handgun competition and had fired a 15-round clip from her Glock semi-automatic when she felt a tap on her shoulder. She turned around, startled. The man ripped the ear protection from her head and put his hand over her mouth. She was taken completely by surprise and for a moment was helpless. He knocked the pistol from her hand and threw her to the ground before she had time to react. Her police training kicked in and she was able to free herself, but the attacker had vanished up the stairs and out the front door. They had arrested the man in less than an hour and charged him with assault, but he only served six months in the county jail.

The man turned and she saw it wasn't who she had thought it was. She took a deep breath and let it out slowly to slow her racing heart.

"Someone you know?" Daniel asked, walking up to the booth.

September flinched, jerked her coffee, and spilled it.

"I didn't mean to startle you," Daniel said. He grabbed a napkin from the neighboring booth and sopped up the coffee.

"I'm sorry," September said. "I don't know where my mind's been lately."

Daniel set his notebook on the table and sat down. He spun it around for her to see the picture.

"I've seen it before," September said.

"Yeah, but have you really looked at it?"

"Are we playing games, now?"

"Take a close look and tell me everything you see."

"I see a symbol, an eight-pointed asterisk written on the floor in your grandfather's blood." She looked up at him.

"You want to know what I see."

"You're going to get around to it some day, I'm sure."

Daniel got up and walked to the other side of the booth and slid in next to her. He bumped her over until he was fully in the booth and she was against the wall. He pulled the computer closer to them. "I uploaded all the crime scene pictures I took with my cell phone and this one stood out. We've been calling this an asterisk, but what if that's not what it is?"

September was feeling a bit crowded and looked at his face. She could see excitement in his eyes, not the piercing glare of a serial killer. She relaxed a bit and decided to play along with him. "You're going to have to give me a little more to go on. It's an asterisk, albeit, not a very good one."

"Bingo," Daniel said. "My grandfather was an artist. There's no way he'd draw such a lousy asterisk. Look at the lettering on "Adele" and even "GODS." Everything is precise, exact. Even in the last minutes of my grandfather's life he could not bring himself to do anything sloppy. Remember, I told you we had an argument about using power tools? It was all about quality workmanship."

The waitress came and they ordered breakfast, giving September time to think about what Daniel was saying. She scrolled the pictures checking each word and then the asterisk. It didn't fit. "You think the asterisk was added by the killer?"

"No, you said the fingerprints in the lettering were my grandfather's."

"But the killer could have drawn the asterisk with your grandfather's hand after he was dead."

"Possibly," Daniel said taking a sip of coffee. "But why?"

September looked at him. "You think your grandfather drew that symbol that way on purpose."

"I do," Daniel said. "And then I wondered what it meant."

"And you think you know."

Daniel got up and went to the counter and asked the waitress for a piece of paper and a pen. He came back and scooted next to September again. He drew an asterisk on the paper and next to it drew a cross. He looked at September, who was watching intently. "What is an eight sided asterisk, but two crosses?" He drew another cross at an angle over the first. "You see this? The asterisk is out of kilter because the crosses are not symmetrical; they have longer legs than arms. And look at this." He drew a shallow "S" on one of the crosses.

September gasped. "A crucifix!" She stared at the symbol on the computer screen. It was all clear. There was the cross at an angle and another one with the symbolic figure of Christ on it. She looked at Daniel and her eyes became blurry. "We're looking for a crucifix and a cross? That's what your grandfather was trying to tell us?"

"That's what I thought at first," Daniel said. "I thought the crucifix might be inside the cross my grandfather had carved, but you know where that got us...nowhere. We were stumped at the asterisk." He flipped back to the picture of the crucifix he had sent to his computer from Fr. Rick's office and turned the screen so September would have a better view. "Tell me everything you see."

September leaned into the screen and squinted. "I see an old, poorly-carved crucifix setting on something...another piece of wood."

"Wrong," Daniel said.

"Wrong? There's nothing else in the picture."

Daniel turned to her and grinned. "Oh yes there is." He pointed to the edge of the crucifix. "See that."

"I don't see anything."

"Neither did I at first, but when I looked closer I could see the crucifix is not setting on a lighter wood background. It's setting in lighter wood. The crucifix is inlayed into another object."

September turned the computer toward her and tilted it at an angle. "It's an optical illusion. From this angle it looks like it's setting on top of the background and from another angle it looks inset. But why would he do that?"

"I don't have an answer for that, but I think it's important. I think the crucifix is inlayed in a cross."

"The cross at Saint Mary's chapel at the Grotto?" September asked.

"That would be my guess," Daniel said.

September bumped him to get out of the booth. "What are we waiting for? Let's go back to the Grotto."

"We haven't eaten yet."

"Oh, yeah. Eat fast."

Chapter 18

"I'm tired of waiting. I don't think these two know what they are looking for," the Assassin said, watching the people come and go from Elmer's. "We should get the cross from the church and examine it."

"Like you did the last time? I'm sure you wouldn't be noticed," Fleming said.

"We could break into the church and be gone, but this time we go together."

"Or we can do this my way," Fleming said, "and let the detective and Daniel Tait lead us to the crucifix and then take it from them. There is much less risk that way. Suppose it isn't in the church. We will have exposed ourselves for nothing."

"So your way is to sit back and wait. Something better happen soon."

"Or what?" Fleming asked.

"Or we do it my way. I am sick of the whole thing."

Daniel stood outside the restaurant and waited for September to pay the bill. He had argued with her, but she insisted. Something about she didn't want to owe him. *Women, what happened to chivalry, anyway?* He didn't notice the metallic blue Durango in the corner of the lot.

"Let's take my car," September said.

"In this slush. I think my Jeep is better."

"I hate it when you're right," September said. "We'll go in your car, but I drive."

Daniel shook his head and handed her his keys. "It's not a car. It's a Jeep. You break it, you buy it."

"Get in. Let's hope we beat the Frenchman to the cross."

Daniel climbed in on the passenger side and fastened his seatbelt. "What do we do with the crucifix once we find it?"

"We sure as heck aren't going to give it to the Frenchman."

"I didn't mean that. If the crucifix is imbedded in the cross, I'll bet Father Anderson won't want to give it up."

September pulled the Jeep out of the lot and turned left and entered the 205 Freeway going north. She picked up speed and melded in with traffic. She didn't notice the blue metallic Durango three cars behind her, nor did she see the black Ford Taurus behind the Durango. The Jeep handled well in the slushy conditions and September stepped up the pace and passed a few cars. "You may want to take it a little slower," Daniel said. "The four wheel drive doesn't stop any faster in this stuff than any other car."

September saw the blue Durango pull out into her lane. "Wasn't Fleming driving a blue SUV?"

"Durango. Why?" Daniel asked.

"I think he's on our tail."

Daniel checked his side mirror. "That's him. I ditched him earlier this morning. I'm surprised he found us this fast."

"I wish you would have told me. I would have been looking for him."

"I forgot."

"You forgot," September said, glancing at him. "You had Fleming on your tail and you forgot."

"That's what I said. For your information there was a black Ford Taurus waiting outside my work early this morning. I ditched them, too."

"Great," September said, checking the rear view mirror. "We've got both of them on our tail now."

Daniel looked in his side mirror again. "That's the one. What, have we got a beacon on us or something?"

"How good is this thing?" September asked. "Can we lose them?"

"It's got four-wheel-drive and a Hemi engine. It'll out run either of them on dry pavement and, in this stuff, no contest. Put your foot in it."

September did just that. She pressed down on the accelerator and the Jeep lurched forward to fifty and then sixty. The all-terrain tires spewed a wake of slushy snow 20-feet on either side of them as she maneuvered in and out of the slow-moving traffic. She slipped into the slow lane and took the next off ramp, turned left and another left and entered the freeway going the opposite direction. As she pulled onto the freeway she could see a line of traffic where she had just been. Apparently, they had stalled due to the wake of slush she had left on the windshields of the cars she had passed.

"Looks like our tails are stuck in traffic," September said giving the Jeep's padded steering wheel a triumphant tap with the palm of her hand.

"Where'd you learn to drive like that?" Daniel asked.

"Traffic school. We even got to play on sheer ice. Now that's a kick in the britches."

Daniel's knuckles were white from gripping the handhold on the front window column. "You think, now that we've lost them, you could slow down a little?"

September backed off the gas immediately. Her adrenalin was flowing so fast, she hadn't realized she was doing seventy in driving conditions more appropriate for thirty. "Sorry." She turned off the freeway and headed cross-country toward The Grotto.

September pulled the Jeep into The Grotto parking lot and stopped short. "I wonder what's going on here?"

A uniformed officer walked over to the vehicle and September lowered the window. "What's going on officer?"

"I'm going to have to ask you to move your vehicle. The Grotto is closed."

September slipped a hand in her Jeans pocket and came out with her identification. "I'm Detective Gale, Portland City Homicide," she said, looking the man in the eye.

He took the identification and nodded and handed it back to her. "You can pull your vehicle over there." He pointed to several other vehicles in the lot.

September pulled the Jeep next to an Emergency Response Vehicle. She looked at Daniel and smiled. "I wasn't sure he would buy it."

"What now?" Daniel asked.

"Come with me. Let's see if we can find out what's going on." She removed the keys and opened the door.

Daniel hesitated.

"You can stay if you want, but this could be interesting."

"Okay, but I don't want to end up back in jail."

September had already left a trail of footprints in the snow as she walked toward a long string of police tape. Daniel caught up with her.

"It seems everywhere we go, something happens. What do you think it is this time?"

"Let me do the talking. You stay beside me and listen."

Daniel nodded. "I won't say a word."

September approached an officer who was standing next to the gift shop inside a string of crime scene tape. "What's happening, George?"

The officer saw her and lifted up the tape. "I didn't know you were on the case, September."

"I'm not. Just happened to be in the neighborhood. This is Daniel Tait." She ducked under the tape and waited for Daniel. She turned to George. "A homicide?"

"We're not sure. There was a large pool of human blood in the lower lot. We're going for a match now."

"A match. You have a victim?"

George's face became grim. "There was a patrol officer who went missing early this morning. His last call came from the administrative lot below us." He pointed to a flight of stairs that led to the lower levels where the maintenance shop was located.

September grabbed Daniel's hand and led him down two flights of stairs. She stopped and could see several officers huddled around a patch of blood-stained snow. "Have they found him?" September called out to the nearest officer.

"Near as we can tell," the officer said. "They got a GPS locate on his vehicle. It shows it in the Columbia River. It doesn't look good."

September shook her head. "It certainly doesn't." She nodded at Daniel. "Like I said, we were just passing by. Good luck finding the perp."

"Sure thing," the officer said.

September ducked under the tape and headed back up the stairs with Daniel right behind her. "Look at that," she said.

Daniel saw where she was pointing. A metallic blue Dodge Durango was pulling out of the upper lot just as a black Ford Taurus was pulling in. "I'll bet they got a surprise."

"The surprise may be on us," September said, picking up her pace. "The door of your Jeep is open."

Daniel took off running and was fumbling through the front seat when September caught up with him. "They got my computer."

Chapter 19

Daniel dropped off September at her car at Elmer's Restaurant. The snow was nearly all melted and the sun was peeking from behind large fluffy clouds. Daniel thought it might turn out to be a good day, except his computer was missing. He had another computer at home, but the notebook was smaller and a lot handier for packing around. The worst thing was Fleming had all the information they had. If he could piece it together, then he might be able to get to the crucifix before them.

"Follow me," September said. "It's only a minute away."

As Daniel followed September into the parking area of the Kinsman Apartments, he looked at the stained wooden siding and large elm trees surrounding the structure. It appeared to be about eight units. He followed September up the concrete stairs and waited on the landing for her to open the door. Inside he stood on the brown carpet and waited for her to open the tan drapes. The walls were a neutral beige color and he didn't see any pictures. The room was sparsely furnished with a couch, a coffee table, two chairs, and an end table. A gas fireplace without a mantel was centered in one wall. "You just move in?" Daniel asked.

"What makes you say that?"

Daniel considered that a *no*. "I meant, you don't spend much time here, do you?"

"As little as possible," September said. "It's a place to sleep and occasionally eat. I would have fixed you breakfast, but I'm fresh out of eggs." She was lying and immediately felt guilty for it. "Actually, I was concerned about your girlfriend. We never got around to discussing her."

"What do you want to know?"

September went into the kitchen. "Come in here and I'll put on some coffee."

The kitchen wasn't decorated any more than the living room. There was a dark hardwood table with four matching chairs. The stove was white, as was the dishwasher and the sink. The counters were covered with small white tiles. The room was clean and neat, but without any personality. It reminded him of a showroom at Home Depot, only a notch less friendly.

"Sit down," September said, reaching in the cupboard and coming out with a large container of coffee. "Were you and Elizabeth close?"

"We didn't live together, if that's what you're getting at." Daniel was immediately on the defensive. *What if the police told him September wasn't on the case any more to catch him off guard? What if she was trying to find out something that she could nail him with later?*

Sensing slight hostility in his voice September backed off. "I wasn't prying. You said she broke up with you."

"I guess that's questionable. Your buddies seemed to think she may not have sent the e-mail. It could have been sent from her killer."

"But it was sent from her computer."

"I don't know how they tracked it, but they seemed to know I was in Waldport when I got the message and it was sent from her apartment. It might have been the last thing she ever did."

"By now, you know I don't believe in coincidence, so there had to be a reason for her to die and somehow you are connected." September filled the coffee maker with water and turned it on.

"Don't you think I thought of that? She was probably killed because of me. My guess is she was killed so the police would put me away and not continue looking for the one who killed my grandfather. The best way to get the cops off their tail would be to leave a suspect in front of their noses. Try and pin the murder on me. You said it yourself. You don't believe in coincidence."

"You've been watching too much television. The one who killed...the Frenchman who killed your grandfather could have gotten you framed by planting something in your apartment. If he would have done that, you would still be locked up. He didn't have to kill your girlfriend to frame you."

"Maybe he killed my grandfather first. If he did, then, for your theory to work, his method would have to be traceable back to me. He could have used the same gun to kill Elizabeth and left it in my apartment."

September poured a cup of coffee for Daniel and another for her even though the coffee maker hadn't finished brewing. Daniel tasted it and winced.

"Too strong?" September asked. She took his cup and ran some water from the faucet in it and set it back down in front of him. "I'm not much of a cook. I got it from my aunt. She only cooks pancakes for my uncle."

"Pancakes? Why's that?" Daniel felt like he was walking into a trap and waited for the punchline, but it never came.

"When my aunt and uncle got married, he would incessantly complain about my aunt's cooking, until one day my aunt decided to do something about it." She tasted her coffee and went over to the sink and added some water to it. "Every time my uncle complained about something my aunt cooked, she would never fix it again. It took my uncle years to figure it out. He began to cook more and my aunt cooked less until she only cooked pancakes. I've decided if I ever get married, that's what I'm going to do."

Daniel set his cup down. "Or, you could learn to cook."

September shook her head and smiled. "No, that would be too easy."

Daniel attempted another sip of coffee, tasted it, and set the cup down. "Here's what I think happened with Elizabeth. After my grandfather was killed, the Frenchman went looking for me. He must have been staking out my grandfather and me for some time before he made his move. He couldn't find me, so he tried to get Elizabeth to tell him where I was. He had her e-mail me with the phony message, thinking I would rush home, but he didn't realize we weren't that close. I took the e-mail at face value and believed she walked out of the relationship.

"I don't think the Frenchman is too bright. He should have known Elizabeth and I were not that close, and, while I was hurt, I read the e-mail and let it go. The second thing the Frenchman did that wasn't too bright was he thought my grandfather was a frail old man who would give him the information he wanted, hoping to save his life, but my grandfather was in the war. He told me many times he wasn't afraid to die. For some reason that crucifix was worth saving, enough that my grandfather gave his life to protect it."

September was glad Daniel was volunteering the information. She had not been able to get any information from work and didn't dare call her boss. If she knew September was still working on the case, she would fire her for sure. Then again, they had let Daniel go; that meant they didn't have enough to hold him, yet they were following him. What would that mean if they tracked him to her? "Oh, my gosh!"

"What's wrong?" Daniel asked getting up.

"What were you wearing when the police brought you in?"

Daniel thought for a moment. "Work clothes; a light blue shirt, tan slacks and work shoes."

"Get undressed," September said, standing up.

"What?"

"Remember the bug that was planted on you when we were dodging bullets at The Grotto? If the police have a tail on you, they almost certainly bugged you before they released you."

"The only thing I have on that I was wearing then is my shoes."

"They took your shoes when they interrogated you, didn't they?"

Daniel looked down at his shoes. "You're right. They had me remove them. I remember, I was in my stocking feet and it was freezing in that room."

"Let me see them," September said. "Come on, take them off."

"You sure seem to be in a hurry to undress me," Daniel said, loosening the shoe strings and pulling off his shoes.

"Don't even go there," September said. "I hardly know you, and, you're not Catholic."

"Then you've thought about it," Daniel said. His lips turned into a slight grin.

September ignored him and opened a drawer and pulled out a screwdriver.

"You keep a screwdriver in the kitchen." Daniel said. "Why doesn't that surprise me?"

"You never know when you'll need one," September said, prying the insole out of his shoe.

"Like, what," Daniel said, "you want to whip up a mean batch of pancakes using a screwdriver?"

September started laughing. She pulled the bug from his shoe and picked up the other one.

"You think they have one in there, too?" Daniel was incredulous. "They think I'm going to run around in one shoe?"

September ripped out the insole and pulled out another tracking bug. "Different frequency. They wanted to make sure you didn't get away from them. They are most certainly outside right now."

"Great, now what do I do?"

"We go about our business as usual and plant the bugs on something else. Preferably something that is moving."

"I meant, what do I do for shoes?"

September handed the shoes and the liners back to him. "You're an engineer. You figure it out."

The Assassin and Fleming were in the motel room sitting at the kitchen table with Daniel's notebook computer in front of them. They were staring at the picture of the crucifix.

"See what a little patience will do," Fleming said. "I told you they would lead us to it. Now we know they are looking for the same thing."

The Assassin clamped his jaw. It wasn't often someone got the better of him and lived to tell about it. There was only one living person left in the world who had betrayed him and that was the Grand Master. He wasn't worried about a peon like Fleming. *They called themselves brothers. Cain and Abel were brothers, too, weren't they?* He glared at Fleming. *Yes, Brother, before I go, you, too will be burning with Satan.*

September turned on the lights in her apartment. Daniel had fallen asleep on the couch. September drew the drapes. While Daniel napped, she put a plan together and now that it was dark, she had to go over it with Daniel. She shook him gently and he opened an eye and smiled.
"I was just dreaming about you."
She ignored him. "We need to go over our plan."
"You mean your plan."
"Whatever. It'll be ours before we put it into operation."
Daniel sat up and slipped on his shoes. He had managed to stuff the insoles back in well enough that he could wear them. He tested them out and was satisfied. He walked around the carpet. "What's the plan?"
"Three parts," September said. "First we have to ditch the tracking bugs."
"Why not just leave them here and sneak out?" Daniel asked.
"They are parked by the only entrance to the parking lot. We'd never get past them undetected, unless you want to go on foot. You want to hear the plan or not?"
"What, now I can't even ask questions?"
"Not if they're stupid questions."
"Okay, I'll listen to your terrific plan and not say a word."
"I never said my plan was terrific."
"Well, it must be, if I can't question it."
September went to the kitchen. "Come in here and we can discuss this like adults. If you have a question, please make sure it adds to the discussion."

"You like to live by rules, don't you?" Daniel said, following her.

She sat down at the table. "Don't even go there. You're the engineer who thinks all the wonders of the world can be explained by physics and mechanics. There's a law for this and a theory for that. You don't need God for anything. You've already got it all figured out."

Daniel was taken aback by her outburst. She was even prettier when she was passionate about something, and he could see this was getting to her. "I never said, I didn't believe in God."

"But you don't."

"What's that got to do with anything?"

"Daniel, don't you see? Your grandfather believed in something so much that he protected it with his life. He wasn't afraid to die for what he believed and he wanted you to have what he left behind. He died because he didn't want to give it up to the Frenchman."

Again Daniel listened to her and was moved that she felt so strongly about what she was doing. "I never looked at it like that. I was just looking for something that would lead me to my grandfather's killer. You make it sound like there is a greater plan in all of this. For me it's pretty simple. My grandfather had something and someone else wanted it. They killed him, it happens every day."

September raised her eyes to meet his. "Not like this. This is much more than the killing for money. This isn't someone looking to steal a TV so they can finance their next fix. That crucifix has much deeper significance and your grandfather wanted you to know it."

Daniel looked down at the table. He felt ashamed for not taking his grandfather's faith more seriously. "I loved him so much. For his sake, I just hope we can figure this out. Let's hear your plan."

Daniel and September made no attempt to hide their exit from her apartment. Daniel got in the driver seat of his Jeep and they drove out of the lot fast enough to make sure the police tail was awake to witness their leaving.

"It's three blocks away," September said. "We have about a minute before the bus comes by."

As they drove along 82nd Drive, they saw the Rose City Transit bus pulling away from the bus stop. Daniel pulled the Jeep alongside at the stoplight. September already had the broomstick and the magnetic holder attached to the tip with two-sided tape and, as soon as they stopped, she stuck the magnetic box to the side of the bus. It took only a second and the bus continued along 82nd Drive, while Daniel turned left and entered the 205 Freeway.

"That should keep them guessing for awhile," September said. "The beauty of a tracking bug is you don't have to remain in sight of the vehicle. In this case it works in our favor."

"How do we know they didn't bug my Jeep?" Daniel asked.

"We don't know for sure. I guess if they show up again we'll know the answer." September didn't think they would bug Daniel's vehicle. She didn't think the case was high profile enough to warrant the extra precaution, but she couldn't be certain.

Daniel continued north on the freeway and turned off on Sandy Blvd, heading west. He pulled into a motel parking lot a block away from the Grotto entrance and they walked to the Grotto.

Everything was dark at The Grotto. The parking lot lights were out and the police tape was down. They crept along the edge of the parking area, using dark shadows for cover.

"It's sure quiet," Daniel whispered. "The Grotto must still be shut down." It was a completely different site from the other night when there were millions of tiny lights on all the trees and buildings. Tonight it was as if the world had been turned off.

High in the sky a full moon peeked through clouds giving enough natural light for them to move about with caution. Ahead of them loomed the church, a massive black obelisk against the night sky. They stayed in the shadows of the trees surrounding the

Chapel of Saint Mary and waited at the bottom of the steps. The entrance was in complete darkness.

"What are we waiting for?" Daniel asked. September pulled a small flashlight from the backpack hanging over her shoulder. She held it up for Daniel to see. "The light from this is going to be easily seen, so you'll need to stand behind me to shield it from anyone policing the grounds."

September climbed the stairs slowly. She got to the huge wooden door and stopped short. Daniel was nearly on top of her. "What now?" he whispered.

"It's open," September whispered. "It's supposed to be locked." She lifted a chain that usually was strung through the brass handles for extra security. "It's been cut."

Just then, they heard voices inside the church. September touched Daniel and pointed to the trees by the entry. They retreated to the cover of a large rhododendron bush.

"What now?" Daniel asked.

September touched his lips with her finger. They stayed crouched down and watched. There was a scraping noise and the doors of the church burst open. Suddenly the area was lit up like daylight, as a vehicle jumped the curb of the parking lot and sped past the benches in front of the grotto cave toward the entrance of the church. September pushed Daniel back deeper into the bush and they watched as a man came out of the church with the starburst cross on his shoulder. The gold leaf of the cross gleamed brightly as the man packed it toward the headlights.

September burst from the bushes. "Halt Police!"

Her move was so unanticipated that Daniel put his hands up. She rushed the man with the cross. The startled man dropped the cross and ran for the front of the vehicle as September ran toward the rear. The man grabbed the door on the passenger side and jumped in. September jumped out of the way as the vehicle accelerated in reverse and, with tires squealing, spun around and headed toward the parking area at high speed.

"That was Fleming and the Frenchman," Daniel shouted, running out of the bushes after September. "What are you doing? You never told me this was part of the plan."

September was bent over, recovering from nearly being the victim of a hit-and-run. Daniel went for the cross and picked it up.

"What are you doing?" September asked.

"We need to get this out of here," Daniel said, picking up the six-foot cross.

September stopped him. "Take it this way." She led him along a trail behind the church in nearly complete darkness. They walked slowly for a few minutes. "When are you going to tell me what we're doing?" Daniel huffed.

"Through here," September said, disappearing through the shrubbery. Daniel caught the cross on some wires as he tried to follow and discovered they were Christmas lights that should have been lit. He untangled the cross and ran straight into a wire mesh fence.

"Stop messing around," September said. She was standing right next to him, but in the dark shadow of the church.

He had to focus his eyes to see her silhouette.

"Give me the keys," September said.

At this point, Daniel wasn't going to argue. It was clear that the plan had changed and September was acting on instinct. He doubted anything but an argument would ensue if he tried to give input. He handed her his keys.

"Give me your coat," September said. Daniel was about to ask why, when September added, "I need it to keep me from getting shredded when you boost me over the fence."

She tossed Daniel's jacket over the top of the fence and put her hands on Daniel's shoulders. "Give me a boost. I'll be right back with the Jeep."

September disappeared into the darkness, and Daniel set the cross on the ground and shivered. He looked up at his jacket still draped over the fence and then looked down at the cross. Even in the low light the gold surface reflected the distant rays of a streetlamp. *Grandpa, what have you gotten me into?*

Chapter 20

"You idiot," Fleming said, to the Assassin. "First you kill the only person who knows where the crucifix is and then you kill a police officer, leaving the mess for me to clean up and now, you leave the cross in the parking lot. Is there anything you can't screw up?"

The Assassin slipped his hand into his coat and felt the handle of his weapon. If Fleming would not have been driving, he would kill him right there. It was Fleming who was at fault. He should have provided cover and not let the detective get the drop on him. He had the cross in his hands, what did Fleming expect him to do, stay and get shot? As he sat in the car and glared at Fleming, the Assassin formulated his own plan. From now on he would do it his way. The Assassin sat in silence. He had been the one who stole the computer out of Daniel Tait's vehicle allowing them to know for certain that the crucifix was what Daniel Tait was after.

Fleming glanced over at the Assassin. "I hope I didn't hurt your feelings. Not having the cross for examination, means we are back to my plan of watching Daniel Tait, but we no longer have a track on him. If you want to go back to France, I can take it from here."

The Assassin shook his head. He must discipline himself against his urge to exterminate this man. Discipline...discipline...discipline. He rocked back and forth in the seat, focusing his eyes on the leather grain pattern of the dash. Soon enough Fleming would know the real plan.

Falcon Race pulled the black Ford Taurus sedan to the curb and pounded on the wheel. Daniel Tait and September Gale were up to something and they had successfully defeated his attempt to follow them for the moment. He turned to Judy Jacobs, who was looking in the visor mirror and putting on fresh lipstick.

"What?" Jacobs asked glancing back at him.

"They obviously found the bugs and we've been spinning our wheels in the wrong direction. You got any bright ideas?"

"The last place they went before this was to The Grotto. Maybe they weren't just passing by, like they told George," Jacobs offered.

"That's as good as anything I've got," Falcon Race said. He made a 180° turn in the middle of the block and headed toward The Grotto.

September pulled the Jeep along the side street that bordered the fence where she had left Daniel. She checked to see if there were any lights on in the houses that lined one side of the street. Not seeing any she got out and called for Daniel.

"I'm over here," Daniel said.

September stood looking at the chain link fence. It was a good foot taller than her and had a jagged edge along the top. "Slide the cross over the top and I'll catch it," September said. "Be careful, we want to return it in good shape."

Daniel had already anticipated her request. He was anxious to get out of there. He slid the cross over the top of the fence using his jacket as protection for the shiny surface. "Are you ready? I'll hold it until you get a hand on it."

"Got it," September said. "You can let go."

Daniel took his grip off the cross and it tipped in September's direction. As soon as the cross was out of the way, Daniel grabbed the top of the fence and hoisted himself up. He heard a loud rip as he slid over the top. He landed on his feet, grabbed his jacket and put his hand through the hole. "I don't know if anyone ever told you," Daniel said, "but being around you is hard on my clothes."

"Hazard of the job," September said. "Let's get this in the Jeep and check it out. With any luck we can return it before noon mass."

Daniel was behind the wheel as they hurried across town. "You want to continue with the plan?" Daniel asked.

"Why wouldn't I?" September asked.

"Well, for one reason, nothing has gone according to plan yet."

"We had a minor setback, that's all."

"Minor? We were supposed to examine the cross for any way that it might have a compartment and only remove it from the church if there was some evidence the crucifix was inside. Now it's in the back of my Jeep and we still haven't got a look at it."

"I can't believe you didn't look for a compartment when we examined it the first time," September said. "Head through town and out Sunset toward Beaverton."

"That's a relief," Daniel said. The plan called for them to take the cross to September's parents place for closer examination. They felt both of their places were no longer safe.

September's parents were still in bed when September rang the doorbell. "September, are you in trouble?" Her mother asked when she answered the door.

Daniel was standing beside her with the cross that reached to the top of his head.

"We need to borrow the dining room for a few minutes," September said. She saw her mother staring at Daniel. "Oh, Mom, this is Daniel Tait, the man I was telling you about. Daniel, this is my mother, Maxine."

Her mother stepped back eyeing Daniel suspiciously.

September walked in and motioned for Daniel to follow. "Mom, quit staring at Daniel."

Daniel packed the cross into the dining room and September cleared a place on the table.

"Careful not to scratch the table," September said.

"Daniel Tait," Maxine said. "I thought you were a serial killer."

"Mom!"

Daniel looked up from the table where he was examining the gold leaf on the back side of the cross. "Looks can be deceiving." He grinned. "I don't see anything. It looks like we hit another dead end." Daniel let out a long sigh. "I was really hoping we would find the crucifix imbedded in the cross. I must have read the wrong meaning into the symbol. Maybe it was just an asterisk after all."

Maxine looked at the cross on her dining room table and put her hand over her mouth to quell a gasp. "You stole the cross from the chapel of Saint Mary at The Grotto."

"We didn't steal it," September said. "We saved it from the thieves who were trying to steal it."

"Well technically--" Daniel started to speak, but September interrupted.

"I'm going to call Father Andersen as soon as it's daylight and let him know we have it."

"I'm going to wake your father and we'll all have breakfast," Maxine said, not giving September a chance to protest.

"I'm sorry," September said to Daniel.

Daniel looked at her and could see she was as disappointed as he. He knew she was not apologizing for her mother, but answered as if she were. "That's okay, I am hungry. She's not going to invite your aunt to cook, is she?" He grinned.

"What are we going to do now?" September asked. She still had a concerned look on her face. "I don't want your grandfather's murder to turn into a cold case."

Daniel removed the cross from the table and stood it by the front door. He sat across the table from September. "I know I don't have to tell you, because you have been through this sort of thing before, but my old football coach always used to tell me when things weren't going right on the field to start over from the basics. We both know my grandfather didn't write those things on the floor to pass the time until he died. He told us where the crucifix is, we're just not listening hard enough."

September stared at the table and nodded. "I know you're right."

"Darn right, I am. After breakfast we go back to Grandpa's house and give it the once over for the second time and this time we need to look at it through a new set of eyes."

"We return the cross first," September said.

"Hi, Sweetie," September heard her father behind her.

Daniel looked up at a man with dark wavy hair. He had the ruddy look of a sailor, suntanned skin and deep furrows in his face from protecting his eyes against the glare of the suns reflection off the surface of the sea. He was dressed in a silk, maroon-colored, smoking jacket and had an unlit pipe clamped between his teeth. Daniel could picture him at the helm of a sailing vessel.

"Dad, this is my friend, Daniel Tait." September stood and Daniel did likewise.

Daniel stretched out his hand. "It's good to meet you Mr. Gale."

"Tom," Mr. Gale said. "Do you go by Daniel?"

"The curse of having a formal mother," Daniel said.

An hour later, with the cross in the back of Daniel's Jeep, they traveled through the West Hills tunnel, past downtown Portland and across the Markham Bridge to the East Bound freeway. The sun was rising and cast the snow-covered Mount Hood in a pink glow. They were on their way to return the cross.

"Your mother is a good cook," Daniel said.

"You're wondering how I managed to burn coffee," September responded.

"You know, it's getting difficult to talk to you. You seem to think there's a hidden meaning in everything I say."

"It comes with the job. I'm a detective, remember?"

"Well, I'm an engineer, and if I say I liked your mother's cooking, it means just that."

When they pulled into The Grotto they saw a Portland Police cruiser parked in the upper lot in front of the church. "I run into more fellow officers when I'm off the job than when I'm on," September said. "Let me do the talking."

They packed the cross in through the front door where they could see two uniforms near the altar, questioning Fr. Anderson. He looked up and saw them. "September, I'm glad you finally arrived. I tried to convince this good officer that you prevented a crime. Other than the chain that was broken on the front door nothing else was missing. One of the good Servite Brothers called in the crime."

They set the cross on the floor by the altar and Daniel began hooking up the wires. September explained what had happened, leaving out the trek through the brush, the scaling of the fence and the examination of the cross at her parents' house.

"There were two men inside when we got here," September said. "We startled them and they dropped the cross and ran. We took it with us for safekeeping. We would have had it back here sooner, but my mom insisted on feeding us breakfast. That's it, nothing else to report."

"Are you going to press charges?" an officer asked.

"I don't see any reason for that. We have problems from time to time. The thieves probably thought the cross was solid gold. As you can see, it's covered with gold leaf, hardly worth stealing. I'm happy to have it back."

"Be sure and replace the chain and you might want to consider a better lock on the electrical panel. They cut the power to everything including the security camera with a single pull of a lever."

"I've already called the locksmith. Thank you for the quick response." Fr. Anderson escorted them to the door and returned to help Daniel position the cross at the proper height. "September, you need to come clean with me, why were you two here at three o'clock in the morning?"

September spent the next fifteen minutes filling the priest in on what had happened.

"Well, I'm glad you finally ruled out this cross as a suspect," the priest said giving her a knowing look of guarded disbelief that she was being completely honest. "Daniel, I'll pray that you find what you are looking for."

Daniel wondered at Fr. Anderson's comment. *He thinks I'm looking for something in addition to my grandfather's crucifix.*

Falcon Race had caught the call on the radio concerning the Chapel of Saint Mary at The Grotto. He and Jacobs waited in the parking area not far from Daniel's Jeep. "It's just a stroke of luck, they returned here," Jacobs said.

"From here on out, we do it the old-fashioned way. We stick to them like pitch on a pine tree," Race said.

September waved at Race and Jacobs when she got into Daniel's vehicle. "Might as well get used to them," September said. "They aren't going to let us out of their sight from here on out."

"That sounds like a challenge," Daniel said, pulling onto 82nd Avenue and gunning the Jeep.

September grabbed the handhold by her window and looked over at him. "You don't need to kill us in the process of getting rid of them."

Daniel was familiar with off-road areas around Oregon City, and turned off the 205 freeway and headed for the farmlands outside the metropolitan area. Within 30 minutes he had left Falcon Race and his partner stuck in the mud in a wooded area on the edge of Oregon City. He maneuvered undetected back to the 205 Freeway and within another fifteen minutes was pulling his muddy Jeep into the driveway of his grandfather's house.

"I really didn't want them to know we were coming back here," September said. "You'd think the city could put its money to better use than have you followed."

"You mean like trying to find the Frenchman."

"And Fleming," September added. "There isn't any doubt that he's working with the killer; in fact, he may have been the one who killed Father Rick."

"Fleming?"

"Yes, Fleming. He conveniently showed up at The Grotto and I forgot to mention that the bug in your vehicle was

Government Issue. Fleming has his hands all over this thing. I just haven't figured out how to nail him."

"The crime scene tape is down," Daniel said, walking up to the house.

"Normal procedure to allow you access," September said. "But you can bet the room where they found your grandfather is still restricted. It will be until we make an arrest that sticks."

"You mean you're going to stay outside the bedroom and let me do your job for you again?"

"That depends," September said.

They entered the house and Daniel looked at the mess. "I swear, every time we come here the place is a bigger mess."

"Someone's been in here again," September said. "Your grandfather should have installed a revolving door in front. Every time we come here I wonder if we're looking in the right places, then I wonder if whoever else has been here has found what we're looking for."

"There you go with the doubts again," Daniel said. "Remember, we're going to look at the scene for the first time all over again." He walked down the hall and opened the bedroom door. "Let's get down to basics. Have you still got a couple pair of those doctor's gloves?"

They both put on gloves and Daniel said, "What's the first thing you noticed when you entered the room, other than the mess?"

"The bed," September said. "I've never seen a bed quite that unique."

"It's a one-of-a-kind," Daniel said. "Hand carved headboard. Legs from stressed Coastal Pine. I've seen it so many times, I completely overlooked it as a possibility."

"Possibility for what?" September stood up straight and stared at the headboard. "I never bothered to examine it closely." She made her way to it, being careful not to step on any evidence markers. She ran her hand over the carvings. "There's a cross." She said it so softly Daniel wouldn't have heard her had he not been watching.

"It looks thick enough," Daniel said. "Do you have that flashlight with you?"

She handed the penlight to him and he leaned over the headboard and shined it along the back of the board. "I don't see anything."

Daniel started kicking the rails of the bed with his shoe. "This isn't going to work. I'll be right back. He went out to the garage and came back with a screwdriver and a hammer and started dismantling the bed.

Daniel removed a long screw and handed the screwdriver to September. "You get the other one."

They separated the headboard from the rails. "We need to take this out of here," Daniel said. "Can you get that side?"

They packed the heavy headboard out to the living room, where Daniel pushed aside the clutter so they could set it on the floor. Daniel brought a floor lamp over and held it close to the back of the headboard. "I don't see anything, do you?"

"Another dead end," September said. "I'm getting sick of saying that."

Daniel stood the headboard up and held on to it. "Do we want to put it back?"

"It's up to you," September said. "I haven't got anything better to do." She picked up one end.

"Wait a minute," Daniel said, as he picked up his end. A smile crossed his face. He ran a fingernail across an almost invisible seam along the top of the headboard. "My grandfather was good," he said.

"What is it now?"

"See how thick this board is. It's a laminate, several boards thick."

"And that means?"

"It means he could have inserted the crucifix into one board and covered it with another board. It's almost undetectable even when you look closely."

September started for the back door.

"Where are you going?" Daniel asked.

"I saw an ax in the garage. I'm tired of guessing."

"Wait," Daniel said. "I think I know a way that won't ruin my grandfather's work."

Chapter 21

"What are they doing, moving that bed?" The Assassin asked.

Fleming shrugged and watched Daniel and September loading the large piece of wood into the back of Daniel's Jeep. The piece was so large it did not allow for the tailgate to fully close. Daniel secured the door with Bungee cords. He and September drove off with the headboard sticking a full foot past the rear bumper of his Jeep.

"You're sure you're not going to get into trouble for this," September asked.

"This guy owes me a favor, big time. I told him it was worth a case of beer to me and he likes beer."

It was after dark as they pulled up to the guard gate at Space Age Metals. "Jim Bloom should be on his way out to clear us," Daniel said to the guard.

"Wait right over there," the guard said, pointing to a spot beside the gate.

Jim Bloom was a tall lanky man, younger than Daniel, and not nearly as physically fit. He sported a shaggy head of red hair and a face dotted with freckles. He spoke to the guard and approached the Jeep. "Follow me. I only have the machine for fifteen minutes."

Daniel kept his foot on the brake as they idled along after Bloom. When they had rounded the back of the building, Bloom stopped at the side of a huge overhead door and pushed some buttons on a security keypad. The overhead door started to rise and Bloom signaled for Daniel to park in front of it. Daniel and Bloom carried the headboard down a long corridor lined with box-like structures that were the size of a large closet. Daniel explained they were lead-lined digital x-ray machines. They stopped in front of one of the machines and set the headboard on a round table with an adjustable surface. Bloom secured the headboard in place, pushed a button, and the table disappeared through a set of automatic doors which closed after the headboard was inside.

September watched, fascinated with all the machinery and the activity for this time of night. "So this is where you work?" She saw a dozen machines like the one they had loaded the headboard into. Jet engine parts, some the size of a small car, were being moved about the long corridor, some on hand-pushed carts and some by overhead conveyor.

"This is a small part of it," Daniel said. "Someday, if I'm employed after all this is over, I'll give you the grand tour. For now, I want to get out of here ten minutes before we entered."

"Is this what you're looking for?" Bloom asked, tilting a monitor at Daniel to view.

Daniel leaned into the screen. "What do you think, September, is that what we're after?"

September looked at the screen. She could definitely see a cross. Daniel pointed to the lighter image. "This is the cross that's carved into the front of the headboard. See this shadow? The angle makes it a little difficult to see it, but the crucifix is more dense, right here." He ran a finger along the screen. "The wood from the crucifix is a little denser making the image slightly lighter."

"You mean, we found it." September's eyes widened with excitement. "We really found it?"

"Looks that way. Now we can go for the ax." Daniel turned to Jim Bloom. "Can you e-mail me a copy to my home computer and I'll let you get back to business."

"You can forget the beer," Bloom said. "Just get your ass back here. I wouldn't be working this late if you were here."

Jim Bloom ran ahead of them to the guard station and waited while the guard inspected the Jeep for miscellaneous jet engine parts or office equipment. They waved goodbye to him and drove out on the street. Daniel and September were so excited they failed to see the metallic blue Durango pull away from the curb a block behind them.

"It's in the bed board," the Assassin said. "We can take it from them and this will be done."

"We wait until we're certain this time," Fleming said. "We're doing this right from here on out."

"You mean your way."

"That's right. If you have a problem with it, call the Grand Master."

"I have no problem," the Assassin said. He focused his attention on the Jeep ahead of them.

"You're not really going to take an ax to your grandfather's headboard, are you?' September asked.

"I don't think I'll have to," Daniel said. "I asked Jim to e-mail me the x-ray so I can study it closer. I think I saw something that may be a hidden latch, but I'll have to figure out how my grandfather coded it."

"Your grandfather must have been a fascinating man. I would have liked to have known him."

Daniel glanced over at her and nodded agreement. "Me, too...I mean, I knew him, but not nearly well enough. He was involved in things I couldn't have imagined. Maybe if I would have..."

"Have what?" September asked.

"I was just thinking, if I would have been closer to him, more interested in his spiritual life, he might have shared this with me. I'm sure there is a fascinating story behind it, but we'll never know the full story."

September reached over and touched his arm. She fixed her opal green eyes on him. "We're going to uncover as much of the mystery surrounding his death as we can. When this is all over, you'll have a heck of a story to tell your children."

"Thanks. You've been a source of encouragement, a big help."

Daniel backed the Jeep into the driveway of his grandfather's house and stopped close to the garage door. "I'll open the door and you clear off a work bench. The mystery of the missing crucifix is about to be resolved."

They moved the headboard from the jeep, to a cart that was more like a table with wheels. Daniel had September help him turn over the headboard so that the front was facing up. He carefully rolled the cart around several stacks of boxes and stopped under the overhead light in the center of the room. Daniel ran his fingers across the headboard and pointed out some things that September probably missed. "What initially tipped me off was this seam that runs along the top ridge of the headboard. It's almost impossible to hide a seam completely, but my grandfather did it, and it doesn't even show up on the x-ray. Inside is a hidden mechanism, with a metal latch and springs hidden in this area." He pointed to another area along the top of the board. "If we can figure out the combination we can open it and remove the crucifix."

"And if you can't find the combination?" September looked a bit skeptical.

"We take a saw to it and risk damaging something so precious my grandfather gave his life for it."

"Not to mention, destroying the work of art he carved on this. I feel like we're a couple of safe crackers. I don't see any sign of a combination lock."

Daniel worked his fingers along the seam trying to get the back of the headboard to separate. He tapped on it, squeezed it, pushed it, and nothing gave. "I'm going to have to go to my place and get the x-ray from my computer. My grandfather was known to build puzzles and this one might be his best."

"I think we should take the headboard with us," September said. "It's not safe leaving it here."

Daniel looked at the board. "I think it'll be all right. It was sitting in the house and no one touched it. Who's going to steal a headboard? I'll lock the garage."

"I'll help you load it," September protested, grabbing a leg of the headboard.

"It'll be quicker if we leave it and come right back. We won't be gone more than half-an-hour."

September let go of the leg. "It's your call, but if it's gone when we get back, I'm going to say I told you so."

"You see," Fleming said, watching Daniel and September leave. "They don't have the headboard with them. They either have the crucifix with them or it was not in the headboard."

"Then we must intercept it now. If they have the crucifix in their possession we can get it now."

Fleming pulled out from the curb and followed about a block behind. "These two are becoming quite predictable. I think they are headed for his place."

"We can take it right now, not wait to go to his place," the Assassin said, reaching for his gun.

Fleming put his hand over the Assassin's arm, stopping him from removing his gun. "You know what I told you about patience, you haven't learned a thing. Why would they go to his place if they had the crucifix?"

"To hide it from us," the Assassin said.

"Perhaps. I'm inclined to watch and wait for their next move."

The Assassin clamped his jaw tight. Words would not work at this moment. Words would only cause Fleming to become upset and he was the one driving. No, he would wait. Fleming had bought a few more minutes of his life.

They parked under a large fir tree and watched Daniel's Jeep disappear into the parking area in front of his apartment. It was exceptionally dark outside. The heavy rain and the windshield wipers streaking the windshield made what little view they had blurry and distorted. There were only a few cars parked along the curvy road leading up to Daniel's apartment. All the houses along the street were dark.

The Assassin removed his handgun and screwed on the silencer. "You insist we are waiting, no?"

Fleming looked over at him. Before he could speak a bullet had pierced his heart. The Assassin leaned over Fleming's slumped figure and opened the door. The interior of the car lit up and he closed it quickly. He smashed the overhead light with the butt of his gun, got out into the rain and ran around to the driver side of the car, pulled Fleming out and placed his body behind a tree. It took the Assassin less than a minute. He knew the body would be found because it was a well-populated rural area, but the weather was on his side, and if it continued to rain the body may not be discovered for a few days. He climbed back into the vehicle. This time he sat behind the steering wheel. He was running the operation his way from here on out.

Falcon Race and Judy Jacobs had waited several hours for a four-wheel-drive wrecker to arrive and pull them out of the mud. They were told by the wrecker driver that they were stuck in the middle of an obstacle course for monster trucks. They had high-centered and were helplessly stranded. When they had called police dispatch the vehicles that came to their rescue had waited outside the area and not attempted to free them. Falcon Race and Judy Jacobs had finally waded through the mud and waited in the rain until their vehicle was pulled free. Both were soaked to the skin and made a quick change of clothes before continuing their tail on Daniel Tait. When they rejoined the hunt, they were both angry, and agreed that the best way to get Daniel Tait out of their lives was to arrest him on any charge they could come up with, and they had plenty. Eluding a police officer, for one, and if they played their cards right, Falcon Race commented to Jacobs, they could get him on resisting arrest, but for any of that to happen, they had to find him. They routinely checked the places he might be. As they pulled into the parking lot in front of Daniels apartment they saw Daniel's Jeep and pulled their unmarked cruiser into a space next to it.

"We have the story straight?' Falcon Race asked Jacobs, as they climbed the steps to the second story apartment. Race knocked hard on the door. "Portland Police! Open up, we know you're in there."

The Assassin left the Durango and walked along the trees staying in the shadows. He had his collar pulled up on his overcoat and his gun hand hidden in a pocket even though he was not worried about being seen. The only thing on his mind at that moment was to retrieve the crucifix and Fleming, his biggest obstacle, was no longer a hindrance. He heard the police call out and stopped at the bottom of the steps.

Inside the apartment Daniel and September were hunched over the computer. "What now?" Daniel asked, when he heard pounding on the door

"It won't be good, if they find me here," September said.

"Just a minute," Daniel yelled. He turned to September and pointed toward the bedroom. He grabbed his computer and followed her into the bedroom. "The window. I'll follow you."

Daniel handed the computer to September, slid open the window and put his hand through the screen, clearing an opening for September.

September looked at the sloping ground and brush and it looked like a long drop. "I'm not sure about this."

"It's only one story. The worst that will happen is you'll break a leg. You want to sit in the police station all night?" She still hesitated. "Move aside. I'll go first and brake your fall."

Daniel pulled the nightstand next to the opening and used it for a stepstool. He backed out of the window and hung by his finger tips for a second before dropping to the wet ground.

September heard the door of the apartment crash open. "Daniel, catch."

Daniel looked up to see the computer flying at him like a boulder off a cliff. He reached for it, but it was off-target and it continued through his hands, bounced off an evergreen branch and landed at his feet. He didn't have a chance to pick it up before September came dropping toward him. He reached out for her and the two tumbled to the ground tangled in each other's arms in tall wet grass, stopping beside a large fir tree.

"They're in your apartment. We need to go," September said.

"No kidding. You could have given me better warning before you hurled the computer at me."

"I didn't hurl it. Come on, let's beat feet."

Daniel grabbed the computer and they moved along the building and peeked around the corner to see if the path was clear to the Jeep.

The Assassin crept up the stairs. He wasn't going to let anyone get in the way of him retrieving the crucifix. He moved through the door and saw the two detectives going into the bedroom. He looked around the apartment and assumed all four were in the bedroom. He crept up to the bedroom door and slowly reached inside. He found the light switch and flipped the light off. He could see the two detectives silhouetted against the open window.

Falcon Race spun around and fired his weapon, but the shot went wild. The muffled sound of the Assassin's discharge was almost silent in contrast to the detective's weapon. The bullet hit Falcon Race just above the bridge of his nose.

Judy Jacobs had her weapon in her hand and dove for cover between the bed and the window. Falcon Race was crumpled at her side. She could see only dark movements in the room. She reached her gun hand over the bed and was about to raise her head to fire when the Assassin dropped to the floor and fired underneath the bed. His bullet hit the detective in the leg. She screamed and the Assassin fired once more.

September reached in her ankle holster and pulled out her 9mm Glock backup weapon.

"What are you doing?" Daniel asked, grabbing her shoulder.

"I can't leave two fellow officers in jeopardy."

"September, you're suspended, remember? You don't have any idea who they're shooting at."

"Still, I can't—"

"You don't know who fired the shots. You'll get yourself killed."

"I'm sorry Daniel. You go and let me do what I was trained to do."

"I can't go and leave you."

"Then, I suggest you take cover," September said, dashing for the stairs to Daniel's apartment.

Daniel couldn't believe it. He was standing at the corner of the apartment complex with the computer under his arm and September was charging up the stairs toward gunfire. He watched only long enough for her to disappear into the apartment before he felt the gun in his back and heard a voice with an unmistakable French accent.

"We will calmly walk across the parking lot and down the street to the right."

Lights were coming on in the apartments. The Assassin and Daniel walked quickly through the shadows and within less than a minute Daniel was sitting in the metallic blue Dodge Durango. "You have something for me?" The Assassin asked.

September identified herself and flipped on the light in the bedroom. She saw Falcon Race at the end of the bed. She checked for a pulse and there was none. She looked around the end of the bed and a frantic Judy Jacobs stuck a gun in her face.

"Hold it right there," Jacobs said. Her hand was shaking.

"You're hit," September said." Let me help you."

"You are not going to do anything, but wait. I called in back-up."

"Fine, let me check out your leg."

Judy glanced down at her leg. "It's fine. Don't try anything stupid. You and your friend are going to rot in prison for this."

"I didn't do anything. I heard gunshots and came up to make sure you were all right."

"What did you do with the silencer?" Jacobs asked.

September could see she was fading fast. "Put down the gun and let me take a look at your leg."

Judy Jacobs leaned forward and looked at September with glassy eyes. September knocked the gun from her hand and Jacobs fell over. September ran to the closet and grabbed one of Daniel's neckties and used it for a tourniquet on Jacob's leg. As she applied pressure to stop the bleeding she wondered if Judy was going to say she had shot Falcon Race. She heard sirens in the distance. She could rejoin Daniel or wait for the police and be detained for hours answering a hundred questions she didn't know the answer to. "I hope you make it Daniel," she said. She held the tourniquet and saw blood oozing from Jacob's side. *I only have two hands, girl. Hold on.*

September stayed with Jacobs until a paramedic took over. "You did a good job," she said, ripping a bandage open and pressing it against Jacob's side.

"Is she going to make it?" September asked.

"Stand back and let us get her on a gurney."

The more September explained, the more questions it raised until the detective taking her statement got a call from their chief to bring her into the station.

September stood facing Chief Terrell Gordon in her office. She had seen the chief in a bad mood before, but never like this. Her boss was not in uniform, had no makeup on, and her hair was in curlers, those big ones the size of pop cans. Had the circumstances not been so serious, September would have had a hard time holding back a smile. As it was she was nearly in tears. "I've been trying to explain," September said.

Terrell held her hand up. "Did I ask for you to speak?"

September looked at her. "No, but—"

The hand went up again. "You will likely lose your shield for good over this; the most stupid, idiotic, dumb ass thing anyone has ever done under my command. You're damn lucky Judy Jacobs is alive, but her story better not pan out."

"Chief, I'm trying to tell you what happened."

"We'll let the facts speak for themselves. It seems your testimony isn't the most reliable."

"Give me a break. I walked in after the shooting—"

"You better stop right there, detective." The chief lifted some large pictures from her desk. "The facts show you and your boyfriend jumped out the window and you circled around and came back in the apartment and shot Falcon Race, a 27-year veteran with the force, then you turned your gun on Detective Jacobs and shot her twice." She studied the pictures for a moment. "Who belongs to this other set of footprints?"

"Oh my gosh," September put her head in her hands. "The killer must have jumped out the window after us. He could have Daniel."

"Who are you talking about? Don't you go trying to muddy up the water with another conspiracy theory."

"Chief, you gotta listen to me. It's either Fleming or the Frenchman. Both of them have been after Daniel and me ever since we discovered what the Frenchman was after."

"Girl, you just keep on rambling and they're gonna haul your butt to the asylum in Salem."

"Okay, it's obvious you're not ready to listen. What are you going to do to me?"

"Well, I'm sure as hell not going to put you back on the job. You're still on suspension, without pay, until we figure this out."

"Do I need a lawyer?"

Terrell Gordon set the pictures back on her desk. She turned around. "I don't know. Do you?"

"Am I free to go?"

The chief put her hand on September's shoulder. "You know how many heads I butted up against to get this job. I faced prejudice because I was black, because I was a woman, and because I was trying to do a good job in a man's world.

"You on the other hand are about the whitest white person I know. You have light red hair, green eyes and a degree from the university. You come in here and take the job of someone who has paid his dues. I'm not feeling a bit sorry for your little white butt. I'm not feeling sorry one bit. I'm recommending termination. You, my pretty little woman, have disgraced the uniform and everything it stands for."

September couldn't believe what she was hearing. If ever she had a reverse discrimination suit, this would call for it, but there were no witnesses and with all the evidence pointing to her being in the middle of a murder, she wasn't about to open another can of worms. What was important right now was getting back out on the street so she could find Daniel. She needed to stand up and not let her boss interpret the facts any way she wanted.

September fired back a barrage that got the chief's attention. "You want facts? How about ballistics and shell casings? My weapon wasn't fired. Race was dead when I entered the room and Jacobs was hiding behind the bed. She almost shot me because she still thought the killer was in the room."

The phone rang and Terrell Gordon picked up. "Yeah, Gordon here."

"No, not Fleming. Who called in the Feds? How should I know. I'll get a forensics team out there right away." The chief set down the phone. "I hate to say anything positive to you right now, 'cause you are in my sights, but they just found Fleming...dead."

"That's positive?" September asked. "Where did they find him?"

The chief smiled.

"Outside your boyfriend's apartment; where else? That boy is like a dead-body magnet."

"He's not my boyfriend and Daniel Tait is in trouble."

"You're darn right he's in trouble. Killing a Federal officer is way out of my jurisdiction. The FBI is all over this."

"What about me? Are you going to hold me?"

The chief raised her hands as if to dismiss the whole conversation. "You can go, but ballistics better back up your story."

September was out the door and running down the hall when Terrell Gordon yelled after her. "Don't leave town."

Chapter 22

From the passenger seat of the Durango, Daniel glanced over at the Frenchman. "You tried to kill me in my grandfather's garage. What do you want with me now?"

The Frenchman had his gun sitting across his lap pointed in Daniel's direction. "Do not try to engage me in trivial conversation. You know what I want."

"Okay, I understand you want a crucifix, what I don't understand is why you want it."

"It is complicated," the Frenchman said. "You will give it to me and I will go."

"You mean after you kill me."

"It is in the bed frame, is it not? I saw you deposit it in the old man's garage."

"It is not." Daniel said. "I thought it was. I even went to the trouble of having it x-rayed, but it showed only the carving on the front." Daniel needed to buy as much time as he could. Maybe September would figure out what happened and catch up with him.

"Then it is in the cross at the church. I have your computer and have seen a picture of it."

"I thought that, too, but we came up empty-handed."

"That is unfortunate, for you." This time the Frenchman looked at him. His look was not of anger, but neutral, as if it didn't make a difference. "I will have to kill you and look for it myself."

"If you're going to kill me anyway, why not tell me why I have to die."

"Everybody has to die at sometime." The Frenchman turned the SUV into the driveway and up to the garage of Daniel's grandfather's house. He lifted the pistol and pushed it toward Daniel. The silencer was no more than an inch from his forehead.

Daniel closed his eyes. His voice quivered as he spoke. "Maybe I didn't look hard enough at the headboard."

September wasn't sure what her plan was now that she was out of the office, but she was certain it would involve a gun and maybe a telephone, both of which she had hidden in her car. She retrieved both of them from under her seat, climbed into her Prius, and gunned the engine. Saving fuel at this moment was of no interest to her, she had to get to Daniel's grandfather's house before the Frenchman persuaded Daniel to spill his guts, or worse yet, before he added Daniel to his growing list of victims. She reached in her glove box and pulled out a magnetic strobe light and attached it to the roof of the car. Determined to reach Daniel in time, she ignored the dirty looks of the drivers stuck in traffic as she sped past using the emergency lanes when possible. When she was three blocks from the house she removed the strobe, let off the gas and silently crept along on battery-power. She could see Fleming's Durango in the driveway and Daniel's Jeep was nowhere to be seen. It confirmed her worst fear. The Frenchman had Daniel.

Confident she wouldn't be heard, September continued up the driveway and stopped the Prius behind the Durango. With her gun at the ready, she slid along the Durango and up to the open side door of the garage where she cautiously peeked inside. She heard the Frenchman talking.

"You are trying my patience." the Frenchman said.

September was surprised to see Daniel was taking a screwdriver to a seam on the headboard. Daniel looked like he was trying to get the board to split open. He's stalling for time, she thought. He already knows it will take a combination to open it. Some kind of code, he had said. September pushed open the door a little more so she could get a better look. It creaked and the Frenchman glanced over and fired a shot in the same motion. The bullet hit the gun September was holding and the gun went flying. September dove for the gun, but the Frenchman was faster and kicked the gun across the floor. He stood over her with the muzzle of his gun pointed at her head.

"I have been expecting you," the Frenchman said. "The two of you seem to enjoy each other's company."

September rose to her feet and raised her hands. It was only then that she saw the blood dripping from her right hand. A fragment of the bullet must have hit her, she thought, but it wasn't bad. She moved her fingers to make sure everything worked.

The Frenchman motioned her to move closer to Daniel. "You can watch as the young Mr. Tait finds a way to retrieve the crucifix."

"Why not take an ax to it?" September asked, standing beside Daniel.

"You must not destroy the crucifix," the Frenchman said, shaking his head and waving the pistol at them.

Daniel threw up his hands. "I can't open it. I don't know the combination."

"Quit stalling. You would not have the bedboard here if not to retrieve the crucifix." The Frenchman pointed the gun at September. "You will open it or she will be the first to die. You have one minute." The Frenchman looked at the watch on his wrist.

"Don't kill her. I need her help."

"Fifty-five seconds," the Frenchman said. "Forty-five seconds."

"You can't be serious." Daniel frantically looked at the intricately carved figures on the headboard. Along the bottom was a row of asterisks. He had never studied the design before. Each was imbedded in a circle about the size of a quarter. He counted ten asterisks in all. *Why are there ten?*

"Forty seconds."

Daniel stared off into space. There was only one possibility. He had to be right. There had to be significance to ten asterisks.

"What are you doing?" September whispered.

"Thirty-five seconds." The Frenchman started to step closer to September.

"Hold on, I think I can do this," Daniel said, and he started pushing on the asterisks in what seemed to be a random sequence. He pushed the first asterisk, then the fourth, the fifth, the second, the fifth again, the fourth again, the fifth for a third time, the ninth, the first again, the second and the fifth for the fourth time.

September started to back away. *What is he doing?* She watched the Frenchman coming toward her and took a step backwards.

"You are stalling," The Frenchman said. "The girl will die in ten seconds."

"Help me lift this," Daniel said to September.

They picked up the headboard and stood it on the floor. The back of the headboard was facing toward the Frenchman. Daniel counted the asterisks to make sure he had the correct one and pushed the fifth asterisk for the fifth and final time. A section of the front of the headboard sprung opened like a book set on its spine. Daniel could see the crucifix nestled in a perfectly carved slot. With his hands hidden from the Frenchman by the headboard, Daniel removed the crucifix. It was smaller than he remembered. So this is what it was all about. For a moment he forgot the threat at hand as he gazed at the crude object. Then he heard the Frenchman counting in the background. "I almost have it," he said, hoping to buy a few seconds more.

He twisted the base of the crucifix. The shaft of the cross, just below the feet of Jesus, turned and separated into two pieces like a cork from a wine bottle. As he pulled the crucifix apart he was astonished at what he saw and quickly regained control of himself. He must not give the secret away with his stupefied expression. Inside was what he was looking for. What he had seen in the x-ray, but dare not speculate. He held in his hand a tiny glass vial. With trembling hands, he slipped it in his pocket and reassembled the crucifix. The whole ordeal took no more than a few seconds.

"Your time is up," the Frenchman said aiming the pistol at September.

"Wait, I have it," Daniel said, revealing the crucifix from behind the headboard.

The Frenchman started to squeeze the trigger. "I'll take it now, but you both must die."

Daniel tossed the cross in the air and the Frenchman flinched, as he pulled the trigger. The Frenchman reached out for the crucifix that was tumbling over and over in the air. Daniel dove for September but she had already taken advantage of the situation and was diving toward the Frenchman.

The Frenchman tripped over a box on the floor, but was able to catch the crucifix in his left hand and regain his balance. September tackled the Frenchman around the middle and wrestled the gun out of his hand. The headboard teetered, not having any support and slammed down on the concrete floor with a loud bang that sounded like a gunshot. The Frenchman rolled quickly and slipped out of September's grip. He jumped to his feet and was out the door before September could reach his gun that he had lost in the scuffle. She picked up the gun and ran out the door after him.

September heard the crash of the Dodge Durango ramming her Prius before she saw the little car skid across the driveway and stop on the lawn. As the SUV backed down the driveway the rear of the Prius caught the back of the Durango, the windshield of the Prius shattered and the side window glass blew out and scattered across the driveway. The Assassin backed the SUV down the driveway and with the tires smoking and screaming, disappeared down the street.

Daniel caught up with her. "Are you all right?" he asked, seeing the look on her face.

"I tried to shoot him, but I couldn't find the safety on this thing. Who makes guns like this anyway?" She lowered the gun to her side. "I've been waiting to meet him face-to-face and he got the best of me. He got the crucifix and totaled my car. I lost my job all because that man wanted a crucifix enough to kill for it. He got away with the evidence and left us with nothing."

Daniel gently grabbed her shoulders and pulled her to him. "We're alive, we should be thankful for that. Besides, he didn't get away with everything."

"What are you talking about?" September asked, pushing away from him.

"You've got his gun and he didn't get away with this." Daniel reached in his pocket and pulled out the vial.

"What is that," she asked.

"I'm not sure, but it might tell us what all the fuss was about. It was hidden inside the crucifix."

September put her hand over her mouth and reached for the small glass container. "Let me see that."

Daniel let her take it from his hand.

September studied it with astonished respect. It was tiny, about the diameter of her little finger. The glass was green and riddled with tiny air bubbles and imperfections. The top was sealed with red wax that looked brittle with age. She tried to see what was inside. "The glass has too many imperfections to see what's inside. I can't imagine what might be inside. Maybe the bones of a saint. It looks very old."

"Whatever it is, I'll bet it's really what the Frenchman and Fleming were after. The crucifix was nothing more than a box, a container for the more precious cargo."

September handed the vial back to Daniel. "I guess this is yours. Your grandfather died for it. Speaking of Fleming, don't be surprised if the police show up at your doorstep asking questions about him. He was found dead outside your apartment."

"I figured as much. There was blood in the Durango." Daniel took the vial back from her. He held the wax seal up to the sunlight that was peeking through the clouds. "There's a stamp on the cap, a crest of some sort. I need to get this to a lab where I can examine it."

"How did you know that was inside the crucifix?" September asked.

"The x-ray showed something different from the density of the cross. When I was pulling it out of the headboard I noticed a small line at the base of Jesus' feet. The crucifix separated revealing the vial. I was totally shocked. I suspected it, but didn't believe it. Let's see if we can get it to a lab for analysis."

"What are we going to do if the Frenchman comes back after it?"

"Well, I hope you arrest him and put him in jail before he finds out."

"I'm not on the case any more. I'm not even sure I still have a job, but I think I know how to get this mess cleared up."

"How's that?" September lifted the Frenchman's gun. "I have the murder weapon. I'll turn it in and let our forensics lab put the pieces together. Hopefully, there will be the Frenchman's fingerprints on it somewhere. Since you haven't touched it, you will be in the clear. We also can fire it and get the ballistics that should clear me."

"Clear you? What are they trying to pin on you?"

"Didn't you wonder what took me so long to get here? I was hauled into my boss' office and accused of shooting Race and Jacobs. You're lucky I arrived when I did."

Daniel could see she was close to tears. He reached out for her and held her. He bent his head down and whispered in her ear. "Thank you. Thank you for believing in me and thank you for helping me get to know my grandfather."

Chapter 23

The Assassin buried the crucifix deep in his carry-on luggage. He had spoken to the Grand Master and was told to hurry home and prepare for the reopening of the Grand Lodge. He was upset that the Grand Master didn't so much as say, "Merci!" He had traveled half-way around the world and back, had retrieved the precious object the Grand Master was after and would undoubtedly take credit for, and he couldn't even offer a simple, "thank you." As he removed his shoes and lifted his small suitcase onto the conveyor he realized how fatigued he was. He was looking forward to the long flight home. On this flight he would sleep like a baby. *The Croix de Chambery is mine.*

"Please step over here." Two security guards approached the Assassin.

"*Y at-il un problème?*" asked the Assassin. "Is there a problem?"

"We need to check your luggage." They lifted the small carry-on suitcase to a table and opened it. The guard lifted aside some clothing and pulled out the crucifix. "What is this?"

"It is a crucifix, of course. I don't understand."

The guard pulled off the base of the crucifix and looked in the hollow opening. He put the base back on the crucifix and placed it back in the suitcase. "We're sorry for the inconvenience. You are free to go."

The Assassin felt like all the blood had drained from his body. He was frozen and could not move. He stared at the open suitcase with his mouth open.

"Sir, are you all right?"

The Assassin lifted his hand, "I am fine. I felt a little faint. I'll get some water." He gathered his things and sat down to put his shoes on. His mind was racing. *What should I do?* He had failed the Grand Master again and on this, his most important mission.

His face broke out in a cold sweat and his palms became clammy. He waited the hour to board the Air France plane to Paris, all the while his mind was racing. *Think, I have to think. This is God punishing me for all my sins.* He could not get the picture of eternal damnation out of his mind and began to whimper. Never in his 47 years had he felt like he had disappointed all those who put their trust in him, but at this moment he felt totally defeated.

The woman sitting next to him in the waiting area touched his arm. "No matter how bad you think things are, God will never ask you to bear more than He knows you can handle."

He looked over at the woman. She was a frail elderly lady. Her hair was gray and her face creased with years of wisdom. Her legs were covered with a blanket and she was sitting in a wheelchair.

The Assassin forgot his own troubles for a moment and managed a smile. "Thank you. You have given me great comfort." The Assassin put his hand to his face and felt a tear. As he boarded his flight he knew what he must do.

Chapter 24

September stood waiting in the Portland International Airport. She had never taken a vacation in her life and she couldn't believe she was doing this. The airport was crowded with holiday travelers returning home after spending Christmas with their families. She too, had spent the holiday with her father, mother, sister and sister's husband. It had been the best Christmas she could remember. She had her job back with pay for the time she was off. She figured they owed her that since she had never stopped working, anyway. Her father liked the ship in a bottle she had purchased from a museum site on the internet and her mother was thrilled with the gift certificate for a week at the spa vacation she had purchased with her sister. When she told them she was going to spend her week in Europe, they tried to talk her out of it, but when they learned she was going there with Daniel, they were thrilled.

Daniel lifted his suitcase onto the conveyor and watched it go through the x-ray cabinet before walking through the security screening device. He had cleared the puffer station that checked for explosives residue and waited for his shoes and valuables to clear the cabinet. As he slipped on his loafers he could see September standing by a large pillar advertising Samsonite Luggage. She looked fresh and rested. He had not seen her since the day before Christmas when he had given her the round trip ticket to Europe with the catch that he be her guide.

She accepted with the stipulation that they have separate hotel rooms, of course, but he had expected that.

He walked up to her and kissed her on the cheek. September was all smiles. Her dimples were showing and she had a lively glow about her. For the first time since he had known her she didn't look like she was on the job.

"I can't believe I'm doing this. I feel like I'm going to be arrested for having too much fun," September said.

"You haven't heard?" Daniel asked.

"What?" September looked at him suspiciously.

"There's no such thing as too much fun," Daniel said. "Come on our flying carriage awaits."

They boarded the Air Bus A340-300. Daniel knew the plane well. He pointed to one of the four CFM56-5C engines. "One of my titanium fan frames is in the heart of that engine," he said. "Nearly every time I've been to France it was to visit Snecma, who builds the engine in a partnership with GE. Actually this is an older aircraft. The newer ones have Rolls Royce engines."

"Really? Should I be worried?" September looked up at him and grinned. "You should have heard my family when I told them I was going to Europe." She was almost giddy as she spoke.

"They didn't want you to go?"

"No! They were against it until I told them I was going with you and then they were fine with it. My sister even wanted to give me a sending-off party. Can you believe they want to get rid of me that much?"

"I think these are our seats," Daniel said. The business class seats were wide and gave them all the room they needed to stretch out. They ordered drinks and waited for the giant plane to lift off. After take off, when they were high over the city, they could see Mt. Saint Helens, Mt. Hood and the snow-capped peaks of the Cascade Range for as far as they could see.

"I have a feeling the place we're heading to is going to look a lot like this," Daniel said.

September nestled back in her seat. "I can't wait. I'm a Portland girl, not an international traveler, but if the country looks like this, it's fine with me."

"I'll let you in on a secret," Daniel said.

"Secret? I like secrets."

"This is my first trip to Europe when it hasn't been on business."

"Well, you deserve a vacation after all you've been through."

Daniel let out a sigh, like he was letting all his burdens flow out with his breath. "I'm hoping this trip puts some closure on my grandfather's death. I'm happy I can finish the job he started."

"I'm sure he would have wanted it that way. He was trying to do the right thing."

"It's funny, I mean, in a strange way, but I feel like I know my grandfather better than I ever did when he was alive."

September scooted close to the armrest and looked up at Daniel. "There was a time when I thought you were a deranged killer. Now I think you are a puppy dog."

Daniel laughed. "A puppy dog, I think that's the first time anyone ever called me that. I thought you would stick with the deranged killer; after all, the bodies just kept piling up. You don't know how relieved I was when you ended up with the Frenchman's gun."

"That was the nail in the coffin, but I just wish they would have stopped him at Customs. He just slipped through them and disappeared. He's wanted for the murder of Fleming and Falcon Race, in addition to your grandfather and Elizabeth. There's an international warrant out for him."

"I keep thinking we could have been on that list as well, but you forgot Father Rick."

"Oh, I guess I didn't tell you. Father Rick was killed by Fleming. That's how he found out you were looking for the Starburst Cross. He tracked you to The Grotto and caught up with you just below the look-a-like cross."

"I didn't even know what I was looking for when I went there."

September took a sip of wine. "It didn't matter; he had a tracking bug in your jacket, that little trick almost got us killed."

"You know what was the biggest surprise to me?" Daniel asked.

September thought for a moment. "The cross hidden in the headboard?"

"That caught me by surprise all right, but when you think of it, he wanted the cross close to him. He knew it was precious. He might have believed it was what cured him when he was about to die in the hospital, so it stands to reason he would keep it close to him, and it was right where he prayed every night."

"If it wasn't that, then what was it that surprised you?"

"The combination to open the headboard to reveal the cross."

"I saw you punching all those asterisks and wondered what on earth were you doing. I was about to take a bullet in the head and you were pushing buttons on a headboard."

"Not just pushing them. I didn't figure it out until I examined the asterisks on the headboard up close. They were exactly the same as the asterisk my grandfather wrote on the floor.

"You mean the crucifix within a cross?"

"That's right. There were ten of them and that was the second clue. I asked myself, why not one or two or a dozen for that matter, but ten. That was significant."

"What's so significant about ten. It seems logical to me."

"Maybe to you, but to me it meant that my grandfather had thought out the headboard combination very carefully. Ten is a significant number. At first I thought about a combination lock. It could have two or three numbers to make it work, but if you wanted to use the alphabet, every letter could be represented with ten digits. Actually, they could have been represented by only two, but my grandfather would have had to have known computer binary numbering systems to figure that out, but to make a long story short, I'll show you how it works." He took the napkin from under his drink and a pen from his shirt pocket. He wrote a column of numbers starting with zero and ending with nine and then he wrote another column starting with one at the top and ending with ten.

"You see these two columns of numbers? If you start counting, you start with one instead of zero, am I right?"

September thought about it for a second. "Yeah, why would I start with zero?"

"A computer would start with zero, but it doesn't matter. I had to think like my grandfather and he would have started with one like you." He started writing on the napkin again.

"What are you doing now?"

Daniel continued to write. "I'm showing you how I figured out the combination."

He stopped and showed the napkin to September. It had the alphabet written beside each number.

1. AKU
2. BLV
3. CMW
4. DNX
5. EOY
6. FPZ
7. GQ
8. HR
9. IS
0. JT

September narrowed her eyebrows. "I don't understand. It looks like a random bunch of letters next to numbers. I can't believe you made anything out of this."

"Look carefully. You're a detective, you can understand this."

"Oh, I see," September said. "You assigned a letter of the alphabet to each number and started over again when you reached ten...or zero. So each letter could be assigned a number."

"That's right, and assuming I read my grandfather's intentions correctly, all I had to do was figure out what word or words he would use to open the latch and reveal what was hidden in his headboard."

"I don't know," September said, "it sounds pretty complicated. How could anyone figure it out?"

Daniel looked at her and grinned. "It's not complicated if you have a clue, and my grandfather told us what the combination was."

"He did?"

"All the running around and chasing after a cross and the picture in the ammo box were a wild goose chase," Daniel said excitedly. "Grandpa gave us all the clues we needed and everything was under our noses and right there in the bedroom. "Adele de Savoy," the famed "asterisk" and "G-O-D-S". My grandfather was a genius in the simplicity of the clues. The asterisk pointed to the buttons on the headboard. "Adele de Savoy" was the combination to reveal the crucifix, and "G-O-D-S" was the identification of the killer."

September took a long sip of her drink and leaned back in her seat. She was quiet for a long time. When she finally turned to Daniel, she was surprised he was staring at her. "The combination was Adele de Savoy?"

"Actually, it was one-four-five-two-five-four-five-nine-one-two-five-five. When you think about it, my grandfather's crucifix was quite safe. He wrote the combination right in front of the Frenchman and he didn't have a clue."

September leaned in toward him. "You figured all that out in the minute before that man was going to shoot me?"

"Not entirely," Daniel admitted. "You remember the x-ray?"

September nodded.

"It showed just enough of the mechanism, that I knew what kind of lock I was dealing with. Without that, I might have resorted to your solution."

"My solution?"

"The Ax." Daniel leaned his seat back. "Might as well relax. We have a long flight ahead of us."

Chapter 25

The Assassin had been back in Sainte-Mère-Eglise for over a week. Every day he went over his plan and rehearsed what he had to do. He had been given the combination to the safe in the Grand Master's office where the crucifix was hidden for safekeeping. As a reward for bringing the crucifix back, the Assassin had been given the honor of formally presenting it to the Grand Master at the dedication of the new lodge. It would happen right after the Grand Master's speech to the full assembly of the Grand Orient de Savoy. Tonight he would remove the crucifix and carry out his plan. In another day the Grand Masters of GODS lodges from around the world would attend the opening of the new lodge.

Chapter 26

Daniel and September reached the medieval town of Chambery. The view from the taxi on their way to the hotel had been filled with architecture from medieval times. They felt like they had stepped back in time and woke up in the fifteenth century.

"I feel like I'm seeing France for the first time," Daniel said.

The hotel was located along the historic rue de Boigne, lined with architecture from the fourteenth century. The three-story stone block building that lined both sides of the narrow street had high, arched, covered sidewalks that led like a medieval tunnel to the castle complex known as the Chateau de Chambery.

The Chateau de Chambery was a fortified village that once controlled the trade intersection of three roads that led from Lyon, France to Turin, Italy and Lyon to Geneva, Switzerland. It was there Amadeus, Count of Savoy, fortified the site and made it the primary home of the ruling family. It was where the Holy Burial Cloth of Jesus was kept in the chapel built for the purpose to give it a protected home. The cloth was later moved to Turin and became know as the Shroud of Turin. The Chateau de Chambery also housed the nunnery of the Poor Clares, the very nuns who repaired the shroud in the year 1534.

When they had checked into the historic Hotel des Princes, Daniel could not wait to visit the castle and meet with the head of the Poor Clare convent. The vial he had carried with him in a protective box had been in his pocket all the way from Portland. As he lay in his hotel room waiting for the next morning, when he and September were scheduled to meet with the acting Sister Superior, he reflected on the tiny vial that had been the object of the search he and September had been drawn into. Daniel could not sleep even though he had lost nine hours of time on the long plane ride from Portland. He glanced at the pen box containing the vial and removed it to view it for what might be his last time. He was saddened by what he had heard when he had contacted the Poor Clare nuns in Chambery. Sister Amedee, his contact, had said the Mother Superior had been wounded by a gunshot to the head at close range while she was in the confessional of the church. It was only through the grace of God that she had not died on the spot. Deep down, Daniel could feel his gut churn as he believed that it was not an isolated act, but was connected to the crucifix being sought by the Frenchman. Daniel twisted the green glass vial in his fingers and marveled at how it had survived the centuries with the seal unbroken. Even he, with all his curiosity, could not bring himself to break the seal and expose the contents to the contaminated environment of the twenty-first century. Sister Amedee had promised to share the secret of the contents with him when he returned the vial.

Still wide awake, unable to sleep in the excitement, Daniel decided to take a walk. He called September's room on the hope that she, too, was having difficulty adjusting to the time change and was unable to sleep. He checked his watch. It was nearly midnight and he hesitated. What if she's asleep?

After an agonizing two minutes of internal debate, he finally gave into his wild side and called September.

September had gone to her room as instructed. Although she had managed a catnap on the long flight, she could not bring herself to sleep, either. Daniel had said sleeping was the best way to adjust to the time difference. "Get some sleep and wake up to the time change," he had said, but it wasn't working for her. She was on her back on top of the covers, reading "Caldera," a book she had downloaded on her Kindle before the trip and had not had a chance to read until now. The phone beside her bed rang and she picked it up wondering who would call her at this hour. "Hello."

"I'm sorry if I woke you," Daniel said.

"I couldn't sleep."

"Good, do you feel like going for a walk?"

September sat up. "I'm still dressed. I'm ready if you are."

"I'll meet you in the lobby."

It was three minutes to midnight when the Assassin pulled the rented Peugeot 508 Saloon into a parking spot outside the Chateau de Chambery. He had not been accustomed to such luxury in an automobile and felt for someone as poor as he, it was an opulent display of wealth. He had argued with the woman at the rental car company, but she had insisted, they had no other vehicles available and he would not have to pay additional for the driving pleasure of the luxury vehicle. Reluctantly, he had accepted, and on the 12-hour drive from Sainte-Mère-Eglise to Chambery he had enjoyed the comfort of the fine automobile. Yet, in spite of the comfort he was awarded on the drive, he was quite weary, not from the trip, but for what he was about to do. He must enter the home of the Poor Clare nuns once more. The thought of his last visit had begun to haunt him. He had killed on the sacred grounds of the church more than once and knew there was nothing he could do to undo his actions. *You cannot change the spots on a leopard*, he told himself as he made his way in the shadows of the street toward the courtyard where he had played as a child.

As September and Daniel walked from the hotel entrance to the rue de Boigne, Daniel looked at her in the moonlight. She looked radiant in the soft glow of the streetlamps and he stopped and admired her.

"Can't decide which way to go?" September asked.

"Give me your hand," Daniel said.

September eyed him warily and held out her hand. Daniel took her hand in his. "I don't want you to get lost." He started down the street toward the Chateau de Chambery holding her hand and pulling her close to him. The night was crisp and clear. The nearly full moon cast dark shadows that the streetlights could not hide. They stopped at the end of the street and looked up at the towers of the castle and the high stone walls.

"That's where we are going tomorrow." Daniel said.

They continued along the towering walls and rounded the corner. There was no traffic in that section of town this hour of the night and they were the only ones on the street. The city was quiet, and even in the poor light, they could see the steam from each breath as they stopped again and marveled at how massive the fortress was. They turned and looked back along the street from whence they had come. The stone arches covering the sidewalk in front of the shops looked like a long dark tunnel.

They turned back to the castle in front of them. "Look at the size of the gate in the vaulted entry," September said.

"This entire place takes me back in time. You have to admire the skill and workmanship of the people who built this."

"They were dedicated," September said. "The world must have moved at a slower pace than today. I'll bet this took years to build and look how long it's lasted."

Daniel turned to her. "We just flew half way around the world in a matter of hours and when this castle was being built Christopher Columbus hadn't even thought about sailing into the sunset to discover a new route to India."

"Daniel!" September quietly whispered, but her voice was panicked. She pulled him back into the shadows. She pointed at a man across the street. He was standing beside a lamppost lighting a cigarette.

Daniel's mouth fell open. The identity of the man was unmistakable. He was not more than thirty-feet away across the narrow street from them. He was seemingly unaware they were watching him. Daniel held his breath and could hear his heart pounding in his ears. "What's he doing here?" Daniel asked, in a whisper.

"It's him, I know it is," September whispered. She reached in her purse and pulled out her cell phone.

Daniel put his hand on hers and stopped her from activating the phone. "Wait. It'll light up and expose us," he whispered.

"I'd feel a lot better right now if I had my gun," September murmured.

"Let's see what he's up to."

They pressed their backs against the stone wall of the building behind them and breathed shallow until the Frenchman dropped his cigarette on the sidewalk and ground the butt into the pavement with the toe of his shoe. The Frenchman turned and walked toward the high-arched entry which led to the courtyard of the castle. When he had disappeared into the tunnel, September and Daniel slipped across the street and along the castle wall. They stopped at the castle entrance and peered down the tunnel leading to the courtyard. They saw the Frenchman walking along the buildings toward the high steps of the Sainte-Chapelle.

"He's entering the church,'" Daniel whispered.

"I wouldn't have thought of him as a church-going person," September said.

They continued through the tunnel and stopped. The courtyard was well-lit. They would be exposed and possibly putting themselves in danger if they continued, yet their curiosity was overwhelming.

"What do you think?" September asked.

"If we stay to the right we won't be as exposed," Daniel said. "I'd sure like to know what he's up to."

"Me, too." She reached for the small of her back by reflex, searching for her gun that wasn't there.

Daniel took the lead. As he walked along the buildings that made up the inner castle walls, he looked up at the towering church with its high steeple and spires. The door loomed ahead like a dark cavern above four flights of solid stone stairs. He knew as soon as he opened the door they would be exposed to whatever was waiting on the other side. He turned to September who was climbing the third flight of steps and waited. "You want to continue. No telling if he's waiting to ambush us or not."

"I think we need to go back and call this in," September said. "Interpol should already have a warrant for his arrest. I'm not comfortable dying in a foreign country, are you?"

Daniel let out a long sigh. "I was hoping you would say that." He took his hand off the large brass handle. He wondered if royalty had held their hand in the same spot and decided royalty would have their servants perform a menial task like opening a door.

"Hurry up," September said. "Suddenly I feel like getting a few hours sleep isn't such a bad idea."

Chapter 27

It was late the next morning when September and Daniel met for breakfast in the hotel dining room. As they filled their plates with bread, assorted cheeses, cold sliced meat, and boiled eggs Daniel called the attendant over. "You wouldn't happen to have some French toast, would you?"

"Daniel, you be nice," September said smiling.

As they finished their breakfast the attendant, an elderly man dressed like he was going to the royal ball, served them espresso, cream and sugar. September held up her hand. "No cream or sugar. I like mine black."

"*Jeune fille, vous devez le pendre avec de la crème et le sucre*," the attendent said.

"What did I do," September said. "He sounds upset."

Daniel laughed. "He says you must take it with cream and sugar."

September looked at the elderly man and smiled. "Cream and sugar, if I must." When he had gone she stirred the tiny cup of liquid and saw the grin on Daniel's face. "You seem quite amused."

Daniel sipped his espresso. "You'll be happy for the cream and sugar, trust me. Without it...well, you'll know."

"I'll bet you did the same thing the first time you came here," September said. "I'm right aren't I?"

"Guilty as charged, officer," Daniel said. "I always seem to learn the hard way. I actually drank it black. First, last and only time I made that mistake. You think your coffee is bad."

September glared at him. "Don't even go there."

After sipping her espresso and deciding she didn't need caffeine that bad, September finished a glass of orange juice and set the glass on the white tablecloth. "Look at me. I'm in France. I feel like I should be having wine with this meal."

"That would be lunch or dinner," Daniel said. He checked the time on his watch and compared it with a large sculpted clock standing in an alcove along the tiled wall of the breakfast room. "We have to finish our business this afternoon and catch the rail to Sainte-Mère-Eglise."

"That should be fun," September said. "Today we put closure on all that has happened."

Daniel unconsciously reached down and felt the object in his pocket. "It will be all over in a few hours and then we can enjoy the rest of our time in Europe."

September wore a black knee length dress and the camelhair jacket her sister had given her for Christmas. Her red hair showed blond highlights in the morning sun as they walked to the nunnery. They took the same route as they had walked in the midnight hours.

Daniel, dressed in a white shirt, red silk tie, navy coat and tan slacks felt like he was going to a business meeting. The vial in the small pen box was safely stored in his front pocket where he could keep his hand on it. He had not let it out of his sight from the time he had removed it from the crucifix. He had spent the week before Christmas tracing every step his grandfather had made and was anxious to return the vial to the Poor Clare nuns. He had learned that the crucifix had been carved by a priest in 1534 as a container for the vial. He had also learned that the crucifix, while not considered a relic in itself, was a part of the heritage of the nunnery and had been the subject of several legends of miracles, but had gone missing with its contents and until his grandfather had inquired as to its origin, it had been given up for lost. It was with anxious steps that he strode toward the nunnery. He felt like he was about to end a long and arduous journey.

"Hey, wait up," September said. "I didn't wear my jogging outfit."

"Sorry," Daniel said, waiting for her to catch up. They were again standing at the high-arched tunnel that served as the entrance to the courtyard and the castle complex. Daniel stopped again as they reached the courtyard. In the daylight the massive complex was even more impressive. On his left were the four-story-high white stone buildings that had once housed the Duke's army and served as the outer wall of the castle. He felt tiny standing in the entrance and imagined that that was what the Duke of Savoy would have wanted if an enemy breached the walls of the complex. To his right was the church, the Chapelle de Chambery and he admired its towering medieval architecture, with the high, narrow-arched windows and elegant stone carvings over the doors. He had to bend his head back to see the top of the spires. It was a marvel of construction and he couldn't imagine the craftsmanship that it would have required to build such a structure. Suddenly, he missed his grandfather. *You should have been here instead of me, Grandpa.*

"Daniel, if we stop every two minutes, we're going to be late," September said. She climbed the steps and stood with her hand on the brass handle where Daniel had held it ten hours earlier. "You don't think he's still in here do you?"

"Let me do that," Daniel said, grabbing the handle with his hand above hers. For a moment his lips touch her hair and he could smell her perfume.

She turned her head and their faces were barely inches apart. She hesitated.

Daniel swallowed hard. "I wanted you to know chivalry is not dead, even in the twenty-first century." He pulled open the door.

"Lead on, Prince Charming," September said. She could feel the warmth in her cheeks from embarrassment. He was truly a prince and she felt herself wanting to be close to him. It was the first time she could remember since college that a man had had that effect on her.

Contrary to what her sister Tiffany thought, the police force was not a good place to seek a husband. Law enforcement was too demanding a profession for husband and wife. It was not good for children and she couldn't think of a single case where it had not ended in divorce or alcoholism. She followed Daniel into the sacristy, making the sign of the cross with holy water as they stood looking at the size of the church that the Europeans called a chapel. In the United States it would put some cathedrals to shame. She looked up and gasped at the eight-pointed star that was formed by the curved beams that came together high above them. Following the curve of the beams, towering and slender stained glass windows let in a rainbow of light. Along the spine of the arches were ornate carvings in stone, and the walls around the altar were adorned with windows of lavender, blue, and red stained glass, four-stories-high with a depiction of the resurrection of Christ. The stainedglass windows reached high to the ceiling and were framed with sculpted arches that came together forming a peak, which formed a multi-pointed star where they intersected. September looked up in awe and could not imagine attending mass in such an elegant building. *How could I take my eyes off the magnificent ceiling?*

Along the right wall was the door which Daniel had been told led to the nun's quarters. On the other side of the door was a long hallway lined with many doors, which were the private quarters of the nuns. At the far end of the corridor Daniel knocked at an open door.

Inside, sitting at a desk, was a nun dressed in the traditional black habit with a pure white linen wimple that covered the cheeks and neck. The woman wore glasses and smiled as she stood to greet them.

"I am Sister Amedee," the nun said in perfect English. "You must be Daniel Tait." She looked at September.

"This is my friend, September Gale," Daniel said. "She helped me find the crucifix."

September shook the nun's hand.

"Are you Catholic?" the nun inquired, looking at both of them.

"I am," September said.

Daniel slipped his hand in his pocket. "I think I have something of yours that has been missing for a long time," Daniel said.

"Wait," Sister Amedee said. "Before you present the gift, I must assemble the others. I have managed to have Mother Superior moved to the chapel for the ceremony."

"Ceremony? We didn't want a ceremony," Daniel said.

"If you will forgive my indulgence. We have no possessions, except that we all share in the glory of God. You, my son, are the answer to over sixty years of daily prayer by Mother Superior. She was so delighted to get the call from your grandfather."

"Wait a minute," Daniel said. "My grandfather called?"

"Oh, yes. I thought you knew. It was November twenty-second. Mother Superior woke me when she got the news that the crucifix would be returned."

"Then I'm afraid my news isn't so good," Daniel said. "I don't have the crucifix. I only have the vial that was inside."

"Oh, yes. That is what you told me on the phone. Come along." She led them down the hall to the door that led to the church. "You are proof that God always answers our prayers." She paused for a moment holding the door open for them. "In his own time, of course."

They were amazed that an assemblage of nearly thirty nuns had gathered along the wall in front of a marble statue of Saint Francis of Assisi.

"Saint Francis was the founder of our order with Saint Clare, of course, in the year 1212," Sister Amedee said.

In front of the statue that had been obscured until now was a cot in which a nun was reclined and seemingly dead. The nuns surrounding her parted as Sister Amedee approached with September and Daniel. Daniel looked at their faces which all seemed to be beaming. "Am I missing something?" Daniel asked. He pointed to the nun on the stretcher. "She seems near death if she hasn't died already. Why are the nuns smiling?"

"She is with God, but not quite," Sister Amedee said quietly, "but the sisters are happy, for today we have witnessed a miracle."

Daniel was confused. He had not given the vial to them yet. What kind of miracle could possibly have happened?

"Let me introduce you to her," Sister Amedee said. "She has waited her whole life for this moment."

Daniel took September's hand and walked up to the cot. The woman was wrinkled and old. Had he not seen pictures of Mother Teresa, he would have pictured her as this woman, with her eyes closed, seemingly at peace with the world. He looked down at her and clinched September's hand. "She has the crucifix."

September bent down and examined the dark object clutched in the hands of the Mother Superior. From the picture she had seen on Daniel's computer, it certainly looked like the cross the Frenchman had stolen. Suddenly, she could not contain herself and tears started flowing down her cheeks. Daniel, too, was moved to the point of tears. He removed a handkerchief from his coat pocket and wiped his eyes. He reached in the front pocket of his slacks and pulled out the small box. He handed it to Sister Amedee but she refused to take it.

"No, no, no, I am not worthy. Remove it and show it to all of us and then place it into its proper reliquary."

Daniel lifted the vial from the simple box that once had contained a Paper Mate pen he had received as a gift for Christmas. He felt warmth course through his body as he lifted it for the nuns to see. He presented it to each and they kissed their fingers and touched them to the tiny vial. When he was finished he was about to take the cross from the Mother Superior when September, with tears still flowing down her cheeks reached out and touched his arm. He turned, she kissed her fingers and touched the vial as the nuns had done. In any other setting Daniel would have felt self conscious or possibly embarrassed, being in the center of such a spiritual ritual, but he felt at peace. His lips quivered and he struggled to keep from crying, but couldn't hold back the tears that were streaming down his cheeks. He had never felt emotion like he was feeling at this moment, not even when he looked at his grandfather's body in the morgue. He touched his lips and placed his fingers on the vial and then touched the vial to the Mother Superior's lips. He removed the crucifix from the Mother Superior's hands, twisted off the base and placed the ampule in the opening. He replaced the section of the crucifix and gently opened the Mother Superior's hands and placed the crucifix back in her grip. As he folded her hands over the crucifix he said a silent prayer. *May God grant you all that you are seeking in this life and the next. God please help me to be worthy of my grandfather's legacy.* He turned to Sister Amedee, "Do you think she knows?"

Sister Amedee nodded. "She knows, now we must go back to my office."

Daniel wiped the tears away again as he and September followed the nun down the long stone corridor to her office. Inside the nun pulled up two chairs. "Sit and I will tell you a story."

One of the nuns, who had been in the church, brought tea while they waited for Sister Amedee to pull up a chair. "Much of what I am about to reveal to you is not recorded in the history books." She looked at them with pure blue eyes. "It was December 4, 1532 when a fire roared through the very chapel we were just in. The fire raged out of control. Within the church, protected by four sets of locks, in a silver reliquary, was the most precious belonging of the Duke of Savoy, Charles III. It was the Holy Burial Shroud of our Savior, Christ Jesus." The nun swallowed hard at the thought of what she was revealing. "Cannon Philibert and two Franciscan priests summoned the help of a blacksmith to break the locks so they could save the Holy Shroud, but they were too late. The fire had raged with such fierce heat that it had all but consumed the inside of the chapel, and the silver box in which the burial cloth was folded had started to melt and drip molten metal from its edges onto the Holy Cloth. By the time they were able to rescue the box and douse water on it, the Burial Shroud had been damaged by the molten silver dripping on a folded corner of the Shroud.

"There was much grieving within the Duke de Savoy family. One of the Duke's brothers was accused of setting the fire."

"The cloth remained in the chapel and was not allowed to be viewed because of its fragile and burned condition. And then, on 16 April, 1534, in a solemn ceremony, the Holy Shroud was delivered to the Poor Clare nunnery, the very place we are sitting and the Poor Clare's were asked to repair the damaged areas of the Holy Cloth. The repairs were completed and the cloth was returned to the castle. But during the repairs the threads that were trimmed from the damaged areas were collected and given to the Poor Clares. The Sacred Threads were placed in the glass vial at that time. They had been in a place of adoration for close to 400 years, when during the invasion of France by Germany, they went missing. Mother Superior was the only one to see the Croix de Chambery, which contained the Sacred Threads the day they disappeared." She smiled and looked at the bare walls of her office. "And now Mother Superior has the Sacred Threads with her again."

Chapter 28

That night Daniel knelt by his bed and prayed for the first time since he was a child. He slept soundly and was awakened the next morning by pounding on the door. "What is it?" Daniel asked before opening his eyes to the light of day. *It must be late. Why didn't September call?* The pounding continued and Daniel could hear September's voice.

"Daniel, open up. Are you in there?"

Daniel dressed only in his Jockey briefs hid behind the door and opened it against the security stop. "You woke me. What's going on?"

"You didn't answer your phone and I was worried. We have less than an hour to catch the train."

Daniel ran his hand through his hair. "Let me shower and get dressed. I'm sure there will be another train if we miss this one."

"Hurry. I don't want to miss the train."

"I'll meet you in the lobby. Wait, we have to check out. My gosh, what time is it anyway? Give me fifteen minutes and I'll knock on your door and help you with your luggage."

"See, we made the train with five minutes to spare," Daniel said, hoisting September's suitcase up on an overhead rack. The train started to move, and in another five minutes they were settled in a seat sitting next to each other watching the green hills and countryside quickly pass by.

"I couldn't help but feel for Mother Superior yesterday," September said.

"All the while I held the vial in my pocket, I never imagined what it contained," Daniel said. "Can you imagine, the threads in that little bottle actually rested against the body of Jesus."

"Wow," September said. "I never thought I'd ever see you this worked up about anything spiritual."

"Promise you won't laugh," Daniel said. "Something happened when I held those threads. I can't explain it, but I've never felt like that before."

"The real miracle was the crucifix in Mother Superior's hands," September said.

Daniel gave her a quizzical look. "What do you mean? We saw the Frenchman go into the church. He obviously returned it."

"But did you ever imagine a murdering scoundrel like that would have a change of heart and do the right thing?"

"I see what you mean." He gazed out the window. "Pretty country, I told you it would be a lot like Oregon."

September was quiet for a long time. "What are you expecting by going to Sainte-Mère-Eglise?"

"I'm not sure. Maybe something on Adele de Savoy. She was mentioned in the article in the paper my grandfather had hidden in the ammo box. She must have had a big impact on Grandpa. I think she was the one who gave him the crucifix."

"The paper had her listed as a casualty of the war."

"I know, but she must have been someone special for my grandfather to use her name for access to the crucifix."

"Do you think you grandfather knew about the threads?"

"I guess we'll never know, but I'd like to think he did. I still picture him with the cross in his hands, the same way Mother Superior looked. I wonder if she will recover?"

"She's pretty old," September said.

During the quiet times of the trip, September thought about her time with Daniel. She had never met a man other than a priest who could talk about personal things, spiritual things, as easily as Daniel, yet she hesitated to mention it for fear it would make him self-conscious and she didn't want to change anything about him.

After a long time of reflection, September touched Daniels arm to get his attention. "Mother Superior led a good life, but still, you would hope that God would smile on her and let her know He had returned."

"She spent her whole life praying and serving God," Daniel said. "I don't think she would need his reassurance." Daniel thought a bit longer. "I watched my dad and grandfather fight over religion. I thought God was the cause for most of the problems in the world." He swallowed hard. "Until last night I never realized that it was the absence of God that was doing the harm."

"What happened last night?"

"I was lying in bed staring at the ceiling with the events of the day racing through my mind and it dawned on me, that for the crucifix to be placed in the hands of that nun, the Frenchman must have turned toward God, not away from him."

"And that is a miracle," September said.

The Grand Orient de Savoy Lodge was packed with Grand Masters from over thirty countries including the United States and every one of them had to profess their firm belief in the sanctity of man and denounce the worship of a deity in any form. The crucifix had been a symbol of Deity to be desecrated, and today, at the solemn dedication of the new lodge in Sainte-Mère-Eglise, that symbol was to be returned so it could be used in the ceremonies to remind the members of their allegiance to their own power; to the inner strength that did not require a god to solve their problems. The hall was packed with over 200 men.

The Assassin looked out at the assembly with the same calm he had felt many times before he had committed murder at the order of the Grand Master, but there was a difference. This time an inner voice spoke to him. *You are doing the right thing.* The first time he heard the voice was in the airport while he was waiting to catch the plane back to France and the woman in the wheelchair had spoken to him.

The Assassin, dressed in a tuxedo, highly-polished black shoes, and white gloves, entered the lodge through double-doors from the anteroom where he had been waiting for his cue. The ceremony was one that had been handed down in the historical documents of the Grand Orient de Savoy for hundreds of years.

The Assassin kept his eyes fixed on the Grand Master, who was standing behind an altar draped in a black cloth. He marched slowly, as if he were a bride walking down the aisle to her bridegroom. The room was packed with men, all dressed as if they were attending a royal wedding. The Assassin glanced down at the ornate box he was holding, but only for a second. His eyes rose to meet the Grand Master again. He stopped in front of the altar and stretched his hands out to the Grand Master.

The Grand Master took the box and opened it. For a moment there was astonishment on the Grand Master's face, but it quickly turned to panic. He looked down at the timer on the bomb. It was too late to do anything. The Grand Master sucked in his final breath before the entire lodge exploded with such force that it leveled the four-story building.

In their hotel a few blocks away, Daniel and September were rocked awake by the explosion. They had arrived late in the night, had gone straight to bed and had not planned to meet until lunch time. Daniel looked at the clock, which read 10:07a.m. He quickly dialed September. "Did you feel that?"

"It felt like an earthquake. I was just getting up."

"I think it was an explosion. I'll meet you in the lobby in two minutes."

Outside the streets were packed with people frantically looking at a column of smoke rising high above the surrounding buildings.

"Come on," Daniel said, fighting his way through the crowd. He waited long enough to make sure September was keeping up with him, and stopped when he reached the edge of the debris field. He looked up and, as the smoke and dust drifted off in a light breeze, he saw the bell tower of the church with the dummy of a WW II parachutist hanging from a spire. It had been placed there in memory of an American parachutist, John Steele, who Daniel had been told had been a member of his grandfather's unit. He looked down at his feet. He was standing on a piece of smoldering wood with writing on it. *reouverture de la Grande*

Loge "Reopening of the Grand Lodge." Daniel read. He picked up a piece of the sign that had broken off and turned to September. "I think you can read this."

September watched as Daniel wiped away the dust with his hand.

"Grand Orient de Savoy," September read aloud. "We have seen two miracles in as many days."

Daniel's phone rang and he looked at the number. "It's a European code. Who knows where we are?" He put the phone to his ear and listened. He was silent as he put the phone away.

"What is it," September said.

Daniel looked into her crystal green eyes and his eyes turned misty. "After a month in a coma, Mother Superior is awake."

###

About the author

Larry LaVoie was born in a small town in Oregon in 1942. He lettered in football and track in high school. In the summers, as a teenager, he worked in the fields around Dayton, Oregon. Larry graduated from McMinnville High school in 1960 and joined the Oregon National Guard in the fall of 1960. He completed basic training in Fort Ord, California. He spent much of his career as an engineer in the aerospace industry. He has traveled extensively to several European countries. He has lived in several small towns in Oregon and along the Oregon Coast, which is reflected in many of his novels. He now lives in the high desert country of Eastern Oregon. He likes golf and bowling and has participated in several bowling tournaments over the past several years. His writing mainly has a flavor of his small town roots, although a few of his novels take place in larger cities such as Los Angeles, or Portland, or foreign countries. His writings reflect much of his own experience as an engineer and as a person who loves sports and politics. His writings include mystery, thrillers, and action adventure set in interesting places. While many of his novels are written for a mainstream adult audience he has also written for young adult and Christian readers. "I write mainly to entertain," Larry says. "When you read one of my books I want you to enjoy a good story through the eyes of the characters in the novel."

http://www.larrylavoieauthor.com